Mothers

and Other Liars

D0733296

Mothers

and Other Liars

AMY BOURRET

St. Martin's Griffin

NEW YORK

This is a work of fiction. All of the characters, locales, and events portrayed in this novel are either products of the author's imagination or are used fictitiously. While Santa Fe, some other locales, and certain places and organizations portrayed in this work are real, they are used fictitiously and with creative license, including with respect to geography.

MOTHERS AND OTHER LIARS. Copyright © 2010 by Amy Bourret. All rights reserved. Printed in the United States of America. For information, address St. Martin's Press, 175 Fifth Avenue, New York, N.Y. 10010.

www.stmartins.com

Library of Congress Cataloging-in-Publication Data

Bourret, Amy.
   Mothers and other liars / Amy Bourret. — 1st ed.
      p. cm.
   ISBN 978-0-312-58658-4
   1. Young women—Fiction.   2. Foundlings—Fiction.   3. Mothers and
daughters—Fiction.   4. Santa Fe (N.M.)—Fiction.   5. Psychological
fiction.   I. Title.
   PS3602.O8928M67 2010
   813'.6—dc22

                                                            2009046750

10   9   8   7   6   5   4

*In memory of Anne Marie and Estel Henry "Wede" Wedemeyer,
a bighearted pragmatist and a hardworking dreamer who taught
me to believe in daffodils and in love*

ACKNOWLEDGMENTS

During the long journey from blank page to published book, I have incurred debts of gratitude rivaling a small country's deficit. Mere words are never enough, but: to the Dunston's Gang for critique and camaraderie and for never letting me rest on my metaphors. Shout-outs to Paul Coggins for advice on Ruby's legal matters (though any mistake or use of creative license is mine); to David Norman for loving this story enough to take it to Hollywood and for several choice morsels; to Harry Hunsicker for a few well-timed kicks in the butt; and to Will Clarke for easing my way down the road. A special thank-you to Alison Hunsicker, ex-officio member and an early reader who provided spot-on feedback.

To the other critique groups I have had the privilege to be a part of along the way: special thanks to Colleen Rae, who helped me find Ruby's voice, and to the Aspen Writers' Foundation and Catherine O'Connell, who keeps their group going so that a writer's world is a less lonely place.

To JSP for early encouragement and eleventh-hour advice.

To the fabulous Jenny Bent, who talked me down from a couple of ledges with grace and humor. Thank you for "getting" me.

To Jen Weis and the team at St. Martin's for bringing Ruby's story to print with care and enthusiasm.

To the teachers who nurtured my creative spark and hammered on the grammar: Mrs. Bush, Mrs. Krueger, and Mrs. Kessler, and all of you overworked and underpaid teachers out there, know that you do make a difference.

Finally, to my friends and family, who encouraged, cajoled, and supported me through all these many days, and who rescued me when I was spending too much time in my head. I don't know how I would do this writing stuff without you. A special thank-you to Susan Virginia Metcalfe Shores for never letting me forget my long-ago promise to put her name in print, and for never wavering in her belief that I would. And for, well, everything else, my mom, who lies only every now and again.

Thank you, all of you,

always,

amy

The truth is rarely pure and never simple.

—Oscar Wilde, The Importance of Being Earnest, Act I

Mothers and Other Liars

ONE

Ruby Leander's third life ends with the flip of a page. The photo graph catches her eye first. Then the words shriek at her, in stark black and white. Lines of type shift on the page, curl into a tight ball, somersault, gathering sentences, whole paragraphs, gaining momentum. And just like that, on an otherwise ordinary Thursday, this life is over.

She slams the weekly tabloid shut, sandwiching the article between weight-loss ads and pictures of celebrities misbehaving. As her client, Antoinette, approaches, Ruby tosses the magazine aside.

Antoinette bustles up to the nail station, oversized tote bag banging against her curvy hip. Thursday is Ruby's late day, to accommodate the working women. Antoinette has a standing appointment in the last slot. Margaret's partner, Molly, babysits Lark—though nine-year-old Lark would cringe at that word. And Antoinette and Ruby go to dinner. This is their routine.

"Sorry. Sorry. Shakespeare had it right. I want to kill *all* the lawyers." Antoinette plops down on the seat across the narrow table. Her thick hair is tamed into a demure bun, her white blouse closed a button higher than before her recent promotion from the court clerk's office to judge's secretary. She pauses, looks at Ruby. "You okay?"

No, Ruby is not okay. The photograph, the words, are burned into her brain. From a serendipitous thirst, a wrong turn, and a chance meeting—and a big lie—she built this Santa Fe life for herself and her daughter, Lark. This is no sand-castle life that could wash away in the evening tide; this is a mountain life, strong and tall and solid. Yet even mountains erode, and this one is crumbling at her feet. She is definitely not okay.

"Yes. I'm fine."

Without a doubt, that photograph is of Lark; a similar shot sits in a frame in their living room. This life is over, but what she does about the article will define what the next life will be—for her and for Lark.

"You sure you're okay?" Antoinette's voice sounds tinny, as if traveling from a soup can and string, what with having to penetrate that photo before reaching a piece of Ruby's brain. "It's not . . ."

"I'm fine. Really." Ruby tries to ignore the worry creasing Antoinette's brow and avoid meeting Margaret's eyes in the mirrored wall that lines the hair stations. Margaret doesn't miss much in her salon.

"You know you can tell me anything." Antoinette's voice is soft with concern.

The kindness soaks into Ruby's skin, rises to a lump in her throat. "I know."

As Antoinette turns to the rack on the wall to choose her polish, Ruby picks up the tabloid from the floor beside her chair, fans through to the page. She rips out the article, folds it into a tidy square, then gestures to the sudsy manicure dish. "Soak a minute. I'll be right back."

In the back room of the salon, Ruby braces her arms on each side of the sink, fights the nausea pulsing against her throat. She turns on the faucet, splashes her face, the cold water a welcome slap against her hot cheeks. Over the past decade, she has never once thought of herself as a criminal; Ruby did right by that child, even if the law doesn't agree. But now a boulder is careening their way.

TWO

Ruby flings the door open at the first crunch of gravel on the driveway. She gnaws her lower lip as Molly's car parks beside the porch. Clyde bursts from the car first, a flash of four-legged auburn highlights leaping up at Ruby for a quick lick before bounding around the corner into the backyard. Lark's butt emerges next, followed by the rest of the child tugging out a purple backpack.

As Molly pulls away, Ruby waves and mouths "thank you," pretends not to see the questioning look in the woman's eyes. Lark barely reaches the porch before Ruby grabs her, pulls her into a tight hug. Ruby draws in a deep breath through her nose, savors the hint of Larkness buried under scents of horse and a day outdoors.

"Mo-om," Lark says into Ruby's shirt. "You're squi-ishing me."

Ruby loosens her grip, moves her hands to Lark's shoulders. "Sorry, baby."

"What's the matter?" Lark steps away from Ruby and into the house.

Ruby picks up Lark's backpack, follows her inside. "Nothing's wrong. I just needed my Lark fix."

"You were jonesing, huh?"

Even in her terror, Ruby can't help laugh. "Jonesing? Where on earth . . ."

"I'm precocious, remember?" Lark tucks a wisp of angel-wing hair behind her ear.

Ruby crosses the living area, moves to the sink nestled in a corner of the tiny kitchen. Through the gap in the curtains behind the sink, a sliver of the Sangre de Cristo mountains is awash in purple evening light. Reaching past the herb garden and Lark's latest project, an avocado pit suspended over a glass by toothpicks, she tugs the curtains closed against any possibility of prying eyes.

A door slams. Ruby startles. She drops her hand from her throat when she sees Clyde, who nosed open the screen door to the back porch. He pads over to her, rubs his sleek doggy body against her legs. *Normal,* she tells herself. *Just act normal.*

She leans back against the kitchen counter. "You hungry?"

Lark throws herself onto the sofa that they inherited with the house. "We were just finishing our burgers when you called. We were *going* to the movie." Petulance mixes with concern in Lark's voice.

Molly hadn't asked any questions when Ruby called her. Ruby's tone had probably put her off. Back at the salon, Antoinette's face had registered somewhere between hurt and confusion when Ruby asked for a rain check from their regular Thursday girls' night. Ruby didn't intend the edge in her voice, but it cut Antoinette just the same.

Ruby is going to have to explain everything, to Margaret and Molly, to her boyfriend, Chaz, to Antoinette. To Lark. First, though, she has to understand it, believe it, herself.

THREE

"Can we watch one here? A movie?" Lark asks.

Ruby nods. "Your pick."

Lark slides off the sofa, opens the oak armoire, runs her finger down the videocassettes stacked beside the TV—Ruby has yet to upgrade the collection to DVD. *"Singin' in the Rain?"*

"Again?" Ruby says. "Whatever. But bath first. You reek of horse."

"We rode out at Rancho Enchanto." Lark still uses her years-old mispronunciation of Rancho Encantada, the fancy horse stables and residential development just north of Santa Fe. "I got to ride Gus."

Ruby follows Lark into the bathroom sandwiched between the two bedrooms. When the tub is filled, Ruby sits on the toilet lid while Lark soaks the dirt and sweat and summer off her lithe body. Clyde sits at Ruby's feet, his chin resting on the edge of the tub.

"You got camp tomorrow," Ruby says. Lark has attended the twice-a-week Girls Inc. day camp for the last few years, part of Ruby's patchwork of care for Lark while school is not in session.

"Yeah. The image lady is coming again." Already a crisp line divides Lark's legs into the creamy part shielded from sun by her shorts and the bronzed lower limbs.

"Images?" If Ruby can keep Lark talking, she might be able to fake her way through a cheery bath time.

"Of us. Girls. Last time she showed us pictures from magazines and stuff. And asked us what we thought the pictures said about the girls in them. She showed us how the people who make the clothes put us into either 'Girly girl' or 'Naughty girl.' Like the T-shirts that say 'Boys Will Be Toys.' The ones you won't let me wear."

Ruby shakes her head at Lark's bubble beard. Sometimes the kid is nine going on forty, sometimes nine going on four. "The ones you wouldn't be caught dead wearing."

"Well, anyway, we're making our own shirts. Tomorrow we get to draw what we want on them and then she's going to take the pictures and put them on the shirts." Lark pauses to scrub her face with the washcloth. "We're supposed to draw things that show who we are. Like it's okay to use 'Princess' or 'Flirt' if we want, but what else are we?"

Lark washes her "toeses," chanting the "Moses" song from the movie they'll watch after her bath. "Do you think the other kids will think I'm a total nerd if I put old movies on my list of things I like, on my shirt?" Her elfin face is earnest.

"Some of them might." Ruby folds her arms in her lap. "You can't control what other people think, baby bird. Sometimes you can't even control what you think. You can only control how you act."

"Rinse, please." Lark tilts her foamy wig backward, ropy collarbones jutting out, the shampoo aroma a halo of that peculiar mix of strawberry and banana that the makers call kiwi. Ruby fills the plastic cup again and again from the faucet, and pours it over her daughter's corn-silk head. "Besides. Why would you care about the thoughts of someone silly enough not to like old movies? Okay, stand up." Ruby holds up a blue towel. "Just be your own wonderful self."

The phone rings as Ruby enfolds Lark in the towel. A second ring, a third, shriek. Ruby rushes to the kitchen counter, picks up the receiver as if it might bite.

"Hello?" Her voice is old-man gruff as much from fear as the instinct to disguise. "No, no. There's no one here by that name."

Slamming the receiver onto its cradle, she lays her hot forehead against the cool counter. A telemarketer, just a pesky telemarketer asking for Mrs. Levy.

She raises her head, clasps her hands behind her clammy neck, then she hurries into the living area. A yank on the cord beside the large picture window sends the rarely closed blinds crashing to the sill. Coughing through a cloud of sparkly dust, she leans over the sofa, peers through the slats, down the street, looking for cherry-topped cars or big, black government sedans.

Ruby's brain scoffs at her flailing heart. *They're not going to call first; they're just going to kick in the door.*

FOUR

In the shed, Ruby works her grandfather's special concoction into the weary bones of the wood. Mineral oil, carnauba wax, and lots of elbow grease.

This slab of wood gets a rubbed-in dose of Ruby's fears, too. The furniture she makes is not typical Santa Fe, no pine and antlers but rather clean lines and Midwestern sensibility. Hers is a rescue mission, salvaging used and abused planks from castoffs, painstakingly removing nails, and caressing life back into their arthritic joints. Fur-*nurture*, she thinks of it.

A splash of white moonlight from the door mixes with the yellower overhead light into a lurid square on the workbench. Ruby rubs and rubs the oil into the wood, as if quenched grain will reveal the future like tea leaves scattered in a cup. Yet she sees only the past, all those hours spent in the basement watching, and helping, her grandfather work.

He died when Ruby was twelve; she has coopted the story of his fall from an ornery John Deere tractor to explain the absence of Lark's father. After he died, Nana avoided his corner of the basement as if it were a pit of snakes, but Ruby fiddled there now and then, kept his tools from rusting. And all those basement lessons come flooding back to her with the tang of sawdust and turpentine each time she steps into this shed.

She listens to her grandfather's music when she works, old standards she finds only on AM and only on a clear night like tonight. What would he say, what would her grandmother say, about this mess?

You've made your bed, Nana's voice whispers in her ear, and Ruby thinks about all those moments that added up to make this particular bed. She never even considered that someone was out there looking for Lark. Ruby could have made it right, back at the beginning, but now, now she isn't sure anything can be right ever again.

From the shelf above the workbench, a toddler Lark stares at her. Picking up the ceramic frame, Ruby traces Lark's face with a finger. Cow eyes, that's what her grandmother would have called those huge pools of knowing. Lark has always been cautious, watchful, as if she knew from the start that life, even mountain life, was not to be trusted.

Back then, Ruby thought of life as a cosmic crazy quilt. Like maybe on the way to being born, a person was handed a gunnysack full of scraps to be pulled out one by one. At the time, the pieces might seem totally unrelated to each other, ugly even. A person might come across a piece that didn't make any sense, or hurt someone terribly. Yet at the end of her days, she would be able to take a big step back and see that all those raggedy scraps came to be stitched together by time and toil, and tears, into a beautiful blanket that would warm her ancient bones.

Back then, she truly believed it was all some grand scheme. She lost Nana; she found Lark.

Back then, Ruby thinks, *I didn't know squat.*

"Ahem."

Ruby's heart slams against her rib cage as the sound of a voice clearing punctures the quiet of the night. *This is it*, she thinks.

FIVE

She is still calculating the distance to the house, to Lark, when she recognizes Chaz's little-boy chuckle. Her elbows smack the table as her knees sway in her relief.

Chaz swings a white mouth shield from his finger. "You promised to wear your mask."

"But I am," Ruby says under her still-heavy breath. She gestures for him to follow her into the house, motions to the refrigerator as she moves toward the hall.

Summer moonlight shimmers across Lark's bed. Clyde raises his head, his eyes accusing, scolding, then nuzzles back onto Lark's hip. The dog, a stray that Lark brought home a few years ago, is one-quarter heeler, three-quarters God-knows-what, and 100 percent heart. He and Lark sleep each night like embracing lovers, moving in a bed ballet.

All the Larks this child has ever been are here on that silver-washed face, the watchful infant, the four-year-old who ruled the salon, the seven-year-old who played nurse to Ruby when she had the flu, the imp, the old soul, the all-eyes-and-heart kid who tries to rescue every animal in sight. They are all here, a part of the Lark asleep in this bed. Ruby can't imagine a Lark other than this sum total of all the experiences the two of them have shared.

Lark's eyes open, two slashes of obsidian against milky skin. "To the moon and back, Mama," she mumbles in a fairy-tale voice.

"Shh," Ruby says. "Go back to sleep. I love you, too."

Ruby pulls the door shut, crosses to the living area, watches Chaz drain his beer bottle in a few quick swallows. His charcoal hair is finger-raked; he sports a three-day beard.

"I just got off duty. Your message sounded . . ." Chaz rubs his T-shirt at his breastbone. When he removes his finger, the shirt is marked for a second with the indentation of the Saint Christopher medal that he always wears, a gift from his aunt Tia when he joined the police force. "What's going on?"

She plops down beside him on the squishy sofa. "Just the usual."

His dark eyes scan her face.

She reaches out, traces the stubble along his sharp jaw. "Really."

"You always do that, chew on your lip, when something's bothering you."

Ruby shifts away from him, feeling shy, uncertain. Her hand brushes against the bump that used to be her waistline, jerks away. In all her pacing and hair pulling, she has avoided this part of the equation, this lima bean inside her. With her long waist and birthing hips, a baby has lots of room to hide; though she's barely showing, she's four months along.

"I missed you."

Ruby leans against his solid bulk. "I missed you more."

Antoinette had bugged Ruby for weeks to meet her brother. "He's a bit of a player, but, girl, you need some fun." Antoinette kept pestering her, at the salon or over dinner. "Just one drink. Just once."

Ruby hadn't been on a date—a real date—in years. When Lark was a toddler, she went out for a few months at a time with this Bob here or that Bill there. She even had a few sleepovers, at the guy's place, of course, and only planned in advance, with the Ms on hand to baby-sit. She was young still, only twenty-seven, and she was single. She was supposed to be out there hitting the bars. Frankly, she was content with her life the way it was.

But one night, after a couple of margaritas at a favorite hole-in-the-wall Mexican restaurant, Ruby said, "Why not?" Antoinette whipped out her cell phone and called her brother, before Ruby could change her mind, she said. And when Ruby looked up from her enchilada plate, up almost to the strings of lights and hundreds of piñatas hanging from the ceiling, dark-stranger eyes stared at her from beneath little-boy lashes.

At first she thought he was just another too-macho, too-full-of-himself mama's boy. Until he smiled.

"I'm Chaz," he said. He joked about appearing too eager, running like a dog to Antoinette's whistle. But he was pulling double shifts the next few days and wanted to stop by to say hello.

Now, here they are almost three years later. Both of them are still getting used to the idea of a baby, trying to figure everything out. Can they make something permanent work with Chaz's crazy schedule? With Lark? And now, nothing about that *everything* looks the same.

Ruby breaks the silence. "How was your day?"

"Just the usual," Chaz says with a smirk. He is a detective on the Santa Fe police force, heading up the gang-intervention unit. He, too, is a rescuer of children. Yet Ruby is terrified that he will never understand, let alone accept, what she did.

SIX

The first of the summer peaches rest like crescents of sunset in the pie dish. Ruby dots them with biscuit mix, dusts them with sugar, pops the cobbler into the oven.

"So how was camp?" She dumps steaming macaroni into a two-legged colander.

In her bright green Girls Inc. T-shirt, hair a ponytail of white cotton candy, Lark doodles in a notebook at the kitchen table. "Actually, kinda cool." "Actually" is her new favorite word.

Ruby slices the hot dogs into nickels, tosses them into the cheese sauce like coins in a well, stirs in a spoonful of horseradish. After calling the salon to cancel her appointments, she herself spent the day at the library, searching computer databases, chewing on every morsel of the scant information beyond what was contained in the article.

"Mo-om."

Ruby jumps at Lark's bleat. Her hand knocks into the drain board; a coffee cup shatters in the sink. She turns to see Lark pointing at the kitchen counter, at the groceries Ruby has yet to put away. "What, what?"

"The environment? Phosphates? Our rivers? *That's* not the good detergent."

Nestled in a cloud of white—paper towels, a four-pack of toilet paper, a jug of bleach—the bright orange Tide box is conspicuous. For a moment, Ruby is miles, and years, away. "Oh, uh, someone must have put it in my cart by mistake." She knows that she is the "someone," grabbing the laundry soap she hasn't used in ages.

The shards of pottery are Anasazi bronze gashes against the creamy porcelain of the sink. She unwinds a wad of paper towels, scoops up the mess, tosses it into the garbage can. *Pull yourself together,* she tells herself as she finishes preparing the meal.

The blue willow plates are a riot of color, macaroni and cheese, green beans, a smile of cantaloupe with raspberry and blueberry teeth. A regular June Cleaver Ruby is, without the heels and pearls. She sets Lark's plate in front of her, takes the catty-corner seat.

Lark looks down at the plate, over at Ruby. "Thanks, Mom. But what happened to pizza night?"

Lately, Ruby has been so tired by Friday evening that calling in a pizza order is the pinnacle of her culinary ambitions. "I was just in the mood. . . . So what did you draw for your shirt?"

Lark eats a forkful of macaroni and gives Ruby a cheese-streaked grin. "You'll see."

Ruby pushes food around her plate. Playing June Cleaver is one thing; swallowing food is quite another under these circumstances. While Lark eats, Ruby flips through the spiral notebook, pages crammed with self-conscious schoolgirl cursive and guileless doodles.

As usual, Ruby is astounded at the complexity of this child's thoughts. She writes poems full of love and loss and longing, when the biggest heartbreak she has suffered—so far anyway—is seeing a deer dying at the side of a road. "Where do you come up with this stuff?"

Lark kisses a raspberry with an exaggerated smack, pushes it through her cherub lips. "I don't know."

What will these poems look like when her heart breaks for real? Ruby turns her body away from Lark as a single fat tear smacks the page, spattering lilac ink like a bug on a windshield. She remembers reading somewhere that an African language has two different words for rain, the plump round female drops and the sharp needles of males. This tear, she thinks, is definitely a mother tear, a pendulous, pregnant mother of a tear.

Ruby busies herself with Lark's backpack, empties the bottom-of-the-bag detritus onto her lap. A few colored pencils, a crumpled granola bar wrapper, a Baggie of uneaten carrots. She assumes the carefully folded piece of white paper is one of those pop-up Ouija games the kids make, providing sage answers to all the questions of the universe, like will Tom kiss Jane on the playground. *If only,* Ruby thinks. Then she hears the tinkle of metal inside.

SEVEN

"What's this?"

"Nothing." Lark's cheeks flush pink. "Just a present. From the new girl. Olivia. They were her mom's. She gave some to Numi, too."

When Ruby unfolds the notebook paper, a pair of earrings drops into her palm. Dangly earrings, silver and amethyst and pearl. Pierced earrings. She looks at Lark, waits.

"You said I can pierce them."

"When you're eleven."

Lark takes a swig of milk. "But . . ."

Ruby sets her plate on the floor, where Clyde promptly inhales her supper. The plate clinks against the tile as his enthusiastic tongue pushes it across the floor. "You're nine. And these are very grown-up earrings."

She carries the rest of the dishes to the sink and stacks them with the pans and the star-holed colander, then turns back to look at Lark. "Do you really want someone to bribe you to be her friend?"

Lark shrugs her shoulders while Ruby grabs an oven mitt off the counter, pulls the dessert out of the oven. The smell, of golden sugar and syrupy nectar, transports her across miles and years to her grandparents' kitchen. For a moment, she aches down to her viscera to be there, safe amid the speckled white Formica and harvest gold appliances.

A headshake brings her back to Santa Fe. "And are you sure Olivia's mother gave her the earrings? What if she just took them? You know the difference between right and wrong. If she is giving you something that doesn't belong to her . . ."

Ruby's words echo in her own head.

Later, Ruby takes pajamas from the dresser drawer—boy jammies like Ruby's. Neither of them likes to be tangled in a nightgown.

"I'm sorry, Mama." Lark sits on her bed, looking like Clyde after he's been scolded. "Don't be mad. I'll give them back."

Ruby hugs Lark against her chest. "No, baby. I mean, yes, I know you'll do the right thing and give them back. But I'm not mad at you. I'm . . . it's . . ."

She feels Lark's hand patting her back, like she did as an infant when Ruby held Lark against her shoulder, and Ruby strains with every cell of her body to keep from wailing as if she were the infant. She forces her face into a semblance of composure, turns down Lark's bed and fluffs the pillow, straightens the stack of books on the nightstand. Lark devours library books like some kids do candy bars. "You can read for a while."

"Mama?" Lark asks for the daffy song, a ritual she abandoned as too babyish a year or so ago.

As she sings the familiar verses, Ruby tucks the purple sheets along one side of Lark's bony frame. Clyde nestles against the other. Maybe Lark needs the comfort of their old routine because of the earring incident, or because her antennae are twitching at the signal of Ruby's distress. Probably a combination of both.

At Lark's doorway, Ruby pauses. "When you're eleven, we'll pierce those ears. And buy you your own special earrings." And as her mouth says the words, her heart prays that she isn't telling her daughter yet another lie.

EIGHT

The Santa Fe sky is O'Keeffe blue above the Saturday flea market. The light that attracts all those artists to this corner of the world really is different, and the God-skies, billowy clouds backlit and pierced by sunbeams, are amazing. The flea market, though, reminds Ruby of a refugee camp in some drought-ravaged corner of the world. Rows of canvas and plastic awnings tethered to rusted-out campers, rickety card tables piled with the dregs of attics and garages, broken blenders and eight-track tapes and chipped tchotchkes.

One person's junk is another person's, well, junk. Yet if that person sifts patiently enough through the yard-sale rejects, a real treasure can be found, a hundred-year-old reliquary or an ancient African fertility stick. And then, interspersed among the clutter, are the booths of true artisans, the wares of potters and weavers and sculptors and painters worthy of the upscale galleries in town.

Ruby and Jay's booth is down the second dusty aisle, between a rug dealer with heaps of Indian rugs, their reds and oranges flapping on clotheslines in the always present breeze, and a jeweler with three slender glass cases, chunky turquoise displayed on black velvet lining. Across the aisle is Benny, who sells local honey and all sorts of gadgets and tools. In the past, Ruby has marveled at the number of people who can't resist owning a scary-looking dental hygienist's tartar scraper of their own. Today, though, she can barely focus on her own work.

Near the front of the booth, Lark's head shimmers in the sunlight as she lures passersby under the blue canvas awning. Clyde wiggles at her side, greeting each dog like a long-lost sibling. Assorted tables, bureaus large and small, and patio chairs intermingle with displays of Jay's pewter vases and bowls and serving utensils, Arthur Court knockoffs that he brings back from regular runs to Mexico. Ruby's reborn furniture gleams as proudly as the platters in the Saturday sun, and their booth, as usual, is crowded.

This furniture business just sort of *happened*. She made a changing table for Lark from a garage-sale desk, then some patio chairs for the Ms's anniversary and a lamp table for Rosa, a stylist at the salon, from the pieces of an old armoire. Then requests started coming in from friends of friends of friends. Her most popular deck chairs are a simple assemblage of the scraps of wood left over from other projects.

On a regular day, working the flea market makes Ruby's head spin. Today it is in danger of flying off into the stratosphere. Thoughts are fireflies flitting around inside her skull, tiny explosions bursting here and there and there, like the ones she caught as a child and put in a mason jar next to her tall, narrow bed, watching them in the dark until her eyelids were leaden. She deals with customers on autopilot—yes, she makes them herself; yes, they are reclaimed wood; that one there she made from a dining room set she found in an estate sale down in Lincoln; yes, she takes custom orders—while she bashes a useless net around the inside of her head, trying to capture the panic of fireflies.

What should she do? How can she live with herself if she doesn't come forward; how can she live without Lark if she does? She spots Beer Barrel Pete ambling past her booth. Pete, with a face of desert wood and a waterfall of silver hair down to his waist, is a flea-market fixture and purveyor of all kinds of goods, mostly illegal. *Passports*, she thinks. Pete helped Ruby out before; she's sure he would do it again. Maybe Mexico is the answer. Jay has friends and connections down there. Maybe she and Lark could just disappear, start over.

Could she make a new life for them on the run, always looking over her shoulder? Would that life be better for Lark than the alternative? What will happen to Ruby? Lark, Ruby, Lark, Ruby. How will either of them survive? What will they each look like when—if—they reach the other side of this long, dark tunnel?

Ruby understands the marrow-deep determination of that other mother, who never gave up hope. She has that same mother-tiger determination to protect Lark. All morning, she has kept one eye on her daughter, an ear listening for a frantic bark from Clyde. Watching for a suit-clad arm trying to grab Lark from the booth.

NINE

When the tide of people ebbs in the afternoon, Ruby and Lark take a break. Ruby spreads an old quilt on the ground behind Jay's trailer, and they have a picnic in the dust. After Chaz left last night, Ruby fried chicken in the cast-iron skillet. She made potato salad, giving herself a mini-facial in the steam over the stove. The brownies got an extra squeeze of chocolate syrup. And this morning before she woke Lark, she tucked their lunch into the neoprene cooler that staves off botulism so much better than the old wicker basket.

Every moment, every gesture, of these days cries for ceremony, not knowing how long they will last. Toasters come with guarantees, not life. A person never knows when a building is going to crumble to the ground around his ankles or a bus careen around a corner to flatten him like a cartoon character. A person never knows when her daughter is going to be snatched away, shattering her life as surely as bricks and tires.

Lark tears off a piece of chicken, tosses it toward Clyde. He nabs it out of the air, jaws snapping shut like one of those fly-catching plants. The food hits his stomach without touching his mouth; now you see it, now you don't.

"Mmm," Lark says through a mouthful of chicken. "Almost as good as Nana's."

Ruby swats at her leg. "And just how would you know, seeing as how you never tasted Nana's chicken?"

"That's what you always say." Lark shrugs. "Like you're trying to steal her ribbon from the county fair."

Ruby just shakes her head at her wise-beyond-years daughter—and the truth of the statement. All these years and it is still Nana's pan and Nana's recipe. "It's not a competition, baby bird. I'm just trying to do her proud."

Lark unloads a heaping forkful of potato salad into her mouth. "Mmm . . ." She giggles, but her potato-salad smile doesn't fill her big brown eyes, doesn't even reach them. She's definitely putting on a show.

Leaning back on her elbows, Ruby decides just to soak up the moment with her daughter. Maybe Lark's memory will hold on to a crumpled edge of this picnic. Maybe even if she doesn't remember this particular day, a warm, sepia-tinged feeling will wash over her when she picnics with her own daughter someday.

God only knows what is going to happen to her and Lark, but just for now Ruby wants to be selfish and proud that her wonderful sprite is the product of moments like this, moments spent with Ruby.

"Aunt Wonnie!"

Lark's cry yanks Ruby from her ruminations.

"Hey, Larklette. What's the deal, pickle?" When Antoinette plops down on the quilt, Clyde jumps up to greet her. Ruby and Lark both manage to grab their lemonade cups; only the potato salad container and a couple of brownies are trampled in the excitement. "Fried chicken. Fancy."

"Yeah," Lark says. "Mom's trying to bribe me. She just hasn't told me why."

Ruby busies herself, brushing brownie crumbs and clumps of potato salad into her napkin. She averts her eyes from both her daughter and her best friend.

"See what I mean, jelly bean?"

"I see nothin'," Antoinette says. "I know nothin'."

"Then you, Aunt Wonnie, are as blind as my pet bat." Lark's nickname for Antoinette comes from her thinking that when Antoinette first introduced herself, like so many other grown-ups, she was telling Lark to call her "Auntie" something. Their banter comes from years of the three of them taking road trips around the state in search of wood for Ruby's furniture.

"Speaking of blind," Ruby says. "How was your date last night?"

Lark whistles. "Must've been real good for you to come out to the flea market to dish about it."

Antoinette laughs. "You, Miss Sassy Pants, are getting entirely too sassy for your pants."

"But you hate the flea market," Lark says.

"Well?" Ruby asks.

Antoinette shoots Ruby a look. "If only I was blind."

"Beauty's only skin deep, Aunt Wonnie. Skin deep."

Ruby knows Antoinette is not referring to her date. She digs a newspaper sleeve from her tote bag, holds it out to Lark. "Take Clyde on poop patrol."

Lark stomps to her feet. "You always make me miss the good stuff."

Ruby points her thumb over her shoulder. "Go. Then it's back to work for the both of you."

As she and Clyde step around the trailer, Lark calls out over her shoulder, "Tyrant. They have child labor laws, you know."

TEN

This restaurant down off Guadalupe is one Ruby usually avoids. A favorite of hotel concierges, it teems with tourists, though she can't understand why anyone would come to Santa Fe, green chili capital of the universe, to eat Italian. The cavernous glass-and-tile space is crowded and loud, especially on a Saturday evening. But Chaz decided they needed something different, festive, so here they are.

Lark points to Ruby's water glass. "The book says you have to drink lots of milk."

Ruby only recently told Lark about the baby, after she commented on Ruby's blossoming bustline. Ever since, Lark has been reading pregnancy manuals in between Harry Potters. Now she makes a big production of slurping her Coke—Coke that Ruby can no longer drink. Ruby knows Lark is trying to get a rise out of her. She is tired from the flea market. She is hungry from the wait for their table. She is nine.

Ruby is not very good company right now, either. Chaz asks, "Would you like an appetizer?" and she thinks, *What should I do?* Chaz says, "How was the flea market?" and she thinks, *Antoinette didn't buy my anniversary-of-Nana's-death story one bit.*

The plate of antipasto is vibrant against the white tablecloth, like a Santa Fe garden in June. When she first moved here, she had to get used to the unending sea of brown, brown hills Dalmatian-dotted with scrubby piñon bushes, brown roads, brown adobe buildings. Yet Ruby soon appreciated the subtle gradations of brown, and found her craving for color sated in little slashes—lilac bushes heavy with blooms like grapes in a vineyard, windows blue-trimmed to keep evil spirits away.

As she thinks about going to jail, more than hard-core inmates or lack of privacy, the thought of gray walls, gray floors, gray food makes her feel as if her blood is puddling at her ankles. Ruby could face years in prison. A lifetime without Lark. And she doesn't even want to think about what will happen to the baby inside her.

Ruby breaks off a chunk of bread, dabs it in olive oil. Her daughter picks at a salad, which Lark insisted she wanted even though she rarely eats greens. While Chaz makes conversation. He's trying to be sweet, really, the nice dinner, paying special attention to Lark.

Catching his eye, Ruby smiles an "I love you." He squeezes her thigh, his eyes answering, "I love you more."

Chaz doesn't talk much about his work, especially not in front of Lark, and tonight is no exception. But, like the dishes at the kitchen window across the restaurant, he has plenty of topics all lined up. Sports. Sports is always a good one. Lark is a sports fan. He talks baseball stats, he talks football preseason. Lark just moves lettuce around on her plate, and Ruby bites into another piece of bread, a less painful way of biting her tongue.

The waitress takes away the antipasto and Lark's uneaten salad before serving the main course. As she sets a plate in front of Chaz, her arm seems to go out of its way to brush his sleeve. She is pretty, the waitress, young, thin. Reminding Ruby that *she* is not so young, or so pretty, and very soon will be bigger than the table. Chaz smiles up at the girl, one of his Chaz specials, and the waitress's face flushes. Reminding Ruby that her boyfriend is handsome and gets hit on regularly in this man-starved town. He's a consummate flirt, harmless, Ruby trusts. And at least for now, he's her flirt.

Ruby chokes down her chicken parmigiana. Chaz tried to cajole her into ordering the fish special, said that omega-3 is good for the baby, that she needed the protein, until Ruby cut him off with a look that could fell redwood. Then she switched from pasta to the chicken, a boneless breast to throw him a bone. At least the restaurant, despite the chef's special, doesn't smell fishy. She hasn't had any weird cravings yet, but strong odors send her running to the john these days.

Chaz and Lark, she notices, each have their own technique with their spaghetti; Chaz is a cutter, Lark a spinner. Yet they both end up slurping noodles in the end. Ruby thinks there must be something profound in that one, that no matter what, everyone has to slurp noodles in the end. But she is much too tired for profound right now.

Chaz leans back in his chair, looks from Ruby to Lark to Ruby. "Let's just run away."

The clatter of Ruby's fork against her plate echoes across the restaurant. Her mind-reading boyfriend has just voiced the thought that has been screaming in her head all day. "You would . . . could you really?"

"Sure." Chaz grasps Ruby's hand. "You, me, one imp, and an imp-to-be. Las Vegas, baby."

"The real Las Vegas," Lark says.

Chaz nods. "The real one. And after, we can do it all over again proper, with Father Paul and my folks."

"Two weddings!" Lark squeals.

Ruby's rib cage collapses against her gut. Chaz is joking about eloping, not talking about forever running away. A couple of thin gold bands won't solve her mess.

Chaz looks down at Ruby's belly. "They're going to figure it out eventually."

"I can just stay away," Ruby says.

"Right." Chaz chuckles. "As if that won't raise questions when you don't show up tomorrow. Or the next, say, twenty Sunday dinners?"

Chaz's family is tight-knit, Catholic, Hispanic. Four generations of mamas have ruled that roost from the same casita on a narrow lane off Canyon Road. They are everything Ruby isn't, yet they have embraced her, and Lark, in their elbow-to-elbow, something's-always-cooking family. But they don't know about the baby.

Ruby wonders how embracing the Monteros will be when they find out she's pregnant. Not to mention her other little bombshell.

ELEVEN

Early Sunday morning, Ruby steals into Lark's room, whispers to Clyde to keep her daughter safe. Then she slips out of the house. The sun hasn't yet burned away the haze of dawn as she walks down the hill, and the air still holds on to the coolness of night.

The doors are open at the little Episcopal church. Ruby pads down the red-carpeted center aisle and slides into a pew. The few times she and Lark have attended this church, Ruby felt an unfamiliar comfort in the repeated ritual, as if, like the mountains, the ritual gave her something to which she could cling. And she desperately wants to find some of that comfort today.

Growing up, Ruby and her grandparents attended the Congregational church in their Iowa town. Ruby remembers Nana running off with boiled chickens to prepare funeral casseroles in the church basement, or disappearing Tuesday mornings to the ladies' auxiliary. Her grandfather and Nana each had their own Bibles. On summer evenings, they sat on the wicker porch chairs reading them side by side.

Then after her grandfather died, Nana sort of lost interest in the church. She didn't seem mad at God; she still prayed and quoted to Ruby from her Bible all the time. Ruby figured she just couldn't bother to put on her Sunday best anymore.

Ruby didn't mind. She believes in God all right, but she's not sure she believes in organized religion. Over the years, she and Lark have visited many of the churches in town. They have gone with the Ms each December to the Our Lady of Guadalupe church for its namesake saint's festival, arriving before dawn to a chain of farolitos and a candlelit sanctuary. They have never missed attending a Christmas or Easter service *somewhere*. They have even attended a Jewish Seder. She wanted to expose Lark to as much as possible, then let her decide her own beliefs, rather than cram any one denomination down her throat. Especially when Ruby herself has felt closer to God on the mountaintops than she ever has in a pew.

But here, today, she finds herself craving all the organization she can get. As she bows her head, she's not even sure what to pray for. Yet she can't help feel, or hope anyway, that maybe God will hear whatever prayer that surfaces a little better in this quiet, sacred place.

She is still trying to formulate the words of a prayer when a black-robed pastor stops beside the pew. "Can I help?" His tone is soothing.

"I don't know," Ruby whispers.

The pastor sits down beside Ruby, folds his hands in his lap. The heavy silver cross he wears on a chain around his neck gleams red, like an omen, from the sunlight that ripples through the eastern stained-glass window. This man is not the elderly rector Ruby has seen here before; he is young, not more than Ruby's age. His patient demeanor is disarming.

"What if someone has done something that they didn't think was so wrong at the time, but turns out to have been very wrong to other people? What would God say to that?"

"We Episcopalians don't undertake confession as the Catholics do. Here, your confession, and your forgiveness, is between you and the Lord." The pastor pauses, rubs the cross at his chest, as if it were a rosary, as if maybe he wasn't sure those mackerel snappers, as her grandfather used to call the Catholics in their town, didn't have the right idea after all. "Just remember that the Lord always forgives. Always."

One of Ruby's fifth-grade classmates used to tell playground stories about catechism, which the Catholic children attended every Wednesday night for a whole year. Ruby thought it sounded like a pretty good deal: once a week you sit in a booth and tell a priest your transgressions. If you haven't done anything bad that week, or maybe if you don't want to say what you did do, you just say something minor, like that you had bad thoughts about your parents. And voilà!, you were absolved of everything, clean as the day you were born, all for a few Hail Marys and a lecture from a screen-shrouded priest.

The pastor stands, places a hand on Ruby's shoulder. She tries to channel his goodness, his grace, from his fingers, through her shirt, and into her skin. "I'm here, if you want to talk."

After he leaves, Ruby stares into the middle distance. It clings to her like the odor of mothballs on wool, the scent of unconfessed sin. Will everyone else smell it on her, too?

TWELVE

At the Monteros' front door, Ruby drapes her arm across Lark's back and closes her eyes. She is trying hard enough to keep her head above water without wading into this emotional pool. *You can do it*, she thinks. *Just act normal.* Then the door swings open, and she and Lark are swept into the swirling waters of Monteroland.

"Come in, come in." Chaz's mother, Celeste, smells of oregano and affection. She places her hands on Lark's cheeks, kisses her forehead. Ruby flinches just a bit when Celeste hugs her. She's wearing a loose sundress, but she worries that Celeste will notice her expanding bustline and thickening waist.

When Chaz steps into the hall from the living room, his is a photonegative of Celeste's greeting, a big smack on the lips for Ruby, and for Lark a hug that lifts the kid off her feet. "Can you handle spaghetti two meals in a row?"

Lark cocks her head. "As if you really need to ask."

Chaz pulls Lark into the living room, where the men are yelling at the television and elbowing and high-fiving each other. Lark squeezes into a spot on the sofa between Chaz's father and an uncle, her "What's the score?" barely audible over the macho roar.

Chaz's father, after whom Chaz is named, has been saddled with the nickname Chunk since he was a skinny little boy. Like a self-fulfilling prophecy, he has long since grown into the moniker. He is shorter than Chaz and his sisters—their height comes from Celeste's side—as wide as he is tall. He has always been uneasy if not unfriendly around Ruby, but he's taken a shine to Lark. As he ruffles Lark's hair, says something that makes her laugh, Ruby follows Celeste to the kitchen.

From this heart of the house, Celeste is cooking her way around the globe alphabetically. This week they are in Italy; last week, Hungary. Ruby takes a seat on a stool at the counter and lets the voices and aromas wash over her. Chunk's great-grandparents built the original house. Its bones, and grace, have been well preserved through several updates. The history, the legacy, are layers of the thick adobe walls.

The older women jostle each other as they dance between stove top and oven and counter, putting finishing touches on the meal, pulling bright colored platters and bowls from the pine cabinets. Across the room, the younger generation, Antoinette and her cousins, set the long farm table with Fiestaware the colors of the New Mexico heavens: sunset red, sunrise yellow, big sky blue.

They all talk at once, voices in a perpetual game of rock, paper, scissors, Antoinette's new job at the courthouse, a cousin's new boyfriend, an aunt's old pains. Sunday dinner at the Monteros' is as much a ritual as morning Mass.

"Off your tush." Aunt Tia pokes Ruby, points to the refrigerator. "Get the salad on the table." Despite her redundant name—Tia is Spanish for "aunt"—she is Ruby's favorite of Chaz's aunts. Tia and two others are Celeste's sisters; one is Chunk's sister.

"Grab the water pitcher while you're there," Antoinette calls. Her own sister, Linda, holds the bucket of ice.

Ruby is grateful that they assign her these tasks, making her a part of the family rather than treating her like company. As she pours water in each heavy blue goblet, she tries once again to imagine growing up in this house, surrounded by abundance and mess and boisterous relatives, so different from the quiet space she and her grandmother inhabited.

All conversation halts as, in a grand crescendo, Celeste dumps a mound of pasta into the biggest bowl, steam rising like a choir of angels. In the time it takes Ruby to refill the water pitcher and return to the table, the TV is muted, children's washed hands are inspected, and the throngs crowd around the table for grace.

Antoinette grabs one of Ruby's hands in her slender fingers; the other is clasped in the farting uncle's dry, meaty palm. Lark is across the table, between Chaz and Linda, the baby of the family and the only one of the three siblings who is married. Ruby likes her fine, but her suburban life down in Albuquerque is very different from Ruby's or Antoinette's.

Chunk says grace, adding an entreaty for God to watch over the Dallas Cowboys as they train this summer. The amens are whispered, mumbled, spoken, then punctuated with the traditional Montero squeeze. Antoinette holds Ruby's hand a moment longer, gives it an extra squeeze, making Ruby feel all the guiltier for lying to her.

The dinner table looks like a crowded bazaar, platters circling, arms reaching, Chianti flowing. Ruby watches in awe as the prodigious amount of food disappears from the table. Even the mountain of pasta, which in most universes would be bottomless, is chiseled down to the platter in Monteroland.

Throughout the meal, Ruby thinks she's faking it just fine. No one seems to notice that she doesn't touch her wine, and for the first time in days, she is actually hungry, lustily munching warm, buttery garlic bread, shoveling in the rigatoni drenched in better-than-any-restaurant Bolognese sauce.

Then from across the table, a snippet of conversation wafts toward her. Lark and Chaz. Discussing soccer.

"When the community league starts up next spring," Chaz says, "how 'bout I help out with coaching your team."

"That would be awe-some, Chaz."

Ruby feels the color drain from her face. *Next spring.* There might not *be* a next spring. Her stomach flails. Ruby covers her mouth with her hand, pushes back from the table, overturning her chair. She runs to the bathroom, falling to her knees at the toilet just in time.

Chaz opens the door as she stands at the sink, mopping the sweat from her forehead with Celeste's guest towel of the month, cheery yellow with an embroidered beach umbrella.

"Well, that was one way to make the announcement," Chaz says. "Maybe a bit dramatic, but hey . . ."

Ruby stares at him a moment, not comprehending his words. And then it hits her. "Oh, God. Oh, no." The hot color floods back to her face. She buries her head against Chaz's chest. "Oh, no."

And he doesn't even know the real reason she puked.

THIRTEEN

"It's okay." Chaz chuckles. "They were going to find out anyway. Come on." He takes Ruby's hand and escorts her back to the big eat-in kitchen. The faces staring up at her range in expression from glee (Celeste and Tia) to amusement (Antoinette) to shock (most of the aunts and uncles) to embarrassment (that would be Lark) to what Ruby can only read as disgust or utter disappointment (Chunk).

Amid the chatter of "Are you okay?" and "When are you due?" and "Saltines worked for me," one comment stands out, the farting uncle's words sloshing in wine. "S'a disgrace, what it is. A kid of mine gets knocked up, I'll do some knocking around."

Ruby motions to Lark and heads for the front door before the shushing and hand slapping is over. As they reach the gate across the small courtyard, Chaz grabs her arm.

"Ruby, wait."

"You go back inside," Antoinette says to Chaz when she steps in beside him. "Deal with them." As Chaz retreats, she pulls Lark and Ruby to the bench swing that Ruby made for Celeste and Chunk's anniversary. "They'll come around."

Through the screen door, gruff voices collide with one another.

Show her some respect. Chaz.

Respect? The farting uncle.

Like she respected the sanctity of marriage? Chunk.

Like she's the first—like I'm the first in this family. Chaz again.

The swing glides back and forth as Antoinette pushes her feet against the ground. "He was my protector, you know, when we were in school. Worse than my dad when it came to checking out the guys. Gave one a black eye."

Ruby tries to imagine growing up with a brother who would punch a guy out for you, a brother or sister at all. She is too raw for any of this.

When Chaz returns, he motions to Lark and Ruby. "Come on, let's blow this taco stand."

"Do you really want to say *blow*?" Lark chirps.

FOURTEEN

Lark has morphed into one of those creepy ancestral paintings. From the sofa, her questioning eyes follow Ruby around the room. Ruby paces, opening drawers, sifting through Mrs. Levy's gadgets—garlic presses, apple corers, slicers, dicers, ricers, and a few items Ruby has yet to identify. While Lark watches.

Ruby had been shocked to learn that Mrs. Levy left the house and all its furnishings to her. The old woman was a difficult client to put it mildly, never happy with her hair, her nails. Ruby had just shown her the respect and kindness that had been ingrained in her, making house calls during those last weeks of withering. But Mrs. Levy had no family, and she had been very clear in her desire for Ruby to have the house.

This house has been a nest for her and Lark, safe, secure, since they moved in several years ago. Ruby usually relishes her Mondays off, puttering, cooking, spending time with Lark. Today, though, the house feels more like a cage.

"Why don't you take Clyde for a walk?"

On the sofa, Lark scratches behind the dog's ears. "That's okay."

"Molly dropped off some new paints and canvases."

"Maybe later."

Perhaps Ruby will make soup. Making soup is her winter therapy, arranging all those bright vegetables in tidy rows on the cutting board, dumping them into a stockpot aswirl with simmering spices. The soup won't make Ruby feel better; if only this were some physical ache or a simple summer cold that would cure itself with a week of chicken broth. But at least her hands would stay busy. *Idle hands,* Ruby hears Nana's gravelly voice say. Almost a decade gone, and the old sage still speaks to Ruby, maybe now more than back when she was alive. And always in those half phrases, letting Ruby's own mind complete the maxim.

"Can I—may I—have some gum?" Lark asks.

"Sure." Ruby fills the metal watering can, walks out to the back porch to quench an urn of geraniums. Clyde slinks around her, lifts a leg on a scraggly lilac branch, scurries back inside. He, too, knows something is going on.

Why does it always come back to the *if onlys*? If only Antoinette hadn't been late; if only the previous client had left any magazine but that one at Ruby's station. The only *if only* she isn't willing to entertain is the one about her actions nine years ago.

As she steps back into the kitchen, the sharp words slice into her soul. "Is this me?"

Lark stands in the living area, holding the tabloid page. On the old trunk that serves as a coffee table, Ruby's purse gapes open. The dog stares at Ruby, accusation brimming in his rheumy eyes. And all she can do is wish that her idiot brain had thought about what was in her purse when she told Lark she could have a piece of gum.

FIFTEEN

Lark grips the article in both hands, reading it over and over as if she will be tested on the facts someday. From the side table, she grabs a framed photograph—one of the first pictures Ruby snapped of her—holds it next to the newsprint. Her chocolate-syrup eyes shoot up to Ruby's face, registering the finest details, the pain, the fear, and, yes, the betrayal. Tossing the article and picture frame on the table, she stomps down the hall to Ruby's bedroom.

Ruby follows, Clyde padding beside her. Lark digs through the wide bottom drawer of the dresser, pushing Ruby's sweaters and winter socks aside. Stirring the drawer, Nana would call it, making a pot of sock soup.

Lark yanks the stuffed toy out from under the woolens, a limp-necked lavender and blush giraffe, one of the few items Ruby saved from Lark's childhood. Lark jumps to her feet, pushes past Ruby. Back in the living room, Lark picks up the article, studies the photo—an infant sprawled naked on a fur rug, a vivid purple and pink giraffe screaming for attention between pale skin and white fur.

"Is this me?" Lark's voice reeks of anger, confusion, and a little-girl wish for her mommy to tell her another lie.

"Shh. Baby, please." Ruby steps to the window, peers through the slats. The street is empty, but she can feel it out there, the past, the truth, hurtling toward them, a boulder crashing down her mountainside, snapping trees, devastating everything in its path. She twists the cord until the blind slats are snug, though such slight strips of aluminum will never stop that landslide. "Come sit down."

"No." Lark folds her arms against her chest. "Is it? Is it me?" She is small for nine, an old-soul sprite with gossamer hair. A truth this big will be a grenade tossed toward the feeble armor of those two skinny arms.

Ruby feels as if she is teetering at the edge of a flat world, wants to scoop up Lark and run, jump, praying all the way down to land someplace soft, mossy. She takes a deep breath. And tells her daughter about that day almost a decade ago.

For a moment, Lark just stands there. Then she hurls the giraffe across the room, crumples the page into a ball, throws it into the kiva. She trudges to her room with Clyde at her heels, her bony shoulders sag with the weight of it all.

Ruby resists the urge to follow them. Pulling the ball of paper from the kiva, she shakes off the soot, a vestige of the last spring fire that never got cleaned up. *Was this self-sabotage?* she wonders as she smoothes out the creases of cheap, weekly gossip paper. Why else would she have kept the article in her purse, unless deep down she wanted Lark to find it, wanted to force her decision?

She refolds the article, stuffs it into her pocket. From under a kitchen chair, she rescues the clump of faded, overloved giraffe, takes it back to her bedroom, slips it under the winter sweaters in the bureau. The drawer sticks as it always does. With a jerk on one handle, a lift on the other, the heavy wood slams against the frame, sealing this proof of her secret in a vault of layers and layers of time-yellowed paint.

Ruby forces herself to walk steadily back down the hall. The fear and confusion and hurt hang like basement dank outside Lark's doorway. Ruby steps into the room, approaches the bed, tugs at a corner of crumpled purple sheet, tucks the blanket around the tangle of daughter and dog.

"Go away."

Ruby pulls her hand to her side. "Lark, honey."

"Go away."

At the window, Ruby checks the locks, pulls the shade, turns back toward the bed. Clyde shifts, glares at Ruby with doggy reproach. Lark rolls over to face her. The breeze from the ceiling fan ruffles the honey hair around her face.

"You lied to me, Mama."

Ruby would sell her soul to stop the ache in Lark's eyes. If only she hadn't already made that deal nine years ago. The books on mothering, those weepy women on *Oprah*, they are all on the mark. The worst pain in the world is the pain of a mother who can't fix her child.

"Baby bird—"

"Go. Away."

One backward glance, that is all Ruby allows herself at the doorway. Lark lies there under the smoky purple comforter, expensive Calvin la-di-da Klein designer bedding that Lark had begged and begged to get for her last birthday. To think that just a handful of months ago, Lark thought her world would end if she didn't have grown-up sheets covering her little-girl body. To think that just a handful of months ago, Ruby thought she could keep her child happy, safe even, with a sackful of overpriced bedding.

She resists the urge to step back into the room, to tuck those sheets around her daughter's prostrate form and sing the daffy song. *Fancy linens and sentimentality aren't going to fix this one*, she thinks, as she crumples to the floor and sobs.

SIXTEEN

As the white afternoon light shifts to evening violet, Margaret and Molly show up, the greasy smell of Chinese food wafting around them like silk dragons in a parade. Margaret rustles in the kitchen, stashing takeout bags in the oven, while Molly heads down the hall. Strands of Molly's dulcet voice curl around Lark's higher-pitched tones, not quite damping the anguish.

"We'll go for a walk," Molly says when she reappears, herding Lark and Clyde toward the front door, where the Ms' two dogs wait and whine.

Ruby wants to scream "No!" She imagines a black sedan pulling up beside them out there on the road, Molly returning with dog but no daughter. *Be rational*, she tells herself. Even if an article in a weekly gossip rag generated new interest in an old case, they couldn't know Ruby was involved, couldn't have tracked them here. Yet. She swallows the scream in her throat and watches her daughter disappear out the door.

"Okay, spill." Matter-of-fact Margaret. She and Molly, the Ms Lark coined them, have been Ruby's ballast all these years.

The day she walked up to the Jeep in that strip mall parking lot, finding bone-tired Ruby and a whimpering baby, Margaret had taken charge, in her comforting take-charge way. The room she rented out above her hair salon was vacant; it wasn't much, but it was Ruby's if she wanted it while she waited for the car to be fixed. One day turned into two, into a week. Margaret suggested Ruby work off the rent at the salon, keep Lark there with her.

The salon receptionist job gave Ruby the flexibility she needed with Lark, and the "room" above was a light-filled homey studio that Molly had decorated with her own art. When Lark started first grade, Ruby enrolled at the cosmetology school out by the airport and earned her nail tech certificate, and Margaret added the manicure station to a corner of the salon. Lark grew up in that salon, and, well, Ruby guesses, she did, too. They made a family there. They made their life.

A single sharp crack sounds from the kitchen behind her. She flinches, ducks, waits. When she looks up, the cutting board sits on the counter, mocking, after sliding from behind the paper towel roll, smacking onto the tile as it has done so many times before.

And Margaret stares at her, with a combination of alarm and amusement. "Spill."

Ruby hesitates.

"Back porch," Margaret says, and Ruby heads for the side door.

Even with the shield of lilac bushes that encircle the small porch, Ruby feels exposed, naked, beyond the walls of the house. Margaret steps out beside her, holding two goblets of wine. Ruby looks at the glass, looks down at her belly.

"One won't hurt," Margaret says. "It's half full."

"Half empty, I think." Ruby forces a chuckle as she takes the goblet, sits in one of the deck chairs that she crafted with her own hands and her grandfather's tools. She passes Margaret the article.

Margaret's hazel eyes flick from line to line as she reads about the woman whose car was stolen from a gas station in Dallas, a car with her baby inside. Her cropped salt-and-pepper hair shines even in the fading light. "I guess I knew. That day in the parking lot. I just didn't know I knew until now."

And as dusk settles around them like silt, Ruby tells her story for the second time that day.

SEVENTEEN

"But how," Margaret asks. "How did you know what to *do* with a baby?"

"I bought a book. And I shadowed this lady." Ruby tells Margaret about the Wal-Mart glimmering in the dust on the edge of a Texas Panhandle town. As she stared at the rows and rows of baby formula cans, a shopping cart teeming with redheads stopped beside her. Two kids hung on the sides, one curled up underneath the basket, another teetering inside. And a baby about the size of Lark sleeping in a carrier up front. Every kid had the same fire-engine hair. The barest hint of that fire remained in the mother's lank locks, as if the years of child-rearing had leached the passion from the roots.

The woman made a beeline for the yellow formula and tossed several cans into her cart, smiling at Ruby as she loaded up diapers from across the aisle. Ruby waited until the cart careened around the corner, like a biblical burning bush tumbling in a West Texas wind. Then she mirrored the woman's choices of powdered formula and disposable diapers.

"It took me four tries to get the first diaper on." But Lark took to the bottle right away, making the cute smacking noises Ruby remembered from feeding calves on her friend's farm. Lark finished that first bottle right there in the Wal-Mart snack bar, slurping the last drops as if it were a soda-fountain malt, flipping the empty bottle on the table. Ruby read the formula label again, scanned the book's chapter on feeding, shrugged. At the snack bar counter, she asked the pimply kid to fill it halfway with water, afraid the baby might explode if overfed. Lark drank the second bottle at a more leisurely pace.

After the meal, they got back in the car and headed toward California and its beckoning ocean. In Albuquerque, they hit rush hour, traffic on the freeway creeping along through a maze of orange barrels to the spider web intersection of highways. Ruby didn't realize she had been spun north, not west, until just outside the San Juan Pueblo. Then before they reached the next exit, she spotted a sign that said Las Vegas was just one hundred and twenty miles ahead. She had watched enough entertainment news to know that Las Vegas wasn't far from Los Angeles; surely she could find a route to California from there.

As the last shards of sunlight were soaking into the mountains, the Jeep crested the hill above Santa Fe, and the persistent whine that Ruby had ignored since the big hill up to Cochiti mutated to a metal-on-metal grate. Taking the first exit, she steered the car toward a swarm of lights, like fireflies frolicking in the valley, and coasted into a strip-mall parking lot.

The baby woke before she could even think about the car. And as she was snapping Lark back into her sleeper, this time fastening the diaper, not backward, not sideways, on the first try, the voice pierced the crisp air. "Hi, I'm Margaret. Let me guess. You thought our Las Vegas was the one in Nevada."

She watches Margaret watching her, tries to imagine the view from Margaret's eyes. While Lark was growing from infant to adolescent, Ruby grew from a too-tall, mousy teenager to the confident mother she is today, or was yesterday anyway. The mousy is still there in her appearance, mousy brown eyes, mousy brown hair that Margaret trims once a month into short layers that feather around her face. If she were asked yesterday, though, she would have said that her demeanor isn't mousy anymore, but today she's not so sure.

"But why?" Margaret asks.

"I was nineteen and stupid." Ruby smirks at her belly. "As opposed to almost thirty and stupid." She takes a sip of the wine. "I wanted to be a wild child. Like my mother." She remembers so little of that first life. But she remembers this, the wildness. A photograph in her underwear drawer shows her parents standing by that shiny red car, laughing and hugging each other. And in a picture in her mind she sees herself in the backseat, car top down, her father driving, her mother riding shotgun, laughing, hair whipping in the wind.

"I had just lost my grandmother," Ruby says. "I had no one. I wanted to go back there, to California. I guess I thought maybe I could find my mother, some of her, there on the beach."

Margaret leans back, crosses her denim-clad legs. "And then?"

"And then came Lark. And you." Ruby gestures to the mountains, fading to purple beyond the backyard shed. "And this."

Back then, Ruby thought that what she wanted, what she needed, was that wild life, unrooted, washed clean every day by the tide. Such a change from the careful Iowa life, cultivated in tidy rows, that she had with Nana. The life her mother had fled.

But the truth is, Ruby is not her brave mother. She is timid, fearful, afraid of even the idea of constantly shifting sands, foam swirling around her ankles, tugging her out to sea. The craggy edges of mountains give her something to hold on to, and she needs something to hold on to.

She fills her mouth with the last of the wine from her glass and swallows as if she's trying to down a pill. "I've still never seen the ocean."

EIGHTEEN

"Are you ready to talk?"

Ruby's question is met with the murderous look perfected by girls long before they turn nine. She enters Lark's bedroom without an invitation, sits down on the floor beside the bed. Lark stands at her easel, scribbling furiously in black marker over the painting she has been working on with Molly. "Hey, I liked that one."

"I. Messed. It. Up." Lark spits her words. "It's ugly."

"Well, I liked it. Guess that means I like ugly, huh."

Lark shoots Ruby another glare, rips the page off the easel, and crumples it up.

"We're going to have to talk about this," Ruby says. "About what it means."

Lark throws the wadded paper to the floor. "It means you lied."

Ruby grabs her daughter by the wrist, tugs her to the floor beside her. They sit side by side, each of them with knees pulled into her chest, arms wrapped around shins. Clyde sprawls in the doorway, keenly watching his humans.

"You *lied* to me, Mama."

"I lied to everybody, baby."

Lark rests her head on her knees, with flexibility Ruby lost long before she was pregnant. "So my dad wasn't killed by a tractor?"

Ruby shakes her head. "Nope. Your great-grandpa was, though."

"I wasn't really born in Iowa?"

"Nope."

Clyde whines, plods over to them, brushes Ruby's knees as he darts in to lick Lark. Lark stays folded up, scrunches her face at the dog's tongue until Ruby manages to yank him away. Lark wipes her cheek against her arm, tucks her chin into the hollow between her bony knees. "And . . ."

Ruby tips her head against the mattress edge, as if bouncing her words off the ceiling will soften the blow to Lark. "And even though you didn't come from my body, I'm still just as much your mother."

"Okay." Lark jumps to her feet, picks up her crumpled artwork, tosses it into the wastebasket in the corner.

"Okay?" Ruby lifts her head, watching her daughter warily.

Lark steps back to her easel. "Okay." She picks up the marker, replaces its cap, drops it into her tackle box of supplies. "Okay, I forgive you. But you should have told me I was adopted."

Ruby lets her head fall back against the bed; her brain too heavy with thoughts to balance on a mere human neck.

"Mom, I said okay. But if it'll make you feel better, I can ground you."

NINETEEN

Later that night, Chaz sits on the blue cloud of sofa, beer in hand.

On the surface, their backgrounds couldn't be more different. Chaz holds a degree from the University of New Mexico; he goes to Mass with his family every Sunday of the world. He is rough-and-tumble, law-and-order. He owns a gun. Yet Ruby found a gentleness under those muscles, and his values were the same ones that Ruby had been steeped in, like she was a bag of Lipton in boiling water.

When Chaz walked her to the Jeep after they met at the Mexican restaurant, he pointed up to the half-full moon. "My little sister's right. You hung that one for sure."

And Ruby thought to herself, *Yes. And I'm over it, too.*

She still is over the moon about this man. If what she tells him, if it drives him away . . . she can't imagine facing whatever is to come without him beside her.

Chaz places a finger on her lip, gently rolls it out from between her teeth. "What is it?"

And for the third time that day, she breaks her news, knowing she will break another heart.

For Chaz, Ruby includes logistics. A few discreet questions out at the flea market, and she was pointed to Beer Barrel Pete and his backroom forgery business. A week later, a birth certificate for Lark Ann Leander was in Ruby's hands. She doesn't tell Chaz that the date, December 6, was her grandmother's birthday, or that Annie was her mother's name.

"What are you going to do?"

"I'll do what—whatever—I have to do." She pauses, hesitates. "I can trust you with this?"

Chaz drops his eyes deliberately, blatantly, to her belly. "How can you ask that?"

But she has to ask. He's a *cop,* after all.

As if reading her thoughts, Chaz speaks. "I'm a *cop.* Didn't you ever worry about getting involved with a cop?"

"No." Ruby shakes her head. "That's the thing. It never crossed my mind. I never thought what I did was a crime. And it's not like that day was always on my mind. You think other mothers are constantly reminiscing about their labor or the long road of adoption? After a while, your kid is just your kid."

Now, though, Ruby does think about it. By telling him, she's making him compromise his values, risk his job. She has to know how much this man will give up for her. Would he run away with them, leaving his family behind forever? Would he raise their child on his own, wait for Ruby to get out of jail?

Chaz sinks lower into the spongy sofa, rests the beer on his knee. "This is what I do, bring kids home." His voice is chalky; his eyes look everywhere but at her.

"Bangers," Ruby says. "Druggies, messed-up kids."

"They're still kids. They still have mothers."

"I *am* her mother."

Chaz looks her in the eye, finally. "No. You're not. That's the problem, Ruby." He sets his beer on the table, stands, wipes his hands on his jeans.

"Don't," she says. "Please."

"I need some time."

As he walks out the door, Ruby wonders if he is walking out of her life.

TWENTY

This office doesn't look like a TV law firm. The lawyers have converted an old adobe home off Paseo de Peralta into an airy workspace. A woman—secretary, receptionist maybe—leads Ruby to the doorway of what must have been a corner bedroom, closes the French doors behind her. Two walls boast twin sets of windows that seem to pull the ash trees inside. The other two walls are lined with glass shelves that hold a collection of pre-Colombian artifacts; the glass and precision lighting create the appearance that the pieces are levitating under an ancient mystical spell.

A fiftyish man, poet's beard, jeans and white turtleneck, sleeves pushed up to the elbows, steps from behind the drafting table centered between the windows on the far wall. "John Brainard," he says. "John." The hand he extends is calloused, not the hand of someone who sits behind a desk all day. *A gardener,* Ruby thinks. She tries to still the quaking in her own hand as she holds his.

"Angela was a little vague about what you need." He motions her to a low-slung leather chair next to an old chunk of wood—probably a piece of gating or a window shutter—that serves as a coffee table. He takes the seat next to her, picks up a crisp yellow pad and pen off the table. "What can I do for you?"

Ruby clasps her hands in her lap, sits ramrod-stiff in the slinky chair. "It's confidential, what I tell you. Right?"

"Unless it involves a future crime—say you tell me you're about to murder someone and tell me exactly who—then, yes, I am bound by attorney-client confidentiality."

She looks around the room, trying to get a fix on this poet-lawyer-antiquities-collector-gardener, whether to put her trust in him. Her grandmother used to say something about faith, about jumping off a cliff and building your wings on the way down. Ruby isn't sure that she can craft wings big enough for this mess, but she doesn't know what to do except jump.

TWENTY-ONE

For so long Ruby had been alone with that macaroni necklace of a center line, tugging her through the void, away from Iowa and Nana's too-fresh grave, away from what she considered her second life, even if she could barely remember the first. Then, just as the blackness was fading to purple, the oasis appeared, a rest stop right there beside that sorry excuse of an interstate. Her parched throat urged her to exit.

She steered past three slumbering trucks, their amber bulbs glowing like animal eyes in the half-light. Two drivers in gimmee caps stood to the side, jumped back in mock terror as Ruby maneuvered up the narrow lane. At the top of the hill, she stepped out of her shiny new Jeep, stretched to reshape her body from a question mark into an exclamation point, then walked behind the rented trailer to give the padlock a quick tug.

The vacant pavilion wasn't much of a rest stop, just a couple of picnic tables and a bathroom ripe with bleachy stench. But it did have vending machines, and after feeding them with lavender-scented coins scavenged from the bureau drawer and administering one swift kick, Ruby held a sweaty can of Coke and a Clark bar. One person's pin money was another's breakfast.

Down at the bottom of the hill, engines coughed and yellow lights lit up the humps of the semis, modern-day camels leaving the oasis to cross an asphalt desert. She stood there for a moment, feeling very alone in that breezeless Oklahoma air. Then she drained the can in a few gulps, the burbling stream trickling down the desert of her throat with a burn comforting in its familiarity.

If Ruby hadn't been such a strident litter-loather, she would have missed her entirely. But when she tore off the end of the candy wrapper, a bit of paper clung to her fingers, still moist with condensation from the can, so Ruby stepped right up to the mesh barrel—tilted for drive-by tosses—to flick the scrap into the mound of trash.

"Holy shit!" Ruby's voice was a rifle shot through the still of dawn as she jumped back from the barrel. "Ho-ly shit." She stepped closer, peered into the pile of trash. Maybe it was dead, so unblinking were those saucer eyes. She looked back at the pay phone, where a receiverless cord hung next to an empty, blue phone book jacket. She looked down at the entrance ramp, hoping to see another car, someone, anyone, who could deal with this horror instead of her. Then she blew a whisper of air at the face, which was answered with a jerk of pink-clad limbs.

A baby. What kind of mother would just throw away a baby like it was a half-eaten Big Mac? The papers had stories about this kind of thing. Young mothers, poor mothers, desperate mothers leaving their babies in church doorways and outside hospitals. Did this baby cry one too many times on a nerve-frazzling drive? Maybe it was sick or something. Maybe it had some awful birth defect that the mother just couldn't handle.

Ruby surveyed the few bits of baby not shrouded in jumpsuit; all body parts looked to be intact and appropriately apportioned. Except for those impossibly huge eyes. Maybe that was the deal breaker; maybe the mother couldn't stand one more second of those eyes peeling away the layers of her soul, seeing all the ways she was sure to disappoint them in the years to come.

"Damn, damn, damn." Ruby rubbed at her gritty forehead, trying to force her road-weary brain to think. The broken telephone was not going to help. And flagging down a passing truck would take more nerve than she could muster. The baby just lay there, not making a sound, clutching the neck of a purple and pink toy giraffe in one tiny fist. Wisps of pale hair framed the narrow face, and those disconcertingly soulful eyes stared back at Ruby as if waiting for her to come up with the answer they already knew.

Tucking the candy bar into her jeans pocket, Ruby reached in and plucked the baby, carrier and all, from the nest of fast-food wrappers and soda cans.

TWENTY-TWO

John picks up a pair of dime-store reading glasses, twirls them by one stem. "Have you checked this out? Are you sure it's the same baby?"

Ruby nods, incapable of further words. Telling this story again, to an outsider, even one bound by confidentiality, has deflated her. Tears threaten to leak from her eyes like the last breath of air from a punctured tire.

The lawyer stands, moves to one of the displays, makes minuscule adjustments to the position of a few artifacts. *He is kind,* she thinks, creating busywork to give her time to collect herself. If nothing else, at least this lawyer is kind.

That day at the rest stop, Ruby had thought of all kinds of reasons why a baby would end up in a trash can. Except this one: that a couple of drugged-out teenagers would steal a car from a gas station in Dallas, a car with a baby inside. That the girl would sober up just enough somewhere in Oklahoma, hear her boyfriend crazy-talk about his plans to get ransom by sending the parents the baby's ear. That she would sneak the baby out of the car when her boyfriend stopped to take a leak, hoping he was still too coked-up to notice the baby wasn't in the backseat. That the girl would find Jesus in rehab nearly ten years later, track down the mother through archived news reports, tell her story. Just the third step of the twelve she was climbing.

"This says she left the baby on a picnic bench as a trucker was pulling in."

Ruby nods. "Maybe she was too stoned to remember. Maybe she didn't want to admit she threw her in the trash." This detail, the one that Ruby hopes Lark never learns, could be too horrible for the girl to retain, let alone speak. "I don't know, but I know it's Lark."

"What about the truckers you saw? Do you remember anything about them, in case we need to locate them?"

As if scrutinizing the room today will help her peer across the years, Ruby scrunches her forehead. "The trucks were from the same company. It was barely light, but I remember a slogan, something Christian, across the backs." She doesn't add that she remembers this because it bugged her, that someone would use religion as a marketing ploy. *Jesus is my copilot, so I'll drive your stuff, what, faster? Better?*

"I can make some inquiries, discreet, of course, with the federal prosecutor down in Albuquerque." He steps back toward Ruby, pretzels himself into his chair. "I know her. We were in law school together at UNM. She's a straight shooter and a good lawyer. She trounced me in moot court."

He picks up his yellow pad and starts scribbling. The *scritch scritch* of pen against paper fills the quiet of the room. Then he lays the pad on the table, leans forward, hands clasped at his knees. "It is possible, given the circumstances, that we can negotiate a deal for you, but . . ."

The "but" swings through the air like a wrecking ball. There is always a "but"; Ruby just doesn't know which part of her this one will crush.

"You understand what it will mean. We could try to fight for custody, prove the biological parents are somehow unfit, or argue best interests of the child."

Here it comes, Ruby thinks. Here comes the soul-obliterating "but."

"I think we have a good shot at avoiding jail time for you, but . . . you understand that if you come forward, you undoubtedly will lose custody of your daughter?"

There. The words are spoken. Sometimes a person has to hear them out loud to make them real. And the surprising thing is that they don't change the resolve that has come almost like a sense of peace. Ruby still knows, all the way down to her obliterated soul, that even if Lark hadn't found the article, she has to do what is right. And at least he called Lark *her* daughter.

She can't manage words, answers him with just a nod.

TWENTY-THREE

"Let's go for a walk," Ruby says to Lark.

"But . . ." Lark has been bristling against Ruby's need to keep her close, keep her indoors, these past few days.

"It's okay. Fresh air . . ."

"Fresh perspective," Lark says, finishing Nana's saying.

They head out on one of their favorite loops, up Artist Road, across Gonzalez, down Palace and back over to Artist Road. Clyde nudges between them, bounds off to investigate odors and chase critters, circles back and shoves between them again. The air is cool, God-washed, after a spectacular afternoon storm.

Neither of them speaks as they walk through this older neighborhood. Lines of scarred adobe walls tease them with glimpses here and there, of gardens choked with poppies, colorful bottles on blue-trimmed windowsills, religious statuary. Ruby reaches out, squeezes Lark's shoulder. She is answered with a flash of worried, scared eyes. Ruby forms practice sentences in her head as Lark scuffs her sneakers along the roadside, kicks at rocks. What words does a mother use to break her daughter's heart?

As the sun dips below the mountains, leaving a smear of rainbow sherbet in its wake, they reach the foot of Palace Avenue. They cross over to a little park beneath the rustic wooden cross planted on a hillside—Santa Fe's version of the Hollywood sign. They sit in the grass, lean against the trunk of an ancient tree, Clyde blanketing their feet.

Ruby pulls a dented tin bowl and a couple of bottles of water from her backpack, fills the bowl for Clyde, tosses the other bottle to Lark. She peels a juice-heavy orange, pries the segments apart with her fingers, hands Lark the little bites of sunshine from the center. Angel kisses, her grandmother called them, and Lark needs all the kisses and angels she can get.

"We need to talk about what happens next."

"Nothing is going to happen." Lark takes a swig of water as if she were swallowing an antidote. "You said no one else knows."

"But now we know. And those people, your other parents, they deserve to know, too."

Lark studies the tiny moue of orange in her palm. "You could write them a letter, tell them I'm okay. Then we could go somewhere and hide."

Mexico, Ruby thinks again. Could she possibly subject this child, and her other one, to a life on the run? She holds out another segment of orange. Lark shakes her head, but Clyde noses in and gulps it down. "Do you really want to live like that, always having to lie about who you really are?"

"But if you tell . . . what happens?"

Ruby sits up taller, crosses her legs. "I've already told." She watches Lark's eyes flash from milk chocolate to fancy dark Swiss. "I talked to a lawyer. And he's talking with another lawyer down in Albuquerque, trying to work things out. But I might be in a lot of trouble."

"No." Lark tosses the last of the angel kisses aside. "Tell him you made a mistake, made it up." Her face darkens in shadow. "I'm sorry I looked in your purse. I promise, I promise I'll keep the secret."

Ruby scootches Lark over to her, pulls her into a stiff embrace. "Oh, baby bird. No. This is so not about you knowing the secret. It's just, before, *I* didn't know. And now that I do, I have to do what's right."

When Ruby pauses to take a breath, Lark turns her head away, presses her chin into Ruby's ribs. "The charges are pretty serious, baby. The judge could make me go to jail."

Lark flings out an arm, wraps it around Clyde. "But you saved me. You loved me." Her voice catches on her anxiety. "You didn't know. . . ."

"Love." Ruby cups Lark's chin in her palm, raises her head until Lark's eyes meet hers. "I love you. That won't ever change. But what I did, it was still wrong."

The ramifications sink into Lark's face like water on a thirsty garden. "If you go to jail? Will I, and my sister, will we live with the Ms? Or with Chaz?"

The baby. Ruby can't even think about what will happen to her right now. First she has to do this, the hard part. She would climb into the trunk of this noble tree and pull Lark in with her if she could, and stay there, protected, forever. She looks up at the cross, which memorializes some priests who were slaughtered in a pueblo revolt four hundred years ago, prays for the strength to massacre her daughter's heart. Again. "Your other parents, they will want you to go live with them."

Lark crosses her arms, hugs her chest. "I won't go." Ruby can feel Lark's voice digging its heels into the ground. "I'll just say no."

"It's not that easy," Ruby says. "I wish, I so wish it were." She holds Lark tightly beside her. "The judge, he can make you go."

"It's not fair," Lark wails. "I didn't do anything wrong. Don't let them take me away." She crumples like a tissue into Ruby's lap, her tears washing over Ruby's bare legs. Ruby's own tears soak her collar as Clyde stands, moans, licks and licks and licks at his humans.

Lark's body feels boneless, a puddle of hurt in Ruby's lap. The fissure in her own heart is jagged, like a lightning scar in an old-growth tree.

TWENTY-FOUR

Antoinette looks like an old-church Madonna painting when she cries. All she needs is a fat Baby Jesus in her lap.

"I'm sorry," Ruby says. "I'm so sorry. I couldn't tell you Saturday. I had to tell Lark first, if I was going to tell anyone at all."

Antoinette swipes her nose with her sleeve in a very un-Madonnalike move. "I'm not crying because you lied to me. I understand that. I'm crying because the whole thing is so . . . so royally fucked-up."

Well, that totally blows the Madonna thing, Ruby thinks. She's heard her friend use the naughty F word, as Antoinette calls it, only a handful of times, usually occasions involving extreme bodily pain. Ruby walks past Lark's closed bedroom door to the bathroom, returns with a box of tissues. "Here. I thought I saw a booger, but it's snot, as Lark would say."

"How can you joke. How can you even . . ." Antoinette pauses to blow her nose.

"Talk? Walk?"

"Breathe. How can you even breathe?"

Ruby sits down on the sofa beside her. "I don't know. I don't know how I'm going to do any of it. But in a weird way, I'm breathing easier now, now that I made up my mind, now that I've told all of you."

"He's good, your lawyer." Antoinette combs back her hair with both hands, loops it into a knot. "I asked around. But it's not too late to pull the plug."

Ruby shakes her head. "What kind of example would that be, for Lark? What kind of life?"

"These people, they'll be reasonable. They'll want what's best for Lark."

Again Ruby shakes her head. "My lawyer says—"

"I know. I know they'll get custody. But surely they'll want to go slow. Surely they'll let you visit."

"That, my friend," Ruby says. "Is the thought that keeps me breathing. But do stop calling me Shirley."

TWENTY-FIVE

"Go. Be with your daughter," Margaret says. "I had Zara cancel your appointments for the next couple of days."

Ruby nods. She knows she hasn't been able to focus, that she's doing her clients a disservice. Fortunately, this last client needs only a polish change. Ruby wouldn't trust herself with cuticle trimmers another time today.

As the client curls her hands into careful Cs in front of the small fan clipped to the edge of the manicure table, Ruby folds and stacks the thin white towels, places the pink finger bowls on top of the pile, as if she can make order out of her messed-up life through a tidy workstation. Out of sight in the back room, she tosses the towels in the hamper, places the bowls in the sink. And wipes the hot tears from her cheeks as she walks out the door.

She sits there in her Jeep, waiting for her brain to command her arm muscles to drive. It is all too much; everything is too much. She wants—no, needs—to spend every moment with Lark. She also needs to make money to pay for lawyers and court costs and potential fines. And the legal fees are just a slice of the ugly pie. The money that remained from the sale of her grandparents' house after Ruby bought the Jeep ran out years ago, but she has the small fund that Mrs. Levy left her to pay property taxes and maintain the house. She can work overtime at the salon, make more furniture. But all of that will be a drop in the rusted bucket of what Ruby will owe. And she's not going to be doing nails or making furniture in jail.

Money isn't the only thing driving her, though. Even if she had all the cash in the world, Ruby is afraid that if she doesn't keep doing these regular things, if she doesn't keep putting one foot in front of the other through the dailiness, she'll never move again.

Finally, she manages to engage her brain and put the car in gear.

At the house, Molly greets her with a shrug. "Come on, Daisy," she says to her black Labrador. "Playdate's over. Let's go spring Dudley from the doggy salon." Clyde follows them outside, to re-mark his territory around the porch, no doubt.

Her daughter's eyes bore into Ruby before she crosses the room. "Why did you have to tell?" Lark sits stonily on the sofa. "Why couldn't you just pretend you didn't see the article? Why did you do this to me?"

Ruby knows that Lark isn't really looking for answers; her daughter just needs to vent. Still Ruby tries to comfort her. "Oh, baby bird. I didn't do this *to* you, to hurt you. . . ." She sits on the sofa next to Lark.

Lark flinches when Ruby reaches toward her. "Why didn't you just tell someone back then? Why didn't you give me to the police?"

Ruby lays her arm across Lark's shoulders anyway. "That was my plan, at first. But then, then the way you looked at me . . ." She tells her how infant Lark puckered her satiny mouth into a little pink heart and made a pitiful kitten mewl, how Ruby reached over to brush a tress of duck-down hair across that velvety forehead, how Lark grabbed her wrist, wiggled her fingers into Ruby's palm, and didn't let go.

"I looked into your precious baby face and I saw . . ."

"What? What did you see?"

Ruby can't speak this part, especially not to Lark, how at that moment, a flash of memory from many years before pulsed at her from a cobwebby corner of her mind. With that memory searing her scalp and baby fingers gripping her hand, only one thought was possible: *save this child, protect her.*

Now Ruby rubs her eyebrows with her knuckles, as if she can manually push those unwanted pictures back into that dark corner. And she feels the same steely resolve.

Somehow, she's got to protect this child.

TWENTY-SIX

That evening, Ruby kneels in the garden. She's always been able to find solace wrist-deep in soil; this time she finds only dirt. The weeds bear the brunt of her emotions.

Inside, Lark is making beaded bracelets with Numi. Ruby didn't hesitate when Numi's mother called to ask if she could drop off Numi while she ran some errands in town. Lark needs a friend right now.

Ruby is not deliberately eavesdropping; Lark knows she is weeding below the open bedroom window. So Ruby supposes that what Lark tells Numi with a pinkie swear is what she wants to tell her mother instead.

It's like my whole life 'til now has been a ginormous game of pretend. And now I go live with people I don't even know. A whole different house with whole different parents. In a whole 'nother state. That's not really my bed. This isn't really my room. My mom's not really my mom. I'm not even really me. I don't know who I am.

The bird clock tweets 7:00 P.M. shortly after Numi leaves. "I think I'll just go to bed," Lark says.

She hasn't gone to bed this early since she was a toddler. With a sigh as heavy as her sorrow, Ruby follows her into Lark's bedroom, trying to think of how to tell a child that you have to do what is right, even if you hurt her in the process.

Lark flings off her clothes, yanks on her pajamas. She slams shut the drawer, stomps down the hall, carrying around her own little cloud of anger like Pigpen carried his stink. *Anger again*, Ruby thinks. *Now if I can just get Lark through the other—what, five, seven?—stages of grief before—*She chokes off the rest of her thought.

The rush of water against porcelain drowns out Ruby's soft sob. Lark manages to make even toothbrushing an act of anger, bristles scraping gums with vigor.

"Baby." Ruby tries again as Lark trudges back to her bedroom. As Ruby reaches out to give Clyde a good night pat on the head, Lark turns toward the wall like a sulking spouse. "Am I just a manicurist or a woodworker? No, what I do isn't who I am. And where you live isn't who you are, either."

Ruby sits on the edge of the bed and waits, for questions, maybe tears. All she hears, though, is Lark's breath slowing, deepening, in rhythm with Clyde's mucousy snores. "Good night, sweet dreams, I love you . . ." Ruby pauses, finishes Lark's part of their nighttime send-off herself. "To the moon and back."

When Ruby stands and moves toward the bedroom door, Lark finally speaks. "I wish you had never found me. Why couldn't you just leave me there to die?"

TWENTY-SEVEN

Later, Chaz arrives. Ruby checks to see that Lark is sleeping soundly, then fills him in on the events of the evening and reports from her lawyer. John checked out the story from the magazine. The police did follow up with the girl, but no charges were filed against her because she was fourteen at the time and was just along for the ride, so to speak. They also tracked down the boyfriend—to a cemetery in East Texas.

That means if anyone is going to pay for the crime, it will be Ruby. John contacted his friend, the federal prosecutor, and they have "begun a dialogue." She's reasonable, he said, has no ax to grind.

As for Lark, Texas's Child Protective Services will have the ultimate say, but John and the prosecutor both agree that gradual turnover would be best, to give Lark time to adjust. "Turnover" they call it, negotiating details as if Lark were a pretty necklace being returned to its rightful owner. Nothing is *right* about any of this.

Chaz seems to hear her thoughts. "She'll be all right." Next to her on the sofa, he rubs his chin against Ruby's neck. She bristles as much from the comment as his stubble.

The problem is Chaz really believes everything is going to be all right. Yes, Lark is going away, but she's going to her real parents after all, so everything will be all right. Ruby won't go to jail; his family has been lighting candles and making novenas to make sure about that. Law-and-order Chaz, emphasis on the order. He wants the order back in his life; he wants this part to be over. And Chaz and Ruby will just tootle along as if none of this ever happened.

"I know it's hard." He wraps an arm around her, pulls her to his chest.

His impatience is thick between them as she slips out of his embrace. Chaz isn't one of those guys who thinks that buying a girl a meal is a green light to play in her pants, but he does like his alone-time with Ruby.

"I'm sorry," she says.

Even Chaz's skin tightens as irritation replaces impatience. "I'm trying here." He stands, strides to the refrigerator, returns with another beer. "It's hard for me, to get past it."

"Get past what?" Ruby looks in the direction of Lark's bedroom. She struggles to keep her voice low. "The disruption to your life? The fact that I saved, loved, who I thought was an abandoned child?" She tugs at her hair in frustration. "How is that so different from what you do, saving kids from the streets?" She pauses, points to her belly. "Or can't you get past the idea that your pregnant girlfriend may go to jail?"

"No." He collapses onto the sofa as if the burden of Ruby's deed is too much for even his sturdy legs. "I don't know how I can get past you not telling me. Before now."

The sour mood stinks up the room as much as the reek of days' old Chinese food that followed Chaz back from the kitchen. "I never told anyone."

"I'm not just anyone. Or at least I didn't think so."

"I thought about it, going to the authorities." Every now and then she would read about some child being abused and worry that the monster who tossed away Lark might be mistreating another child. With DNA testing, they might find that mother, protect her other babies. They might take Lark away, too, though, put her in "the system."

And then that other memory, from Ruby's own childhood, would burble to the surface like oil from summer asphalt, and the risk of coming forward would become untenable. If she had known that someone loved Lark, was out there looking . . .

Chaz points his beer at her. "I'm not talking about authorities. I'm talking about me. You never told *me*."

Ruby's anger dissipates like mist in a breeze, replaced by weary sorrow. "I don't expect you to forgive me." She takes a breath, tries to swallow the emotion. "I can't even forgive myself."

"I'm sorry, I'm sorry. I know how hard this is." Chaz places a hand on her belly. "But don't shut me out."

The next words cut Ruby to her core. "So that's it? You get rid of me because you're having your own baby?" Lark stands in the doorway, glistening eyes visible even in the dim light.

Ruby looks down at Chaz's hand, back at Lark. Like a game of freeze tag, no one moves. Even Clyde is a statue beside Lark, one paw in midair.

Lark breaks the spell, spins, storms back to her room, door slamming in her wake.

TWENTY-EIGHT

Her grandmother called Monday "holy day." Laundry day, cleaning day, holy day. At the time, when Ruby was doing her own assigned chores, she didn't get it, especially during summer break. Nana said that the whole cleanliness-is-next-to-godliness thing means exactly what it says, that a person can find God, find the sacred, in the mundane tasks of chore day. She said she felt like she was scouring her own soul clean as she scrubbed the linoleum floors. Ruby tried to tell her grandmother that she herself felt much closer to God sitting down by the river. But Nana would have none of that.

Even in the dark of night, this house is gleaming brighter than it has since Mrs. Levy's thrice-a-week cleaning lady had her elbows in the suds. The wood floors have been mopped and buffed and conditioned. Every inch of kitchen—appliances, cabinet faces, that grimy seam around the stovetop—has been assaulted with toothbrush and toothpick. Ruby has beaten and vacuumed rugs and carpets, bundled newspapers for recycling. And she has cried.

She keeps waiting to feel some of Nana's holiness. She can feel her raw fingers and elbows and knees. She can feel the itchy sweat on the back of her neck and down between her boobs. And she can feel tears carving deep ravines in her cheeks, eroding her face.

Ruby held her own tears until Lark went back to sleep. In part, she held them for Lark. Mostly, though, she held them for herself.

They've been there, every second since she found the article, pressing against her eyeballs like river water against a dam. Ruby has let a few drops squeeze through, but she's been afraid that the dam would break and wash her away. Not even the mountains would be barrier enough to stop Ruby from washing off the edge of the world.

But she couldn't hold them back anymore. The flood of tears burns her skin, clogs her nose, chokes her throat. She has cried and cried and cried and cleaned—a soggy twist on that spit-and-polish thing— and still there is no sign of the swollen waters receding. If God was here in this mess of dailiness, He washed away in the suds and the salt. If the human body is 98 percent water, Ruby is a wisp of her former self. Surely she'll blow away in a gust of wind before she has to face saying good-bye to Lark.

TWENTY-NINE

Antoinette's little blue convertible hugs the two-lane roads. From the driver's seat, Ruby watches the road with one eye, and Lark and Clyde with the other. Child and dog hang their heads out the side of the car, cheek to muzzle in the rippling breeze.

Ruby still feels like a wet rag from her crying spree last night. Yet when Antoinette knocked on the door early this morning, offering her car for the day, Ruby accepted without hesitation, loaded up Lark and Clyde, and headed north under a blue-umbrella sky.

The Jeep is beloved, like a faithful pet all these years. But Antoinette's little Mazda was made for days like this, on roads like these. *Canada*, Ruby thinks. She could just keep driving and driving and driving.

Instead Ruby drives the Land of Enchantment's Chimayo loop. They took Old Taos Highway through Tesuque, stopped at the village market for the best sourdough French toast on earth. The waitresses were their usual small-town selves, all honey this and darlin' that. The French toast looked as beautiful as ever, pale daffodil butter melting on sugar-dusted golden bread. The bacon was cooked crisp, almost carcinogenic, just the way Ruby always ordered it, and the coffee was creamy and hot. But the meal could have been cardboard for all Ruby tasted.

They stopped for a while beneath the towering walls of the Rio Grande Gorge to let Clyde romp around in the river, then they followed its banks farther north on the two-lane highway. Lark is quiet but not simmering. Ruby isn't sure if her daughter has regressed to denial or if this is progress through the tunnel of grief. She's just glad to have a break of sunshine from the anger cloud.

Just before Taos, they crossed over to the high road, followed the snaking asphalt through the rugged hills, past dust-bowl towns shadowed by red cliffs and towering pines, and into Chimayo. Adobe walls older than time bank both sides of the narrow streets of the town. Ruby parks in the lot across from the church, tells Clyde to stay in the car. Together she and Lark cross the open square and enter the little chapel.

After passing through the sanctuary, they walk into a tiny back room where wooden crutches and metal braces and yellowed testimonials are tacked to the walls, evidence of all the miracles that have come before them in this sacred dirt-floored space. Sometimes the town square is packed with tour buses, and a conga line of people squeezes through this room. Today, though, Lark and Ruby have the shrine to themselves, if only until the next belching bus arrives.

"Maybe you could come live in Texas, too." Lark sifts her fingers through the dirt, to which people trek from afar for its purported healing properties. "Maybe you could live right next door." She's now trying out the bargaining phase, it seems.

Ruby plops down on the cool earth next to Lark, leans back against the clammy wall. She doesn't tell Lark that she, too, has had the same thought, that holding on to the idea that theirs will not be a forever good-bye is the only way she's made it this far. *Cell phones, e-mail, airplanes.* Like a mantra, Ruby repeats that trio every time she wants to scream.

She has moments when she worries about how Lark will handle it, straddling a chasm between two worlds. Her grandmother had some saying that Ruby can't quite remember, about a person who tries to be two things ending up being no one at all. But Lark wouldn't be all that different from children of divorce splitting their time between parents. Except that *this* is nothing like *that* at all. It's odd, sending her kid off to live with someone she doesn't know, when all these years Ruby has insisted on meeting a parent before even an afternoon playdate.

"Maybe they won't like me. Maybe they'll send me home."

"You have to give them a chance."

"But maybe . . ."

"Give them a chance, baby bird." Ruby almost smiles as she imagines Lark being such a stinker that those other parents tuck tail and run.

THIRTY

When they return from Chimayo, a plastic grocery bag hangs on the front doorknob. A yellow sticky note stapled to the bag is labeled LARK in black marker, and in smaller blue ink, a scribbled, *We missed you today, Mrs. G.*

"That was nice," Ruby says. "Mrs. Graciella dropped off something from Girls Inc. camp."

Lark snatches the bag out of Ruby's hands and tucks it under her arm as they walk into the house.

"Well? Open it," Ruby says.

Lark tosses a "no" over her shoulder as she heads for her bedroom.

Ruby gives her a few minutes then knocks at the half open door. "Lark, is it your T-shirt? May I see?"

"It's nothing." Lark's voice is choked with tears. "Just some stu-pid thing."

Ruby held the bag; she could see below the knotted handle to the green fabric inside. But she doesn't challenge Lark. Instead, she walks the few steps to the bathroom and strips off her clothes. As she stands under the shower, the road dust slides off her. Yet the worry and sadness cling to her skin like wood stain.

THIRTY-ONE

The galvanized tub radiates the warmth of the afternoon sun. Inside, Clyde shivers with the indignity of bath time.

Despite her best efforts at remaining morose, a tiny giggle burbles through Lark's cherry-candy lips. "That's what they call 'hangdog.'" She lifts Clyde's chin from his chest and nuzzles his soapy nose, water hose writhing beside her. "You'll go with me, boy. *You'll* be my friend."

While Ruby combs burrs and mats from Clyde's tail—the perfect henna color for which Margaret's redhead wannabes would kill—she tells Lark more about that day nine years ago. Ruby talks about seeing the torn Clark wrapper on the seat beside the baby carrier, the C left behind in the rest stop trash bin, the remaining letters leaping out at her like a banner headline. *Lark Leander,* she had thought, now that sounded like the alliterated cheerleader she herself never was. Ruby closes the cap of the shampoo bottle, lays it beside Clyde's brush.

Lark sprays the hose on the dog's underbelly, eyes avoiding Ruby. "Is that what I was to you, a lark?"

Ruby cups Lark's cheek with her palm. "Oh, baby bird. You were—are—everything to me." An early reader and a precocious child, Lark was only six or seven when she pulled out the dictionary and looked up her name. *A bird. An escapade. Mischievous fun.* Impish Lark particularly liked that last one, and for months after, she would sum up any even slightly humorous event—a hunt for misplaced keys, a prank she pulled at the salon—with "Well, that was a Lark!"

Now she turns away from Ruby, busies herself fastening Clyde's collar. "Okay, boy." The dog jumps from the tub, runs circles around the humans, flinging strings of water from his soggy fur, yipping like a puppy. He gambols beside Lark, to the spigot and back.

Ruby pushes back from her knees, sits on her rear, stretches her legs out across the damp grass. So much has happened in such a few short days. John's reports have been upbeat. The case is complicated with jurisdictional issues, but the prosecutor is amenable to a deal with no jail time, and a phased transfer of custody. As Lark coils the hose into a tidy green cobra, Ruby tries to fathom the unfathomable reality that this child could —will—be leaving her soon.

The tennis ball is a bright yellow sun arcing through the sky as Lark throws it across the yard, Clyde dashing after it. At least those other people, the Tinsdales, seem to be decent, John told Ruby. John and the prosecutor have been keeping everything to themselves; he doesn't want the Tinsdales to know anything until every detail is verified and a deal is in place. The Tinsdales don't have to prove anything to regain custody; under the law they are presumed fit until contrary evidence is presented. Yet John's quiet checks into their background have turned up nothing except reports of good people, good citizens. At least there is that. Still, Ruby's whole body feels swollen with grief, turgid even in the dry desert climate.

The shriek of the telephone startles Ruby to her feet. She crosses the yard to the screen door and grabs the receiver off the kitchen counter. The next few minutes happen both in an instant and in an eternity, John's words pushing through her ear, racing through her bloodstream. "No," Ruby says. "*No.*" The word reverberates against her skin.

"Mama?"

Ruby raises her head to find herself on the floor, Lark and Clyde standing in front of her. "*No,*" she whimpers as she curls up on the tile.

THIRTY-TWO

"Ruby." Chaz's voice penetrates the haze. His hand is firm against her shoulder. He lifts her to her feet, holds her steady as she takes wobbly steps to the living area. They have almost reached the sofa when the front door flies open and the Ms burst through. Lark has called in all the troops.

Across the room, her sweet daughter sits against a wall, grasping Clyde. Molly and Chaz bracket Ruby on the sofa while she tries to force her rib cage to expand enough to allow air into her lungs. She hears the ding of the microwave, then Margaret stands in front of her, molding Ruby's hands around a mug of hot tea. When Margaret takes her seat in the chair beside the sofa, Ruby stares into the amber liquid. And the words find their way from her gut to her mouth.

John was apologetic, apoplectic. He and his friend, the Albuquerque prosecutor, were keeping things quiet until Ruby's plea bargain was finalized. But then an assistant in the Albuquerque office called down to Texas to verify certain details of the case, and the federal prosecutor for the Dallas district caught wind of what was going on. The Dallas prosecutor, in John's words, is the worst sort of power-hungry political dog. And he is beholden to some wealthy campaign contributors, who just happen to be Lark's biological family.

"So he's out to make political hay *and* for your blood," Molly interjects.

Ruby nods. "He ran to the courthouse to file the first charges. I don't understand all the rules—jurisdictional garbage, John calls it—but he's now in charge."

"What about the deal John was negotiating?" Margaret asks. "What about the terms—"

Ruby waves her hand. "Out the window. The Albuquerque lawyer has no say."

"The scumbag hijacked the case." Chaz pounds his fist into the sofa beside him.

Punctuated by the four-letter words of the family she has made, Ruby tells the rest. "The Texas guy got a warrant for my arrest. Federal marshals are coming for me." Ruby grabs Chaz's hand, pulls it into her lap. "Tomorrow."

From the other side of the room, Lark speaks up. "And me?"

Ruby swallows. Everyone, even the room itself it seems, holds his breath.

"And me?" Lark's voice is soaked in panic, her eyes dark with fear.

Ruby stands, steps around the coffee table and across the room, slides down the wall beside her daughter. She pulls Lark into her lap, tries to curl every inch of her daughter's body inside her own.

Ruby just sits there, enveloping Lark, Clyde tucked in beside them. Ruby thought she had time, that the cops would take statements, a DNA test. But the guy in Texas decided that the magazine article and Ruby's own story were enough and bulldogged forward. She wants to hold this child forever. Not even the forever of forevers would be long enough. Not nearly long enough.

"You, too," Ruby whispers, not wanting to let the words loose in the room.

Lark doesn't wail, doesn't even whimper. She crawls out from under Ruby, walks to the door, stares out across the porch. "No," she says, "it's not possible." Her phrasing sounds so grown-up. Not a whiny "I dun wanna," not from this kid, not today. Lark spins on her heels, yanks at Clyde's collar, and they march together into her bedroom.

Ruby wants, needs, to go to Lark, but her muscles don't seem to work. And all the while Mrs. Levy's bird clock pecks pecks away at the minutes that remain.

THIRTY-THREE

At the head of Margaret's dining-room table, Lark is queen for the meal. Not guest of honor, Margaret said; Lark will never be a "guest" in her home. The Ms left Ruby's house at noon and had this whole dinner organized by evening.

Ruby wasn't sure she could do this, the whole public-spectacle farewell, even if the "public" consisted of the Ms, Antoinette, and Chaz. But she owed it to them, who love Lark as well, a chance to say good-bye. She will give them this, but she has insisted that she be alone with Lark tomorrow.

The Ms cooked Lark's favorite fancy foods: fried calamari, spinach-and-goat-cheese soufflé, and rosemary chicken. They asked Lark to invite Numi and some of her other school friends, and Ruby encouraged her to do so. But Lark didn't want to. She said why bother to see them now, just to say good-bye. She said it would be better if she just wasn't there, in the classroom, when school started. Ruby tried to convince her to at least telephone Numi to tell her she was leaving, but Lark refused. "I wouldn't get to say good-bye if I just died," she said.

Ruby keeps thinking about the print of *The Last Supper* in one of her grandfather's books. Those disciples all sitting around, drinking wine, making merry, just before they send their beloved off to death. Maybe Lark's comparison isn't so far off the mark.

That first last supper couldn't have been more emotional than this one. Margaret tied individual tissue packets to the napkin rings, but she'll have to break out the big boxes soon. Everyone is trying, for Lark. They tell funny stories, they force their laughter, but in between, though they try to hide it, the sadness flows down their faces. Chaz is gulping and sniffling, and even Margaret, who never cries, dabs at her eyes.

Ruby isn't crying; she's all cried out. She isn't talking much, either, though. She just can't muster the energy for banter. She sits back and watches as this group of people, her family, Lark's family, tries to do the impossible, tries to say good-bye.

"You'll come visit," Molly says. "Or we'll go to Texas to visit you." She moves around the table, taking photos. She told Ruby she is making a scrapbook to send to Lark.

"And when you're older—"

Ruby interrupts Margaret with a glare; she doesn't want Lark thinking about the possibility of coming back, just treading water until she's eighteen. If Lark is going to be healthy, happy, she is going to have to *sink* into her new life.

"Remember when you wanted proof of the Easter Bunny?" Margaret steers her conversation in another direction, tells the story of six-year-old Lark placing a note and a Polaroid camera beside the dyed eggs, demanding that the bunny shoot a photo of himself so she could take it to school. While Lark slept, Molly snapped a blurry picture of Margaret covered in her old curly lamb coat, the sleeves held up like ears. The others at the table chuckle at the story, but Lark doesn't crack the thinnest of smiles.

"How 'bout if Glug sends you a friend to keep you company?" Chaz says, referring to his pet fish.

Ruby holds her breath after that comment. Earlier, Lark had cried as hard as she has cried throughout this ordeal when Ruby had to tell her that she was going to Texas alone, that Mr. Tinsdale was allergic to dogs. Now, though, Lark just responds with a too polite "No, thank you."

Margaret tries again. "Remember when you decided to test nail polish colors on Mrs. Cornwallis while she snoozed under the heat lamp?"

They all join in the "remember whens." Remember when Lark was so smart . . . remember when Lark was so funny . . . remember when?

Ruby wants to etch each moment on her own brain, tattoo it on her skin. Yet Lark will have to pack all those memories into a trunk in the attic of her mind to make room for the new memories she'll make in her new life.

Throughout the dinner, Lark sits at the head of the long burled-wood table, stony, detached. Candlelight dances on the cut-crystal goblets. Sinatra and Cole and Cline sing Lark's favorite songs, a CD burned by Molly, a taste inherited from Ruby. And Lark just sits there.

Finally, Ruby stands, thanks everyone. She steps behind Lark, starts toward the door.

"Hold on there." Chaz kneels in front of Lark, blocking their way. He reaches into his pocket, pulls out a dainty necklace, clasps it around Lark's neck. "This guy'll watch over you, while you're away from us."

Lark picks up the small pendant hanging from the chain. It gleams in the candlelight. Chaz's Saint Christopher medal. He must have gone out today to replace his own thick gold rope with this Lark-sized chain.

"But who will protect you?" Lark asks.

Chaz tucks the medallion under Lark's shirt, lays a hand across her breastbone. "I'll use my magic policeman badge."

Ruby is sure Lark's half-smirk is more to keep her composure than to say she doesn't believe in magic. So she whisks Lark through the line of hugs and kisses and out the room, before either of them can break down. And then she walks her daughter out of the Ms' house like she has done so many times over the past decade, this time for the last time.

They walk to the Jeep under a bright full moon, so bright that the stars are all but obscured. Ruby's grandmother used to say something about faith, that the stars are always brighter on a moonless night, as if God gives you one when he takes away the other, all that doors-closing, windows-opening crap. Tonight Ruby has no faith. The saying that night is always darkest before dawn doesn't take into account that this time, dawn will take away her daughter.

THIRTY-FOUR

Ruby sits on the bed while Lark packs the purple duffel bag she has used for sleepovers and school activities. Ruby didn't realize until just this morning that neither she nor Lark own a real suitcase; they haven't ever gone anywhere. That trip to the California beach that they always talked about will never happen. Their life has run out of time.

A mournful Clyde lies between them. Ruby wishes that Lark would tear into her, pound the pillow, cry, anything. She had thought the screaming banshee hurling "I hate you's" was bad, as if Lark wanted to be so nasty that Ruby wouldn't miss her. But this quiet is unbearable. Acceptance is supposed to be the last stage of grief, not resignation, something that should never shadow the face of a child.

"I'll see you soon. John is working with the people in Texas to set up a visit."

"Whatever." Even distraught, even just while packing, Lark's movements are graceful, balletic. She is like a colt, all elbows and knees, still waiting for that growth spurt that will bring height and proportion. Her little-girl towhead is darkening to grown-up blond, even in the summer sun. A growth spurt likely is not far behind. The reality that Ruby will not be with Lark to see her grow is too enormous to digest; just this little sliver tears her stomach into shreds.

"I'll take good care of Clyde," Ruby says.

Lark swallows, hard.

How many times do I have to break her heart? Ruby thinks.

Yesterday, Ruby wondered what to send with Lark, what to pack.

What was the protocol for this kind of thing? Should she make a list for the Tinsdales, so they know that Lark likes her sandwiches sliced in rectangles not triangles, that she likes her hair brushed for her, even though she pretends she's insulted by the act? All those little details that Ruby doesn't even have to think about. Lark's preferences, that she is scared of heights, the tickle spot at the base of her spine. They are all part of who she is.

But then John called with further instructions. No pets and no truckloads of "stuff." The Tinsdales want Tyler Rose to start fresh in the life she should have had all along. *Tyler Rose Tinsdale*. How ironic that they, too, went for the alliteration, and how utterly precious. Ruby can just picture a little rosebud in place of the dot over the *i*.

Lark smoothes the flap of the duffel, zips it shut. She walks out of the room, leadenly, Clyde moping behind her. Ruby listens to their progress, down the short hall, across the living area, and out to the back porch. The screen door bangs its own opinion about this situation.

Alone in the room, Ruby pulls out the new cell phone and charger and the treasures she hid under the bed this morning: an envelope addressed to Lark and a small framed photo of the two of them up on Chamisa Trail. Ruby crafted the frame in the dead hours of last night, stealing across the yard in the waning moonlight to the shed, wanting something of her own hands for Lark to take away. She unzips the duffel bag and slips the tokens inside.

She sits there for a moment, staring into the suitcase at the spare, neatly folded pile of this life that Lark will take with her. Then she stands, walks down the hall to her own room, and opens the bureau drawer. From under the sweaters, she pulls out the stuffed giraffe.

The other treasures are meant to be a tie between Ruby and Lark. But maybe this, an abused-with-love giraffe, neck floppy from where Lark's tiny hand squeezed the stuffing out of it, will be a bridge between Lark and Mrs. Tinsdale, between her old and new life. She returns to Lark's room and tucks the giraffe beside Lark's rolls of socks.

THIRTY-FIVE

Ruby has vowed to hold herself together, for Lark. Chaz called again this morning, wanting to be here with her. She rejected even her lawyer's presence. She needs to do this alone.

She walks into the living room as Lark and Clyde come in from the backyard. The look that passes between mother and daughter conveys more than words ever could. Yet it doesn't convey enough.

As Mrs. Levy's bird clock coos nine, Ruby hears the crunch of gravel. She and Lark stand in the center of the living area, side cleaved to side, hands melded into one, as the shadows fall across the porch. *I can't do this,* Ruby thinks. The room swirls around her head. Panic and bile clog her throat. *No,* she tells herself. She cannot fall apart.

Clyde growls at the doorbell, steps protectively in front of Lark. Ruby feels like she is watching someone else from far away, a mother shaking her hand loose from a daughter's grip, walking to the door. One man—young, tall, lean—steps in and grabs Clyde's collar, drags him toward the kitchen. Another man—older, red mustache, a doughnut belly protruding over his belt—picks up Lark's duffel and stands sentry at the door. And a young woman, with smooth coffee skin and eyes that haven't seen enough to be cynical, kneels in front of Lark, speaks to her, hand on shoulder, then hustles her out the door.

Ruby doesn't know that she is following them until she feels the yank on her elbow, tethering her to the porch. She watches as the young woman opens the back door of an unmarked sedan, motions for Lark to climb inside. Lark turns back toward Ruby, eyes white like a corralled wild horse. Lark's mouth opens, forms one silent word, "*Mama!*" Then she disappears behind the shutting door.

Lark doesn't shout to Ruby, only mouths the one word. Car doors slamming, engine revving, tires spewing gravel as the car churns down the driveway, none of it makes a noise. Then Chaz is beside her, holding her, bracing her head against his shoulder. And Ruby realizes that the world has not gone silent. She just can't hear anything over her own primal scream.

THIRTY-SIX

The handcuff bites Ruby's wrist as she walks with the red-mustached marshal through the federal building, from the U.S. attorney's office to the courtroom. She concentrates on putting up a barrier between her right wrist and his left, not wanting her nervousness to be conducted through the metal of the manacle. The marshal has been kind; he apologized when he handcuffed her, spouted off a much-worn sentence about his procedural mandate, post-9/11 and all.

John walks a few steps ahead. The halls are fairly empty this Friday afternoon, a few groups of people here and there, office clerks on break, gossiping. They all stop their conversations, turn to watch as Ruby passes. Ruby tries to hold her head up as she walks; she doesn't want to look like one of those dodgy criminals doing the perp walk on TV. Yet she keeps catching herself watching the heels of John's loafers slap against the wooden floor.

Margaret recommended John to her. His wife was a longtime client, and he had helped Margaret out when that Tennessee salon challenged the name of her salon, said they had the rights to *Curl-up and Dye*. Still, Ruby studies those shoes. Shoes tell a lot about a person, and, though she knows none of this is his fault, after yesterday Ruby hasn't quite decided to trust his particular pair.

The courtroom is tiny, windowless; it looks like a classroom, with none of the *To Kill a Mockingbird* grandeur Ruby expected. And it is empty. Chaz, the Ms, Antoinette, they all wanted to come. Ruby couldn't bear having them here, though, to witness her walk of shame.

The deputy and Ruby follow John to a table. The marshal unlocks her handcuff, walks to the back of the room. She rubs her wrist; it burns like the "Indian bracelets" her grandfather used to give her, twisting her skin in his thick palms when they were horsing around.

This morning, Ruby was still screaming into Chaz's shoulder when this marshal tried to pull her away.

"Come on, ma'am," he said. "I have to take you now."

Chaz had waited beside the house all morning, to be there if Ruby changed her mind, to be there when she needed him. And she had.

"Give us a minute." Chaz walked Ruby into the house. Then he stepped back out to the porch. Ruby stood in the living room, her fingers ensnared in her hair, as words volleyed between Chaz and the marshal. *Warrant. Custody. Interdepartmental cooperation.*

"Frank, you have my word, and my badge," Chaz said.

"One hour, Chaz," the marshal replied, "One hour and twelve points on the next fed-city basketball game."

Then Chaz was back inside the house, untangling her fingers from her hair, pulling her arms around him. He sat her on the sofa, called the Ms over. Margaret tried to joke as she helped Ruby dress, cleaning her up, saying it was bad for business if Ruby had bad hair for her mug shots. Molly practically forced a cup of soup and toast into Ruby, after Ruby's own hand shook too much to handle a spoon. Then Chaz drove her to the courthouse, and she met up with John on the steps.

John took her to the federal marshal's office, where she signed papers, was fingerprinted, photographed. The process was surreal, dehumanizing, even under these ideal circumstances. At least she didn't have some prison matron sticking a gloved hand up her rear. Not yet anyway.

And now here she is in the courtroom. The white blouse with the Peter Pan collar that she hasn't worn since her high school senior-class photograph is ironed crisp with lavender linen water. Together with the navy skirt and pumps that Antoinette lent her, the outfit is a bit "Catholic schoolgirl gone bad." And if anyone notices the safety pin that holds the skirt together over her thickened waist, it would be "Catholic schoolgirl gone *really* bad."

The prosecutor, a heavyset woman who looks like she was born in a business suit, enters, settles at the other small table. She will represent the United States at this hearing, standing in for the Texas guy. Ruby still can't get her head around the idea that it is the entire country that she is up against; she keeps imagining all those faces, all those citizens chasing after her with burning brooms.

John motions Ruby to stand as the judge climbs the one step to his riser and sits without any pomp. He looks like Ruby's high school biology teacher, as if he should be dissecting frogs not crimes. Not a judge, John told her, but a magistrate, though Ruby doesn't really understand the difference. This man in a robe still holds her fate in his formaldehyde-soaked hands.

They are here for an extradition hearing. A more involved probable cause hearing has been scheduled in the Texas court in two weeks. John prepared her for what to expect from this straightforward proceeding, told her not to worry. Yet remembering his assurances doesn't ease the overwhelming sense that she is going to pee in her pants.

John nudges her to make her responses: yes, she understands that she is here under a federal warrant for kidnapping; yes, she waives any objection to extradition to Texas. The prosecutor requests the minimal bail to which the Texas guy finally agreed. John already helped Ruby line up the bond with a lien against her house. Still, he advised her to come today without jewelry or valuables. Just in case.

The judge signs a stack of papers, hands them to the bailiff. "We're off the record." He shakes his teacher finger at Ruby. "Watch yourself, young lady. You won't have the home court advantage, and I mean that literally and metaphorically, when you appear in Dallas." Ruby is almost surprised that he doesn't ask her about late homework or hand out a quiz.

She follows John out of the courtroom, heads for the ladies' room a few doors down. Everything went smoothly; everything went as John said it would. But even so she throws up every bite of her lunch.

THIRTY-SEVEN

With John at her side, Ruby walks outside of the cool, dark courthouse and into the blaring sun. And a media maelstrom. The sidewalk is clogged with stiff-haired people, each reaching out a microphone as if straining to touch the sleeve of a matinee idol. Their too-white teeth gnash in their too-big mouths while they jostle one another for position. Behind them stands a circle of cameras, like stanchions fortifying their troops.

John motions her toward the shield of a broad stone column. He steps out onto the walkway and holds up his hands like a TV evangelist. "My client will not be making any statement at this time," he says simply, confidently. Back behind the column, he takes her hand. "Ready?" As if she could ever be ready for this.

They step over a shin-high chain barrier and take quick, determined strides across the courthouse lawn, hand in hand, toward the side parking lot. Ruby's instinct is to run, flee, but John's hand steadies her. "Just keep looking forward, keep calm," he says.

Two reporters leave the sidewalk in pursuit, as if in a race to see who mows her down first. A chubby man huffs up beside John, shirttails flapping and chinos sagging below his bouncing belly. On Ruby's side, a blonde, coiffed hair bobbed at her chin, approaches with mincing steps, legs constrained by a tight scarlet suit. Stiletto-heeled Barbie shoes churn up divots in her wake. "Ms. Leander," she calls, "what do you want to say to the parents of the child you stole?" The voice is barfly-rough, a surprise from such a perky, petite body. "Ruby, what do you have to say?"

Ruby just hums the daffy song and concentrates on John's sure grip of her hand. He weaves her through the scattering of cars left at day's end in the government lot toward an old white Land Cruiser, a spiderweb of cracked windshield sparkling in the sun. John yanks open the passenger door, helps Ruby inside. Before she can buckle her seat belt, he is climbing in the driver's seat, tossing his briefcase in the back.

"Good thing I drove today." The engine spurts to life. "I usually just walk over from my office, but I ran an errand before court."

In the side mirror, Ruby watches the little red reporter pat her helmet hair in place. "Well," she says, with fake cheer, "My grandmother always said life is an adventure or it is nothing at all." Of course the old bird's definition of adventure was trying a new hybrid of tomato plant.

THIRTY-EIGHT

John drives a circuitous route to Ruby's house. He checks the rearview mirror, trying to spot any cars tailing them. Mrs. Levy transferred the house to Ruby through a trust, so it may take the media awhile to locate the address, but they will find it, in this world of computer search engines. Ruby grips the strap above the door as John takes corners as if he were drag racing. Nausea roils in her stomach, yet this is no morning sickness that will pass after a few saltines.

They are all there when John drops off Ruby at her house. The Ms, Chaz, Antoinette. And Clyde. The dog leaps off the front porch, barrels down the drive to greet her, almost knocks her on her can. He jumps up, puts his front paws on her shoulders, gives a quick lick to every inch of exposed skin, then races back up to the porch ahead of her, barking, "She is home, she is home." When he reaches the porch, Clyde spins around on his heels and looks beyond Ruby. The confusion and disappointment register on his face; his other human is *not* home.

The Ms grab Ruby in a two-sided hug; Margaret pats Ruby's cheek with pruney fingers—she hasn't been away from the salon for long. Chaz elbows Margaret aside, jokes, "Hey, you've got your own girl." He squeezes Ruby, lifts her until her feet dangle and the shoes she borrowed from Antoinette fall to the porch. He sets her back on her feet, gives her a loud, smacking kiss. His lips taste of beer and worry.

Ruby steps toward the door, then turns back. She can't do it, can't go inside that Larkless house. Chaz breaks her fall as she crumples to the porch, pulling him down with her. She lays her head in his lap as if she were a child. In the corner of the porch ceiling, Louie, Lark's "pet" bat, hangs upside down, undisturbed by the commotion, sleeping until the prime hunting hours. She wonders if he misses Lark, too.

She doesn't know how long she lies there. At some point the Ms and Antoinette leave, whispering good-byes and promises to call later. With Clyde whimpering beside them, Ruby stays there in Chaz's lap. Her legs fall asleep. Her back muscles tighten into knots of wood. The bat takes off for his night's adventures. And still she can't bear to go inside.

THIRTY-NINE

Under the Calvin la-di-da bedding is a sanctuary. As if she were immersed in water, Ruby hears only her own breath and the occasional deep sigh from Clyde, sees only the shifting light across the plum-and-lilac splashes of the bedding. She breathes in, inhaling her daughter in every breath; she breathes out, Lark wafting across her face like bubbles in the water. Breathe in, breathe out, in, out. This is all Ruby can do, wants to do. In her plum-and-lilac water cave, she doesn't have to think, doesn't have to feel anything but the phone receiver she clutches in her hand.

She ignores the knock at the door, pulls the covers over her head; Lark's covers. She has lain in this bed for three nights and days now, the sweet smells of her daughter growing fainter and fainter until now Ruby relies on memory more than nose, imagining her long body filling, spilling over, a Lark-sized dent in the mattress. She has vague memories of Chaz spooning against her, of voices—the Ms and Antoinette— swirling through the room. Mostly she just tries to remember that scent.

The whole time, Clyde has been beside her, head tucked between his front paws as if he were trying to blindfold himself to the fact of Lark's absence. But even a blind dog would know Lark was gone; her absence is as palpable as Braille. "I know, boy," Ruby whispers.

She groans at the tug of the sheets. "No."

"Get up," Margaret says. "Shower. Eat."

Then Molly's voice. "Come on, Clyde. You, too."

Ruby allows Margaret to roll her off the bed, march her toward the bathroom. She winces at the screech of the shower faucet, more noise than she can stand. The scent of Lark's kiwi shampoo that swirls in the steam wrenches her muscles as if wringing fluid from sodden cloth.

The hot water pelts her skin, each slender needle a stab to her senses. Rivers gush from the showerhead through her tangle of hair. Streams separate into rivulets that weave down her breasts, over her stomach. Just in the past week it seems, the life within her has decided to make a statement, the discreet bump morphing into a flashy bulge, as if the fetus were shouting, "Remember me?"

Little creeks run down the hill of her belly, her legs. When they reach the tub floor, the creeks merge back into rivers, converge in a swirl over the drain. And Ruby remembers.

The enormity of her situation weighs as heavily on her gut as her newly expanded belly weighs on her bladder. Lark is gone, but another life is depending on her. How will she support this other daughter from jail? Who will care for her? She doesn't know how much, even if, she can count on Chaz. Willing her torpor to wash down her body, into the eddy of the drain, she steps from the shower.

The sounds of Margaret's kitchen clatters accompany her as she towels off, and this time the noise hurts less. When she swipes the fog from the mirror, the gaunt face, the football player's black stripes beneath her dull eyes shock her into an understanding. This, she thinks, is how Lark's other mother must have felt in those days after her child disappeared with her car.

Shrouded in the weighty hotel robe Chaz gave her for her birthday, she walks into the kitchen. The window above the sink looks bereft; Margaret has put Lark's avocado pit and the herb pots in the sink to soak away Ruby's neglect. The table looks cheerier. A handful of wildflowers dance in the blue cream pitcher; Mrs. Levy's good china glimmers on top of a much-washed twill place mat. The golden halves of a grilled cheese sandwich are parentheses around a bowl of creamy tomato soup; a tall glass of milk sweats beside the plate. Comfort food, and Ruby is ready, finally, to take comfort, in food and in the sliver of family that remains.

As Ruby sits, Molly returns with Clyde. His walk has not done him the good of her shower. He plods across the floor from the back porch to the front door, flops down, whimpers.

"He misses her," Molly says.

Margaret nods. "We all do."

The Ms communicate a coherent paragraph to each other in a look. They bracket Ruby like the sandwich brackets the soup, make idle conversation—salon gossip, the latest art gallery buzz. Ruby devours the sandwich, a bowl and a half of soup, two glasses of milk. It is a certifiable fact that a grilled cheese sandwich tastes better when someone else makes it for you, but this, this food is biblical.

She wipes her mouth with the cloth napkin, another remnant from Mrs. Levy, sets it beside her plate. "Lap-kin" Lark called it, which makes more sense given where it is used. This memory burns but doesn't char.

Finally, she speaks. She tells them about the phone call the first night, Lark sobbing across the miles. They call her Tyler. They eat in the dining room. Her room is fancy, blue and white, what sounds like toile from her description. White carpet everywhere. She misses Clyde. She misses the Ms. She misses Ruby. She misses Home.

While Lark was talking, Ruby heard a voice in the background. "What is that? What are you doing?" Then a click, and silence. Still.

"They have to understand," Molly says. "They can't just cut you out of her life, pretend the last nine years didn't happen."

"They don't have to understand anything," Margaret says.

After the meal, the Ms leave Ruby with a stocked fridge and promises, threats really, to come get her if she doesn't show up for work tomorrow. Clyde sighs his best doggy sigh, drags his chin down the hall and back into Lark's bedroom. Ruby follows him and makes a half-hearted attempt to straighten the bedding. As she tucks the blanket under the mattress, her hand brushes something. She reaches a bit farther and pulls out a wadded plastic bag.

Ruby extracts a ball of bright green fabric from the bag and unfurls it with a shake. On the front of the T-shirt, the Girls Inc. logo stamped over the left breast. And on the back, a silk screen, text with a border of kid-drawn flowers and dogs and cats. "*I AM,*" it proclaims in Lark's unmistakable purple print.

> *I AM*
> *a bug-loving bookworm*
> *a baseball fanatic*
> *a tree-climbing poet*
> *an old-movie addict*
> *I like art and science*
> *I like to dance and meander*
> *I am a tomboy girl*
> *I am Lark Leander*

Ruby sits at the foot of the bed and hugs the shirt as the words Lark spoke when Ruby was outside the window blast through her head. *I don't know who I* am.

FORTY

This strange magnetic quality seems to have come upon Ruby overnight, as if the Sandman sprinkled her with charged metal filings instead of fairy dust. If she weren't so uncomfortable, she might find it all funny, heads jerking toward her like a dance team doing a domino routine.

Ruby remembers the doorbell ringing several times during the days of fog, and Antoinette left a message to warn her that the local court stringer had picked up the story.

Santa Fe has a reputation of being a town out of touch with reality, out of touch with the world. People might rally around a hot topic like Israel or gay rights, but there is supposed to be an air of not caring, even disdain, for the everyday news. Unless that news is a sordid tale about one of their own.

When she walked into the coffee shop two doors down from the salon to get a cup of herbal tea, she first checked to see that nothing disgusting hung from her nose, that her pants were zipped. In the swirl of whispers, as intoxicating as the aroma of coffee it seemed, Ruby finally got it; she has joined the rarified ranks of celebrity.

Even here in the salon, her magnetic pull is inescapable. The salon is a homey place; Margaret wanted to steer clear of too-trendy austere and sleek, and, despite the kitschy name, from too-cute poodle pink as well. Instead, Molly painted the walls with columns and friezes in soothing tones of gold and amber and bronze. The space looks like a cozy corner of an Italian villa, where you would want to curl up, if not curl up and dye.

Today, however, Ruby feels anything but cozy. Eyes bore into her from the mirrors at the four hair stations and from above opened magazines in the waiting area. Tuesdays are always busy days. But today there is an extra hum in the air. And every woman needs to use the bathroom just beyond Ruby's nail table at least once, walking slowly past her on the way to and fro. If she had a sense of humor at all today, she would make a joke about a contagious bladder infection spreading around like a summer cold.

Ruby's own clients are more discreet. They talk about their weekends, complain about their husbands, but the obvious strain of not talking about Ruby's plight is worse than answering questions would be. One client, who is getting only a haircut today, makes a point of stopping by the nail station, patting Ruby on the head. "I'm sorry to hear about your troubles," she says. Ruby doesn't like this, either. She doesn't like the staring; doesn't like the pretending that nothing is going on; doesn't like the patronizing attempts at comfort. She wants her fifteen minutes to be over.

The fourth appointment is Beverly Sokol, a longtime client whose metabolism was obliterated by chemotherapy several years ago. Beverly has a great attitude; Ruby has never seen her down. She has no breasts. Her hair grew back gray and limp and uncontrollable, when she was hoping for springy red curls. She can't control her weight. But, by God, she's going to control something, if only a perfect ten of passion-pink acrylic nails.

Today Beverly sits in the client chair and promptly dissolves into tears. "I'm sorry," she gasps between sobs. "It's just so awful." Ruby brings her a glass of water, puts a box of tissues on the table. Beverly cries through the soaking, cries through the application of acrylic fill with the paintbrush, through shaping the nails with an electric file. She cries all the tears that Ruby can't shed.

Not until Ruby strokes polish on the first hand does Beverly drop the last wad of tissues in her lap. She puts her other hand flat on the table, sits up straight in her chair. "Oh, my." Her voice is as soggy as the tissues. "It's just . . ."

"I know," Ruby says. "It is. But I finally have some good news. A hearing—for probable cause, it's called—has been scheduled for next week, in Dallas. And the CPS worker has arranged for me to visit with Lark while I'm there."

Knowing when she will see Lark has lifted such a black weight off her that Ruby wonders how she managed to stand upright with it in the first place. Like when a person has the flu. The first day she starts to feel better, she thinks, *Wow, I feel so much better*, and doesn't realize how ill she still felt *that* day until she feels so much better yet the next day. Ruby will never recover from the virus of losing Lark, but at least the days are more bearable now.

Even so, by one thirty, Ruby's head is pounding harder than her heart. The stench of hair spray and ammonia-based dye, the pulse of the New Age music Zara turns a decibel too loud, the glob of turkey sandwich caroming around in her stomach, all of it ends up in the space between her eyebrows and hairline.

She tidies up her station, sterilizes her tools, throws a load of towels in the washing machine in the back room.

"You're an official tourist attraction." Margaret leans against the counter, speaking between mouthfuls of her own late lunch.

"I'm so sorry," Ruby says. "I know it's a distraction."

"No complaints from me." Margaret snaps the lid on her plastic salad bowl, crams it back in the refrigerator. "We're booked solid through next week."

FORTY-ONE

The doorbell rings soon after Ruby and the dog get home from an evening walk. She turns from the kitchen counter, and the earth shifts beneath her feet. Her heart hammers her ribs as she walks to the door.

"Lark . . ."

Ruby swallows the rest of her sentence when she sees the stricken eyes on the other side of the screen, tries to regain her composure. ". . . Is not here. She's in Texas, Numi." Numi stands there, holding a book in her brown arms. Numi's build is more athletic, the body of a gymnast rather than a ballerina. She is taller than Lark. They couldn't possibly be mistaken for each other, even in dim porch light, except by a parched soul desperate to believe.

"I know. My mom told me." The young girl holds out the book. "This is hers. I didn't get to give it back."

Ruby takes the slender volume from Numi. "That's okay, sweetie. I'm pretty sure she read this one already." Ruby pauses, smiles. "A few hundred times anyway. Would you like to keep it?"

Numi forces her mouth into a class-photo grimace. "No, thanks."

Ruby feels a surge of desire to keep this friend of Lark near. "Why don't you come in?"

"My mom, she's waiting in the car." Numi stares at the porch floor, scuffs her shoe back and forth. Ruby leans out, waves to Numi's mother at the curb, waits.

"I was just wondering." Numi rakes her hand through Clyde's coat. "She's not going to come back, is she?"

Ruby hugs the young girl against her, her large hand a skullcap on the small head. Every time Ruby breaks a heart, hers breaks a little more, too. "Maybe you'd like to come walk Clyde sometime, keep him company."

Numi buries her face at Ruby's hip. "It wouldn't be the same."

"No, it won't. But sometimes, in time, different turns out to be okay, too." Somehow, Ruby thinks, if she can console this child, spread a balm atop her naked wound, then maybe the healing will reach Lark as well.

Numi pulls away, turns from Ruby, swiping an arm across her face. "*That* would take a very long time." As the child slinks down the driveway, Ruby calls out to her. "I'll tell her, when I see her. I'll tell her you said hi." Clyde licks Ruby's arm while she waits until she hears the car door shut, watches Numi's mother drive away.

In the corner of the ceiling, Lark's bat, Louie, hangs undisturbed. Ruby remembers a summer evening a couple of years ago, soon after Lark discovered their front-porch friend. Chaz was grilling—corn on the cob, hot dogs for Lark and Numi, a big steak for him and Ruby to share.

"Louie." Lark's rosy tongue pushed through the gap of four missing front teeth. "Chaz says we should name him Louie."

Ruby remembers Chaz grinning from the side-porch grill, teasing him about being a bad influence on her daughter. "That's just so politically incorrect, naming a bat after Mr. Armstrong. You'll have the antidefamation league after us for sure."

And then the girls giggling. "He's blind, mama. Bats are blind, not deaf."

And Chaz at the same time protesting, "Not Armstrong. Slugger. Louisville Slugger, the *bat*."

Then Ruby dissolving in laughter at the whole Abbott-and-Costelloish confusion, not even trying to explain to Lark and Numi the difference between "deaf" and "defamation."

Tonight, she looks up at Louie and sighs. "This house needs some laughter."

FORTY-TWO

"Come on, girlfriend." Antoinette pushes Ruby out the door. "You need to get out for a while."

Ruby's shoes scrape across the gravel driveway like one of the old men walking the halls at the nursing home where she volunteers. She climbs onto the side rail of Antoinette's cousin's pickup truck, heaves herself into the passenger seat.

"This'll be good for you. We'll find you an old chifforobe or something to punish." Antoinette backs down the driveway, takes Old Pecos Trail, the more scenic route from the center of Santa Fe to the highway.

Ruby slides from side to side on the seat with each turn of the truck. She feels adrift somehow, tightens the seat belt that rests below her belly. She keeps looking over at Antoinette, way on the other side of the cabin, across the abyss that used to be Lark on these trips.

Antoinette tries to fill the void with small talk, about her workweek, how glad she is that the judge she works for decided to close the office while he is on vacation. She talks about her last bad date, her family's latest antics. Then her speech sputters to an awkward stop in the first sentence of a story about her cousin's six-year-old daughter.

"It's okay," Ruby says. "I know that other kids still exist."

"Just remember, in only eight years, maybe seven if the courts agree, Lark will be able to decide for herself where to live."

Ruby looks out the window, at the vast expanse of scrub brush and sand. Eight years is almost as much time as *she* had with Lark. "What if she ends up hating me for what I did? What if she likes being a little rich girl better?"

Antoinette looks down at the space between them. "The Lark I know wouldn't do either of those things."

"A lot can happen in eight years."

Antoinette fiddles with the radio dial, tunes in an Albuquerque country station. "I'm not gonna tell you everything'll turn out all right. But I will tell you I'll be there with you, no matter what."

"Will you come visit me in jail?"

Antoinette takes Ruby's hand. "Oh, girlfriend. I'll be bringing you the cake with a file."

"With your cooking?" Ruby squeezes Antoinette's hand then lets go. "I'd probably die from the cake before I could break out."

"Pot." Antoinette flicks Ruby's shoulder with the back of her hand.

Ruby manages another grin. Her cheeks feel tight, muscles unused to the upward movement. "Kettle."

FORTY-THREE

A smattering of people work their way around the furniture crammed into the back room of the auction house. The owner, Ernesto, waves to Ruby as she and Antoinette enter. Four or five times a year, or whenever the stacks of chairs reach the rafters and any semblance of aisles disappears, he holds these last-chance sales of estate items that have not been sold.

Ruby never bothers attending the first-call monthly auctions; antique dealers and decorators and, especially, novice collectors drive the prices out of Ruby's range at those events. But here, amid the chipped veneer and crap-wood pieces, she has found many treasures. Burled walnut buried under fourteen layers of paint, golden oak planks in furniture too banged up to be useful in its current incarnation.

"It's like a giant furniture purgatory," Antoinette says, as if she's never been here before.

"No," Ruby says, "purgatory is the county dump where the stuff goes from here. This is limbo, one last chance to get it right."

Antoinette weaves between a row of dining tables stacked face-to-face, running her hands down legs in a variety of styles. "I always feel like I'm at the dog pound. I want to rescue them all."

Ruby pauses in front of a tall piece, a sturdy cabineted base with a bookcase-like top, two wide screen doors opening to narrow shelves.

"What is that?" Antoinette asks.

Ruby picks at the faded blue paint. A thick chip breaks loose. Underneath are layers and layers of several colors, like the sandstone cliffs at the ancient Anasazi Indian pueblos. She tugs at two drawers. One has a rotting bottom; one won't even open it is so warped. "A pie safe." She tips open a tin-lined drawer below the shelves of the top. "This is where they stored the flour. And here"—Ruby yanks out a wooden cutting board hidden above the drawers of the base—"is where they rolled out the crust. Then, after the pies were baked, they cooled on the shelves."

"Cool," Antoinette says. "What are you thinking you'd make out of it?"

"Here, help me." Ruby motions to Antoinette to tug at the heavy base while she slips a hand between the piece and the armoire it stands against. She knocks on the back of the pie safe; it is solid wood, not cheap plywood as on so many modern pieces. "I don't know. I let them tell me. Sometimes a table stays a table, sometimes it becomes something else."

"Oh, Ruby." Ernesto—as always in shiny black cowboy boots, dark dress pants, and starched western-cut shirt—walks up to them. When he shakes his head, his trim beard scrapes against his collar, jiggling the strings of his bolo tie. "That one, she's a lot of work for not so much wood. And Lord knows even what kind of wood is beneath all that paint."

"Ah, but she speaks to me," Ruby says. "We're kindred spirits."

Ernesto shakes his head again, his tie strings swaying. "You and your talking wood." He opens one of the upper doors; its rusty screening sags forlornly. He reaches into the back corner, and two of his sausage fingers appear outside the top, waggling in the air like bunny ears. "Did she tell you she come with her own mouse hole?" Ernesto laughs as he extracts his hand. "I know you the furniture doctor, Ruby. But this, she need one heck of a salvage operation."

Ruby scrapes her fingernail across the flaking paint. "Like I said, we're kindred spirits."

FORTY-FOUR

The biggest draw of the season, Indian Market, is still a month away, yet the flea market is crowded with fat tourists wearing bright T-shirts and fanny packs, and skinny locals wearing smug disdain. Anyone who doubts the reports of rampant obesity in America need only spend a Saturday morning in Adobe Disneyland. Of course this is an exaggeration—there are lots of skinny tourists and fat locals, too.

Fortunately, the media have lost interest. Another child goes missing, another wife is axed, and the storm is over as quickly as it started. *Lark who?* Their story, praise God, just didn't have "legs."

Several of Ruby's clients stop in, each with a dog beside her. Two golden Labs, one regal Bouvier, and a snuffling pug in a sun hat. Everyone and his dog, literally, are at the market today.

All the humans have heard the news, offer their support. "Oh, Ruby," they say. "Oh, dear." All the dogs offer licks. Ruby keeps from drowning in sympathy by reminding herself that the visit with Lark is next week. Even though she knows no visit will ever be long enough, at least she'll get to *see* Lark, see for herself how her daughter is doing in her new life.

Beer Barrel Pete sidles up to Ruby just after noon. His watery eyes dart over her shoulder, scanning the aisle. He looks like he's jonesing for caffeine, or something more sixties. Pete has been wearing the same pair of jeans and woven hippie shirt for the past decade. His hair is a wilder, longer tangle of gray, and the road map of hard days is etched more deeply on his face. He, too, has heard, but he hasn't come with words of support. "You didn't get it from me," he whispers. Ruby can taste the Winstons on his breath.

This man only looks like an addle-brained derelict; he remembers every single one of his customers and what he supplied each of them. And he wants assurance that Ruby won't tell the authorities where she got Lark's birth certificate all those years ago. Pete need not worry. John didn't exactly advise her to burn evidence, but he did make sure she understood that the federal crime was for *possession* of a forged document.

"Get what?" Ruby says with theatrical confusion.

"That's my girl." Pete spins away from her and melts into the crowd.

Just before closing, as a nice couple from Minnesota arranges for the shipping of Ruby's last pair of porch chairs to their lake house, John comes into the booth. "This stuff is gorgeous." He wanders around the booth, running his hands along the surfaces of the few remaining pieces until Ruby finishes her paperwork. When the Minnesotans leave, he gestures behind him. "Let's take a walk."

He leads Ruby down the mostly deserted aisle, past the vendors packing up their wares in trailers and trucks, disassembling their tents. Her blood has stopped flowing altogether as she imagines all kinds of horrors. "Is it Lark?" Her voice sounds like it is coming from very far away, farther than even Lark is right now. "Tell me."

"She's okay." John puts a hand on Ruby's back. "They wouldn't let me talk to her, but their lawyer assured me she's okay."

"But?"

"The prosecutor presented your case to a grand jury and got an indictment. That means there is no need for the probable cause hearing. And we have a trial setting, for six weeks from now."

"That's good, though, right?" Ruby asks. "I mean, you said we'd lose the probable cause hearing anyway. At least this moves it along. I want it to be over. And I can still go next week, for the visit with Lark."

John's shoulders sag. "They rescheduled the visitation for the day of the trial."

The hubbub around Ruby becomes a blur. *Six weeks.* How can she possibly hold on that long? They loop their way around the perimeter of the market, past the concession stand reeking of popcorn and hot dogs cooked too long, and back down Ruby's aisle, as she tries to absorb the reverberation of this latest blast.

Then John reaches into his pocket, pulls out a cell phone. The cell phone Ruby gave to Lark. "They sent it to my office. They don't want Lark to call you."

FORTY-FIVE

"At all?" Ruby takes the phone from him. "For *six weeks?*"

John explains that the Tinsdales got a court order barring Ruby from any contact with Lark. Phone calls, even letters, interfere with the reestablishment of their bond. And they'll refuse delivery of any more packages from the Ms as well. "They want their child back, and they want her to themselves."

"They lost *their* child that night at the gas station," Ruby says. "Lark is not that same child. There is no bond to reestablish."

"Hey," John says. "You're preaching to the choir. I'm the good guy, remember?"

Ruby tries to take a deep breath, but a ball of air and dust catches at the back of her throat. "I'm sorry."

"There's more," John says as they reach Ruby and Jay's booth. "They will produce her for the visitation prior to your hearing, as CPS recommended."

"But?"

"But the Tinsdales are 'unreceptive,' as their lawyer put it, to the idea of any form of visitation, beyond the one visit."

Anguish rises like morning sickness in her throat. Ruby lied when she told herself she was preparing for this. She could never be prepared for this. "So that's it? One visit and good-bye forever?"

She walks across the booth, sinks onto the little folding stool that she never seems to find time to use while the market is open, drops the phone in the dirt at her feet. *Not forever,* she tries to remind herself. Seven, maybe eight years before Lark is old enough to decide for herself. But what if the Tinsdales poison Lark's memories of Ruby, turn Lark against her for keeping them apart? Her hands land on her belly, and the realization that this child may never know her sister spins around in the dust at Ruby's feet.

Jay shoots her a worried look, then turns back to packing up the last of his serving pieces into the milk crates he "recycled" from behind the Albertson's at the edge of town, with an ear cocked toward Ruby and John.

"We're not giving up yet," John says. "We can still file a petition for visitation in family court. A lot will depend on what happens at the trial."

"You mean if I go to jail."

"Let's not even go there right now."

Ruby puts her hands on her knees, drops her head between them, trying to make the ground and sky stop their dance. Jay gives up all pretense of not listening, gives her a bottle of water.

"Can I try?" She lifts her head up, looks at John. "Can I try to talk to them."

"With the protective order, and the trial pending, that wouldn't be appropriate." John shakes his head. "Let's just give this some time, see if it settles down a bit."

"And if it doesn't," Ruby asks. "If it doesn't *settle*?"

John shrugs, shakes his head.

The first thunderhead of an impending afternoon storm speeds across the sky, a solitary ship on a vast azure sea. Across the field, the imposing structure of the Santa Fe Opera is barely visible over the hill. That's another thing Ruby didn't get done this summer. Since Lark was five, they have gone to an opera each season, either in the nosebleed cheap seats or with up-close tickets that a client happened to offer her. There just wasn't enough time; there could never be enough time to spend with Lark.

Beer Barrel Pete galumphs past and gives Ruby a conspiring look. Maybe she *should* steal Lark back. Sometimes doing the wrong thing is the only way to make something right.

FORTY-SIX

Dawn doesn't break so much as seep. Shiny obsidian fades to streaks of deepest purple, then lavender. Stark slashes of trees flesh out into trunk and limbs and leaves. Ruby is as road-weary as her Jeep; neither of them has driven much beyond Santa Fe in the past decade. She took the back route, through Galisteo, down to Clines Corner, picking up the interstate to Amarillo then state highways to Wichita Falls, interstate down to the city. All towns are ghost towns in the hours before sunrise; the strip malls of larger cities as ethereal as the cotton gins of the hamlets.

Then she reached Dallas. This neighborhood is a pocket of verdancy in the midst of all the cement, houses set back on large lots, parkways stretching their long green legs behind them. The house is plunked down between two cottages-on-steroids that look like they grew from irradiated seeds in their own gardens. Next to them, the Tinsdales' newer Tudor seems ill at ease, as if company is coming and it must be on its best behavior. The yard is immaculate, not a sprig of a shrub or a blade of grass out of place. The stone is scrubbed-with-a-toothbrush clean. Windows and gaslights gleam in the silver light, and a massive Martha Stewart wreath chokes the front door. This is not the house of an accidental housekeeper.

Ruby stares at the windows, but she sees no evidence of life beyond the fancy draperies. The house doesn't breathe, let alone laugh. She can't imagine her sprite of a daughter springing like Tigger through its hallways.

The tears come unbidden with a startling new thought: *what if*

Lark is better off here than with Ruby? What does Ruby have to give? She hasn't amounted to much in her uneducated ragtag series of lives. These people can offer Lark so much that Ruby can't. Maybe a Tiggerless life was what Lark was meant to live all along.

Ruby crumples over the steering wheel as the weight of it all comes crashing down on her. The pain of losing Lark will never go away. Ruby *knows* this, because she has lost so much, too much, already. The hurt may wane, even scab over for a time, but it will be there, always. And now the wrenching guilt of having deprived Lark of who she was meant to be. It is all too much for one body to contain. If Ruby can't live without Lark, yet Lark shouldn't live with her, then how can Ruby live at all?

The rap on the Jeep window penetrates Ruby's hiccups and gasps. Her head jerks, arm flails against the door handle.

"Ma'am, I need you to step out of the car please."

Ruby wipes her sleeve across her face. She looks out at a paunch stuffed in beige, then an irritated mouth comes into view. "Ma'am?"

The rest of her day is interminable. Alone in a cell in a police station, Ruby sits on a bench bracketed to the wall. Her body is wrung dry of tears. She feels crazed in the exposed cage, even in a clean, rather *Mayberry* cage. If she were to be sentenced to prison . . . she'll end up in a mental ward.

Midmorning, a polite young officer brings her a sausage biscuit, and a few hours later, a fried chicken platter. "Bubba's finest," he says. Ruby is amazed to find she is ravenous, devours everything, sops up cream gravy with a flaky biscuit.

She tries to doze, but phones ring incessantly. And she can't stop the screaming in her head. Finally, the cell door slides open and John stands in front of her.

"*What* were you thinking, Ruby?" He waves his arm. "No, don't answer that, not here."

An officer leads them through a series of hallways to a courtroom. Dark wood paneling, movie-theater seats. Ruby sits beside John as he talks to the judge, more a conversation than TV-courtroom banter, like buddies chatting over a pitcher of beer. Technically, she is not in violation of the protective order; she didn't attempt to contact or communicate with the child in any fashion. And though she is on bond in the federal matter, she did not cross state lines with the intention of fleeing.

The judge has thick white hair and a country-club tan. "What do you have to say for yourself, Ms. Leander?"

"I just needed to see it, where she is living, so I could picture her *somewhere*."

After more talk and admonishments, Ruby is released into John's custody. They will fly back to Albuquerque; her Jeep will be shipped to Santa Fe.

Anger reaches the brim of John's voice as they leave the courthouse. "You are damn lucky those folks live in Highland Park and not the city of Dallas. Separate cities, separate jails. You'd still be just some number in a cell for sure." He tells her she screwed up royally, that this may impact the outcome of the federal case.

"I wasn't going to take her," Ruby says. But she's not altogether sure what she would have done.

FORTY-SEVEN

Ruby's arm muscles ache. Her hands are raw, knuckles scraped of a layer of skin for each layer of paint she has scraped off the old pie safe. Tonight she sits on the shed floor, maneuvering around her belly to scour drawer faces between her splayed knees.

The final layer of paint simply dissolves under steel wool instead of loosening and lifting in pieces like a typical strip job. None of the usual chemical solvents even penetrated this last layer; Ruby spent many frustrating hours trying to chip through it with her scraper. And now, after all that work, the stubborn stuff just liquefies with plain old vinegar. Milk paint—made with actual milk way back in the day. She hadn't come across that one before, but fortunately one of her grandfather's books held the answer.

All her labor has done nothing to dull her other ache. The loneliness is unfathomable, this Lark-sized hole in the world. Like a bird knows where to fly south for winter, like a tree knows to reach for sunshine, Ruby knows she has made the biggest mistake of her life. Lark was right; Ruby shouldn't have told. They should have run if they had to. Sometimes doing the right thing is worse than doing nothing at all.

A memory fizzes to the surface, Mrs. Olestein, the high school health teacher, scratching yet another of her many lists on the chalkboard. The seven warning signs. *A sore that does not heal.* This Larkless life is a cancer. Eating away her heart, her soul. This sore will never heal; it is a gaping wound.

She trudges through her days. Each morning, she rolls out of bed, chokes down her vitamins. She goes to work at the salon, home, then here to the shed until her legs refuse to support her body any longer. Then she lies in bed, clinging to Lark's "I am" shirt, a piece of pure Larkness, her Lark, not some Tyler the Tinsdales are determined to reclaim. She watches through the window as light shifts through a spectrum of gray, while she thinks up unthinkable plots to kidnap her daughter all over again.

Clyde's bark alerts her before Chaz steps into the shed. His bulk absorbs a wedge of the fluorescent light. She sets aside the vinegar bottle as he steps behind her, slips his hands at her armpits and hoists her to her feet.

He keeps a hand on her shoulder until she stands steady then turns her to face him. "Wow," he says to the belly that brushes against his belt buckle. The struggle is there in his eyes, to comprehend the reality, the overt actuality of this other life. "Wow."

An angry welt rises from his cheekbone. Ruby reaches out, stops short of touching it.

"It's nothing," Chaz says. "The kid got in a cheap shot."

Ruby's struggle to comprehend *this* reality is like pouring that bottle of vinegar straight through her veins. Chaz's job is not only unpredictable; it is dangerous. If something were to happen to him . . . Ruby doesn't know how she can possibly make this relationship work, with the chasm of the secret she kept from him and the void of Lark between them. But she doesn't know how she can *not* make it work, either. The scent of Chaz, lime and musk, mixes with her acrid workshop smells.

Ruby knows only this, she knows that she loves him. "I just worry."

"I know. But don't." Chaz walks over to the radio, tweaks the ancient dial, trying to bring in the oldies station more clearly. He doesn't mind her taste in music, but he can't stand the static. Maybe because his work is anything but, he does everything he can to make the rest of his life static-free.

"I missed you," Ruby says.

"More." He gives up on the radio, runs his hand across the rough and warped base of the pie safe. "This poor thing is a mess."

"So am I," Ruby says.

Chaz folds his arms. "I'm sorry I haven't been here for you. First the conference, and then two shifts back-to-back."

"It's okay. I understand."

"But are *you* okay?" He steps over to her, pulls her into an embrace. "Look at you." He leans back, hands on her shoulders, eyes on her belly. "Look at her. Are you eating? Taking care of both of you?"

Ruby pulls him outside the shed, down onto the cool grass, rests her head on his shoulder. The night is full-dark, the stars as sharp as the scent of pine in the air, as if she could reach up and pluck them like apples from a tree. "I'm lost without her."

"I know."

"I just want her back." Ruby sits up, clutches a fistful of Chaz's shirt. "We could do it. We could go to Mexico, with Lark and the baby. Start over—"

Chaz takes Ruby's face in his hands. "Look at me. Enough. That's crazy talk."

She stretches out on the lawn. "I know. I just miss her . . . so much." She tells him how she thinks about that other mother, what she went through. "This is unbearable, even knowing where she is. I can't imagine what it would be like if I didn't know that she's safe."

Chaz traces circles on her forehead, rakes his fingers through her hair. She breathes in, still surprised after all these years to find crisp, clean oxygen with not even a hint of Iowa rendering plant. His words, *everything will be all right, everything will be all right,* are a lullaby. And finally Ruby drifts off to sleep under the stars, with Chaz's lap as pillow.

FORTY-EIGHT

When she opens her door, Celeste laughs, places both hands on Ruby's belly as if she were a preacher healing the wounds of the world. Chunk stands inside the doorway, fidgeting as Ruby and Chaz enter.

Inside the house, the Monteroland clan swarms Ruby and Chaz. Even the auntsunclescousins are on the welcome committee, either as recompense for the last dinner's debacle or in deference to Ruby's pain. Like a square dance, they swirl and whirl around Ruby and Chaz, until Chaz has been do-si-doed to the living room with the men and Ruby has been spun off to the kitchen with the women.

The air is rich with spices; jars line the counter like toy soldiers marching toward the stove top. Cumin, coriander, saffron, ginger, cinnamon, paprika. Celeste is up to Morocco on her world gastronomical tour. Ruby missed Japan through Lithuania, yet Celeste, Ruby is sure, hasn't missed a bit of what's been going on.

"Don't worry." Aunt Tia pats Ruby on the back. "We're not eating with our fingers."

Ruby eyes the water pitcher; she is anxious to keep busy. Antoinette must notice, because she fills the ice bucket and motions Ruby toward the table.

"So your court date got moved up." Antoinette reaches past chairs, dumping scoops of ice cubes into water goblets.

"Yeah, the judge had a hole in his schedule." Ruby pours water slowly, as much to stretch out the task as to protect Celeste's table. "If it means I see Lark sooner, if it means the trial will be over sooner . . ."

"If I were your lawyer . . ." Antoinette has talked about applying to law school since Ruby has known her.

"You should, you know," Ruby says. "You'd be good, *do* good."

"I just wish I could fix it, just this one thing, you know?"

"I wish you could, too." The clank of ice cubes against glass sounds like wind chimes as she gives Antoinette the latest news.

John told her just yesterday that the Tinsdales are now screaming about a civil suit, suing her for damages for keeping Lark from them. Like when a wife sues her husband's mistress for loss of conjugal rights or parents sue a hospital for wrongful life. Not that Lark shouldn't have been born, but that she didn't get to live the life she was supposed to have lived, that Ruby gave her the wrong life. *Civil lawyer,* Ruby thinks, *that is definitely an oxymoron.* She is in the unfortunate situation of facing both a criminal prosecutor and a civil trial lawyer who have political aspirations, John explained, and they will seek the spotlight at every turn.

Ruby's own attorney is a jack-of-all-crimes and will represent her in both the civil and criminal proceedings at a fraction of his usual fees. "Margaret offered a lifetime of free salon services for his wife," Ruby tells Antoinette.

"He's probably getting the better bargain."

First Lark was treated like property. Now the value of trying to keep Ruby out of jail is being measured in shampoos and sets. "His wife *is* addicted to hair spray," Ruby says.

FORTY-NINE

Buffered between Chaz and Antoinette in the circle of faces around the table, Ruby is touched when Chunk adds to his prayer a plea to watch over her in "her trials and tribulations." She is also relieved to see Chunk's sister remove the wine goblet from her husband's place setting; the farting uncle apparently has been conscripted to the wagon. He looks down at his lap when Celeste holds up the wine bottle. Ruby is not the only reluctant teetotaler at this table.

"Today's pairing is an Australian shiraz, to complement but not compete with the Moroccan spices." Clearly, Celeste has been watching too much of the Food Network.

By an edict from Celeste, no doubt, the meal chatter is kept far from anything to do with Lark or Ruby. Tia's daughter is grilled about her new boyfriend until an uncle asks Chunk about the rash of residential construction in the south of the county. This topic carries them well through the plates of roasted lamb with a tomato-onion glaze, steaming couscous the color of autumn, stewed vegetables with chickpeas. Chunk has worked for the county roads department forever, from the grit and grime of pothole detail to his current position as supervisor of all the crews, and he is the resident expert on land development.

The dinner table is a storm, flooding wine and snowdrifts of food. Ruby eats slowly to avoid any chance of a repeat of her performance art at the last meal. She chews chews chews each bite of lamb so tender that neither silverware nor teeth are necessary. And at some point during the meal, she realizes that she feels almost *good*. The grief of losing Lark is a tight twist of second skin, like the ripples and welts from a third-degree burn. She'll walk around with those scars forever, but she *will* walk around.

Finally, dessert, a honey-soaked pastry stuffed with apricots and almond paste, is passed. Every culture, it seems, has its own burrito. After she has eaten enough to look like she has eaten enough, Ruby elbows Chaz.

"Sorry, Ma," Chaz says. "We gotta go. I want to crash a pickup game at the park basketball court. Try to bond with the street thugs."

"The dog, he's still not eating," Ruby adds. "I need to check . . ."

Before Ruby and Chaz reach his car, Celeste hurries through the gate. She thrusts a grocery bag full of leftovers into Ruby's arms, smooshes the bag and Ruby in another embrace. "We'll all keep lighting candles. You, Lark, your baby girl. The dog, too. You're all going to be all right."

FIFTY

"What on earth?" Chaz stares down at the bucket of pink glop and the crowd of lidless brown bottles on the newspaper that is spread out on the back porch.

Ruby stirs the mixture with a wooden spoon, squeezes a few drops of red food coloring from a tiny plastic bottle. The drops splat into the bucket, swirl into the mixture, then disappear, barely deepening the shade of pink. "I bought all the single bottles at Albertsons and the Plaza market, but it still wasn't enough." Ruby gestures to the stack of small rectangular cartons beside her. "So the Ms went back and bought up the variety packs as well."

"We're the food-coloring cavalry," Margaret says from a deck chair.

Chaz squats down beside Ruby, brushes away the strands of hair that have escaped the elastic band, places a hand on her neck, "But why are you using food coloring in the first place?"

"Because I didn't have time to pick berries." Ruby scratches her brow with her forearm.

Chaz's face registers a *huh?* as he sits down beside her. The dog lumbers over and licks Chaz's cheek.

"The milk paint." Ruby waves her wooden spoon toward the dismantled pieces of pie safe strewn around her—bottomless drawers, cabinet doors, shelving, and the empty husks of the base and upper half. The inside of the upper casing is painted white; the rest of the wood is bare. "I wanted to replace the original finish."

"So you're making paint." Chaz picks up a box of instant milk, pours a few flakes into his hand. "From milk."

"Yes," Ruby says. "Hence the name *milk* paint." She picks a dog hair from the mixture, flicks it onto the newspaper.

Molly laughs. "Duh, Chaz. What did you think, that the pioneers rode their horses over to Sherwin-Williams?"

Chaz shakes his head. "I don't think I ever thought about that at all."

"Neither had we. Of course, the pioneers used milk straight from the cow." Margaret pauses to drink from her goblet. "Ruby has allowed herself a few modern shortcuts in her quest for authenticity."

Ruby pulls the red-coned top off another little bottle, squeezes it over the bucket. "I have to get it red enough, then I can add some blue to tone it down. I just didn't know it would suck up this much tint."

"We suggested wine." Margaret refills Molly's glass then her own from the bottle on the table. "Berries, grapes, what's the difference?"

Chaz picks up a roll of mesh wire, fingers the mesh. "This for the doors? I'll cut it for you."

"No!" Ruby grabs the screening from him, places it out of his reach. "I need to do this one by myself." She can hear the streak of mania in her voice, can read Chaz's wary look. He often helps her, screwing legs and armrests onto chairs, even sanding if he's really bored.

A flash of memory sears her mind, Lark at two, shoes on the wrong feet, struggling to find the armhole of her shirt. "By myself. All by myself," she would demand.

"Don't be offended," Margaret says. "She yelled at us, too."

"Okay, then," Chaz says. "Can I at least keep you ladies company?"

Molly gestures to the wine. "Grab a goblet. Join us for the show."

Ruby realizes she is acting crazy, but this one, she needs to do by herself. She needs to put this warped, rotted, mouse-holed pie safe back together before she goes on trial. Somehow, she just needs to salvage this one piece.

FIFTY-ONE

The wooden bowl of popcorn rests on the ball of daughter that used to be Ruby's lap. Clyde sits at attention beside her, his head following the movement of her hand from the bowl to her mouth, waiting to catch any pieces she drops. Popcorn and orange juice, together, what an odd craving.

Casablanca fills the TV screen in all its black-and-white glory. Ruby keeps waiting for Lark's pure-honey voice to chime in with her favorite lines. *Will they always have their Paris?* she wonders. Will Lark even remember her after a few years?

When the reflection of headlights swooshes across the wall, Clyde leaps from the sofa and lands almost at the front door. Ruby, however, needs several attempts to heave herself out of the sofa sinkhole. In the process, she elbows the bowl, and popcorn showers the room like confetti shot from an air gun. She opens the door as the Ms step onto the porch.

"We were in the neighborhood." Molly's grin is sheepish.

Ruby looks back and forth between Margaret and Molly. "You guys making sure I haven't crawled back under the covers?"

"Of course not." Margaret whistles to the dog. "Hey, Clyde, let's go for a walk."

Clyde pauses his popcorn snarfing, looks to the door, to the floor, to Ruby. "Tough decision, buddy," Ruby says.

The Ms' terrier mix darts around Margaret, grabs a puff of popcorn, dashes back out the door. Clyde's tail swats Ruby's leg as he shoots past her in hot pursuit of the small dog, leaving behind, amid the popcorn, a swath of rug worthy of a vacuum cleaner commercial.

Margaret nods to Molly. She calls her other dog and follows Clyde and Dudley down the drive. In their wake, Ruby motions Molly inside.

"You throwing popcorn at TV shows again?"

"Ha ha," Ruby says. "Want some tea?"

Molly answers by heading to the kitchen, grabbing two mugs out of the cabinet.

Ruby follows her, fills the kettle, puts it on the stove. She lifts down the acrylic container of tea boxes from the top of the fridge, slides it across the counter to Molly. "Well?"

"Something herbal, I think," Molly says.

"No, why are you here?"

"Since when can we not just drop by?"

Ruby raises an eyebrow, waits for the water to boil, while Molly makes her tea selection like one of Ruby's clients choosing polish from the rack. Ruby pours steaming water into the mugs, and she and Molly walk out to the back porch. These August days are still summer hot, but the taste of autumn is in the night air.

In a deck chair, Ruby holds her mug in two hands. "Okay. What?"

"My grandfather was a bootlegger," Molly says. She tells Ruby how he ran liquor through half of Missouri. Ruby has heard this story before, over bottles of wine, but she tucks a chenille throw around her legs and lets Molly talk. About how her grandfather didn't marry until he was fifty, how he and her grandmother had just one child, Molly's mother. The grandfather was a mean old son of a bitch, but he was a smart old son of a bitch. He put half his proceeds into stocks—just after the big market crash of 1929—and buried the stock certificates in a cast-iron box in the yard. The other half he kept in cash, in an oil drum in his shed, and he supported his family through the Great Depression on periodic withdrawals from the "Bank of Jim Beam."

Clyde leaps onto the porch before Molly gets to her point, no doubt running ahead of Margaret as usual. Molly rubs his head while he licks her chin, and through the kisses she tells Ruby her idea. "It's a karma thing, see, to pay your legal fees with my trust fund. You're in trouble because you did right by Lark. He never did right by anyone. His own daughter was a punching bag. To use his money, it's just karma is all."

Ruby leans back into her chair, puts her mug on the table. Clyde moves over to her, lays his head in her lap. This is big. This could be Ruby's answer, at least to the financial end of her problems. Molly's generosity, though, is just too big.

"Please. You and Lark—you're family." Molly talks with her hands. Freckles of paint, yellows and greens, dot her cuticles, lie under her nails, mirror the freckles that splash across her nose. "Let me do this. At least think about it."

Margaret's voice comes out of the shadows of the driveway. "Oh, she'll let you, for damn sure."

Ruby can't help grin. Maybe Celeste's candles are working. Because for the first time, Ruby actually does think that everything could turn out all right. Of course, that thought usually precedes her world turning to crap.

FIFTY-TWO

Ruby hasn't been on an airplane since that day long ago, the day that marked the end of her first life and the beginning of her second. And now she's flown twice in a month. She leans her head against the cool glass of the window and stares down at the swipe of land far below. The odd alien circles and sewing machine–straight roads are like the repeating patches and seams of that crazy quilt that she pictures as her several lives.

She squirms against the upright seat, anxious for the trial to be over, anxious for it to start. Anxious in its correct definition, definitely not as a substitute for eager. And eager doesn't begin to describe how she feels about seeing Lark.

Beside her, John does a crossword puzzle. He fills in the squares, line by line, in confident blue ink. Ruby tries to absorb some of that confidence.

The pilot announces the descent into Dallas impossibly soon after the takeoff from Albuquerque, and the hemstitched land is replaced by car-clogged highways and shopping centers and houses with turquoise patches of backyard pools. House after house in tidy rows, as if they had been planted, crop dusted by Butch from her Iowa hometown.

The plane touches tarmac as smoothly as a busybody neighbor running a glove across a dusty mantel, and Ruby and John join the conga line of people and black roller suitcases and strollers down the jetway. When did people start wearing their chore clothes to travel? she wonders. She remembers a Sunday-best atmosphere on that other flight so long ago.

She herself is dressed for her appearance in court. John urged her to look young and sweet. And pregnant. The makers of maternity clothes made the sweet part easy. This stretchy lavender top and dotted skirt were on the unsweet end of the spectrum. Lark's image lady would have barfed over all the girly pink ribbons and bows.

The idle chatter of the airport gate area distills into a steady buzz as they approach the security point, excited whispers, heads craning side to side. *Maybe it's a proposal,* Ruby thinks; she read about one of those in a celebrity magazine at the salon.

As they approach the narrow exit from the secured area, microphones and cameras and people press against the glass wall. The crowd parts like Moses' sea as she and John step into the glare of lights. Not a proposal, she realizes; this is a perp walk. And she is the perp.

"Shit," John says under his breath. His expression is somewhere between pained and totally pissed off. "That asshole lawyer," he mutters.

A uniformed agent runs interference inside the secured area, but once they cross through to the main terminal, they are on their own. John leans over Ruby like an umbrella, trying to protect her from pelting questions. "Keep your head down and your mouth shut," he hisses over the din.

Ruby stares at the carpet fibers sliding under her feet, trying to ignore the microphones waving around by her ear. Shoes. Lots of shoes. Down-in-the-heels Hush Puppies, shiny loafers. And a pair of black-and-white Barbie heels. She recognizes these shoes; in her peripheral vision she sees a slash of tight crimson skirt—Little Miss Red Suit. John whisks Ruby down an escalator, past merry-go-rounds carrying baggage instead of horses, and out the door into a furnace of Dallas air. He waves to a taxicab parked at the curb, and when it pulls forward, hustles her inside.

In the backseat of the cab, she leans her head against cracked vinyl, closes her eyes and breathes the pine-in-a-can air, in out in out. Beside her, John sputters an apology, says his "soon-to-be-latest ex-receptionist" must have given out their flight information to a cunning caller. Up front, a scrawny dark-faced driver shouts into a cell phone in a gutteral language, competing with the crackles and squeals from a CB radio and the pulsing bass from the dashboard radio.

Ruby tunes out all of it. She scrunches her eyes against the spectacle etched on her lids and breathes.

FIFTY-THREE

The courthouse conference room is icebox cold. The cramped space smells of sweat and fear and anger. Ruby sits on a scarred wooden chair at a scarred wooden table. Across from her, John reemphasizes points about the hearing to come, talking in the comforting tones of her obstetrician just before he puts her feet in the stirrups. But all Ruby can concentrate on is why her precious daughter has not come through the door.

John's words are hard to hear through the tick of the clock in Ruby's head. He gripes about having to relinquish his cell phone at the metal detector, looks at his watch. "This is ridiculous. They're playing games." He stands. "It's a bit like running to Daddy, which can be trouble in someone else's jurisdiction, but I'll go check with the judge's clerk."

Ruby puts her head down on the table. And waits.

She jerks up at the click of the door handle, turns to receive John's update. Instead she sees five and a half feet of slickness, a too-shiny suit, a bad comb-over, a self-important sneer. The Tinsdales' civil lawyer, she guesses, the bulldog street fighter with his eye on a slice of political pie. Then Lark rushes past him and into her arms.

Ruby hugs her daughter, still her daughter, always her daughter, sinks her face into Lark's hair. She runs her hands down arms, across hips, wanting to touch every molecule of her child. Behind Lark, John reenters the room, glares at the short stack of smugness. "Let's give them some privacy." John practically shoves the other lawyer into the hall and closes the door behind them.

The miracle in front of her requires all of Ruby's focus. She lays her hands on Lark's pale cheeks, winces at the charcoal smudges beneath Saint Bernard eyes. "Oh, baby," Ruby says, "Oh, my sweet baby bird."

Lark's eyes brim, but the tears don't spill over. Ruby pulls Lark's head onto her chest, presses her daughter's forehead against her own breaking heart. They stay like this for several minutes until Ruby catches movement from the corner of her eye. On the other side of the gritty window, a matronly court clerk, a stack of manila file folders wedged in the crook of her arm, gestures to John, points down the corridor.

The door opens and John steps in. "I'm sorry," he says. "We have to go. Now."

Mr. Smug sidesteps his squat form past the clerk, around John, tugs at Lark's shoulder. Lark raises her head from Ruby's chest; her noodle arms drop to her side. She inches her face closer to Ruby's until they are almost nose to nose. And Ruby looks into those same soulful eyes that stared out at her from that rest stop trash barrel almost a decade ago. Those same eyes, peeling away the layers of Ruby's soul, begging her not to disappoint them. Again. "*Do* something," Lark whispers before she shakes off Mr. Smug's meaty hand, turns, and walks out the door.

FIFTY-FOUR

The U.S. attorney for the Northern District of Texas looks like a television star—tall, trim body, a face a sculptor would love. His eyes burn with the fervor of a man on a mission; unfortunately this particular mission is to slay Ruby on his way to being elected the state's attorney general. John warned her about this, that the chief prosecutor would first-chair this media-ripe trial instead of handing off the case to one of his assistants. Even his name, Stanwick Noble, is marquee material.

He plays this day to a full house. Every bench in the room is crammed with reporters, some with sketch pads, some with notepads, all rapt in anticipation of the spectacle. Thankfully, because this is a federal proceeding, cameras are prohibited in the courtroom, which itself looks like the set of a television drama—rich, gleaming woods, polished marble, a crisp American flag that has never suffered the indignities of sun and rain and wind. In the marble behind the judge's platform, four words are etched. IN GOD WE TRUST. God, her lawyer, a supposedly merciful judge, the superpowered crystal that Zara, the woo-woo salon receptionist gave her, which Ruby stashed in her bra for good measure. Ruby will put her trust in any of them, all of them, if only she had enough trust to spread around.

A young woman walks through the low swinging door from the gallery, a box crammed with notebooks and files banging against her suit skirt. She hefts the box on the table next to Noble, sorts its contents into stacks, takes the seat beside him. His second chair; John told her to expect this, too. The one who does all the work while Noble reaps the spotlight and the glory.

Ruby steals a glance to the seats behind the young prosecutor. A fortyish blonde, tousled hair bigger than she is, sits next to an older man, sixty maybe, silver hair slicked back from a tan forehead. He looks like an ex-quarterback for whom exercise, and appearances, are religion. His arm encircles the woman's shoulders as if she is his property. The Tinsdales.

The archived newspaper articles reported their ages, but the difference, here in front of her, is striking. The couple is flanked by a younger blonde, a sister perhaps, and an older woman with dyed-brown hair, shiny face-lift skin, and daytime pearls. Ruby sees nothing of Lark, her Lark, in any of these people. Before Ruby turns back, Darla Tinsdale looks toward her. Her expression is hazy, unreadable.

"Oyez, oyez. All rise."

John grasps Ruby's elbow as the bailiff speaks, steadies her to standing as the judge enters with all the pomp she expected the first time. The judge is gray-haired and ruddy complected. The charges against her—kidnapping, the lesser included offense of transporting a minor across state lines, possession of fraudulent identification documentation—barrel out of the bailiff's mouth, bounce around the chamber. Ruby still can't quite believe that she is the person this clerk is talking about. It all sounds so, well, criminal.

At John's nudging, she enters her plea. "Not guilty."

"You may be seated." The judge's voice sounds younger than he looks; perhaps being a federal judge, like the American president, ages a person in fast-forward. He greets the lawyers, then raises a palm. "Before we bring in the potential jurors, I see that the room is full of our dear friends from the media. Let me make one thing perfectly clear: I will not allow my courtroom to devolve into a circus. I'm not going to clear the courtroom, because I don't believe it is warranted. Yet. But I remind you that there is a young child, an innocent child, involved here, and I will brook no nonsense, absolutely none. Have I made myself clear?"

Both John and the prosecutor stand. "Yes, Your Honor," they say in unison.

The judge leans over his tabletop, picks up a pen. "Okay, then. Let's get on with this."

And at that precise moment, it hits Ruby. All that she has lost, all that she has at stake. She thought that she could—that she needed—to do this alone. But she wishes she hadn't made Chaz and the Ms promise to stay in Santa Fe as the echoes of loss and doubt and fear, Ruby's own and all those defendants who came before her, ricochet off the marble walls.

FIFTY-FIVE

The rest of the morning passes in a blur of John and the prosecutor taking turns questioning members of the jury pool, moving to strike certain prospects, telling the judge that this one or that one is acceptable to his side. Throughout, Ruby sits, hands clasped on top of the defense table. So much hate and violence and fear and intimidation is embedded in the grain beneath her palms, so much bitterness that even she couldn't give this miserable wood a new happy life. She tries to shutter her discomfort, radiate innocence and goodness in her body language, on her face, for the jurors who study her as if she were an extraterrestrial species, as if they could never imagine themselves in this chair.

And all the while, Lark's voice whispers in her head. *Do something.*

Just before noon, John and Noble settle on the twelve individuals who will determine Ruby's fate, and the judge swears in and gives instructions to the jury, then dismisses them for lunch. Ruby watches as they file out, five women, seven men, five African American, five Hispanic, one Asian, and one lone Caucasian. The jury of her peers who will judge her as surely as Saint Peter at the Pearly Gates.

Over sandwiches at a deli in the office building across from the courthouse, John tells Ruby he feels good about the jury panel. He had been concerned about women; while they may be sympathetic to Ruby's motive in wanting to protect Lark, they may also be sympathetic to the Tinsdales, have suffered the loss of a child, in some form or other, themselves.

Pieces of tuna cling to the roof of Ruby's mouth like barnacles that the tide of her bottled water must labor to wash away. She readjusts her headband—Margaret's contribution to the young-and-sweet package—so that it digs into a different part of her scalp. At least the throbbing behind her ears reminds her that she is alive; the rest of her feels numb, detached. John talks more about the jury, what to expect this afternoon. And Ruby struggles to hear him through the noise in her head.

She follows John through the throngs of worker bees, out of the deli. Walking outside is like stepping into the tenth circle of Hell. Angry heat slaps against her shins, burns through the soles of the navy pumps she again borrowed from Antoinette. No wonder the sidewalks are as deserted as if under siege; summer is war in Dallas. Ruby follows John across the street, walking in someone else's shoes, wearing someone else's clothes, makeup. Living her own nightmare.

FIFTY-SIX

Back in the courtroom, Ruby can feel the press of press as the judge calls the court to order, spouts some legal stuff, procedures and mandates and timetables. Her head feels as if it has been stuffed with peanut butter. The judge's words buzz without meaning, compete with the echo of Lark's plea. Do *something. Do* something. *Do something.*

She clasps both hands across her belly as if in bedtime prayer. *Here is what matters*, she tells herself again and again and again, her daughter-to-be. And Lark, wherever she is in this huge, overwhelming city.

As the judge calls for opening statements, the prosecutor buttons his suit jacket, steps out from behind his table. He starts in about a heinous crime, a grave injustice. This poor, poor couple, their only child abducted in the dead of night, the anguish of not knowing her whereabouts for almost ten years. His church-choir baritone thunders with indignation, injustice.

Ruby stiffens against the wooden seat; John places a cautioning hand on her knee. "Nine birthdays, nine Christmases. Nine *years* of not knowing where their child was, whether she was even alive." Noble nods toward the jury on each "nine." "These parents, their child, deserve the justice that we are asking, that you *must* mete out today." His words hover around the courtroom like barroom smoke after he sits, until they are crowded out by the scritching and scratching and rustling from the crowd.

The judge motions for John to make his statement. He stands beside Ruby and places a hand on her shoulder. He stays there behind the table, beside her, radiating a quiet dignity. His statement is simple: "We have every sympathy for the pain of the parents, but, with respect, Ruby Leander did not steal that car in Dallas. She rescued a baby abandoned in a *trash can*. Her only intent was to protect that child, and she has done so, admirably and with deepest love."

With love. Truly Ruby loves every inch of that child. This morning, the only sensation that penetrated the ache of losing Lark was the thrill of seeing her again. Even though that joy was tempered by the agony that after today, Ruby never may see her daughter again. Yet now she can't even find her own pain, so consumed is she with the despair on Lark's ashen face.

Ruby's focus clarifies as Philip Tinsdale is called to the stand. He strides across the floor, leaving a vapor trail of too-flowery cologne, and climbs into the mahogany witness stand, a man used to getting his way. He wears his Italian suit like as if it was made for him, which it probably was. He straightens a tasteful silk tie, unbuttons his jacket, a paragon of cool in the hot seat. The prosecutor asks him to describe the circumstances of that fateful night, and he launches into his own well-rehearsed oration, about his sweet wife driving a teething baby around and around—

John stands, interrupts. "Objection, Your Honor. Hearsay."

Before the judge can respond, Tinsdale interjects. "My wife is in no condition to testify. She . . . she's never forgiven herself." His voice tinkles with razors and broken glass. As if his wife actually had something to forgive; as if it were he who could not forgive her. As if maybe Mr. Cool was in fact a hothead in a Mr. Cool suit.

The judge cautions Noble to control his witness, says he's inclined to sustain the objection.

"Your Honor," Noble says, "Mrs. Tinsdale was hysterical when she called her husband that night, told him what had happened. As such, her statements to her husband are admissible under the excited utterance exception to the hearsay rule."

"Then, Your Honor," John chimes in, "we would further object to this testimony on the grounds of relevance. The prosecution is not suggesting that Ms. Leander had anything to do with the carjacking incident itself, so it is irrelevant to the charges before the court."

Noble jumps in place as if he were goosed from behind. "Chain of custody, Your Honor. This testimony is relevant to establish that the victims lost possession of their child through no fault of their own, that they never relinquished custody to the defendant."

The judge pauses, sips from the glass of water beside him. "I'll allow it."

The trial, Ruby thinks, is like a tennis match, spectators' attention bouncing from lawyer to lawyer to judge. On this court, *in* this court, though, the ball being whacked around is Ruby.

FIFTY-SEVEN

She zombies out again as Noble continues to question Tinsdale. A few words here and there pierce the dense fog in her head, Darla distraught, bedridden, the agony of the unknown, unable to conceive another child, adoption agencies turning them down. A few head-shaking objections from John.

Like Molly, Tinsdale talks with his hands; Ruby follows the shiny square of light reflected from his shiny gold watch as it bounces from the ceiling to the back of the court reporter's head and up the wall again. He's a lefty, Ruby notes; the watch bands his right wrist. That may be the one trait he and Lark share; she's as left-handed as they come. Ruby can't seem to process the words flying around her, but this she notices, this and the fact that her observations are so ludicrous.

When Noble finishes, John stands, approaches Tinsdale. "Mr. Tinsdale, I am sorry for the ordeal you and your wife have been through. I have just a few questions for you. Do you have any reason to believe that Ms. Leander had anything at all to do with the horrific carjacking where your daughter was taken?"

Tinsdale leans forward like a bully. "No, but—"

"And when your daughter returned to you, was she well nourished?" Ruby doesn't cringe when John again calls Lark their daughter; by law and DNA, Lark is their child.

"Yes."

"Educated appropriately for her age?"

This time Tinsdale almost spits the "yes."

John shifts his body toward the jurors, makes eye contact with a few of them before turning back to Tinsdale. "So she appeared to have been well cared for, loved even?"

Noble jumps to his feet like his football team just fumbled a ball. "Objection! Mr. Tinsdale is not a psychologist."

John clasps his hands, tilts his head as if humoring a petulant child. "I'm not asking for a psychiatric profile, Your Honor. Just a parent's impressions."

"Overruled." The judge scribbles on his pad. "The witness will answer the question."

Now Tinsdale looks like the petulant child. "I don't recall the question."

John steps toward the witness stand again. "Is your impression, as a parent, that Ms. Leander took good care of the physical and emotional health of your daughter?"

"Yes, but—"

"That's all, Your Honor," John says.

After Tinsdale glides back to his seat in the gallery, Noble attempts to call several more witnesses, neighbors, friends of the Tinsdales. Each time, John objects to the relevance, and the judge agrees. Finally, the judge admonishes the prosecutor, "Mr. Noble, this is what we call 'piling on' where I come from." His voice takes on a twang that hasn't been present before. Ruby has noticed this phenomenon in bars in Santa Fe; perhaps exasperation, like alcohol, brings out the long-buried true self in a person. "Do you have any witness who can provide new information, facts actually relevant to the case at bar?"

Noble slides back behind his table. Ruby can almost see the idea that this was going to be *his* day in court sliding down his perfect suit to puddle on the floor. "Your Honor, we would offer into evidence a document marked Exhibit A, an affidavit of the superintendent of Santa Fe public schools, attesting to the fact that the child in question currently is enrolled in school in New Mexico. Since the child started out in Texas, ipso facto, she was transported across state lines—"

John interrupts before he even stands this time. "Your Honor, the defense stipulates to the facts at bar."

"Well, then." The judge folds his arms on the benchtop.

Noble riffles through the papers on his desk. His assistant hands him a thin plastic sleeve. "Your Honor, as to the charge of possession of false documentation, we would offer into evidence this document marked Exhibit B, a copy of the counterfeit birth certificate the defendant presented to the Santa Fe school district to enroll the victim's child in school, with attendant affidavits establishing authenticity and custody of same."

John stands again, repeats what he said earlier about stipulation.

Noble tugs at his jacket, throws back his shoulders. "The prosecution rests."

FIFTY-EIGHT

"Your Honor," John says, "at this time the defense moves to dismiss the kidnapping count. The prosecution has failed to establish the required elements of the offense with which Ms. Leander has been charged." *With which*, Ruby notes, no dangling preposition; her high school English teacher would love this guy. "Specifically, they have failed to show that Ms. Leander possessed the applicable mens rea at the time she rescued that infant from a garbage can."

John has explained all this to her, the legal maneuvering. He will make this motion; in all likelihood the judge will deny it. Judges are generally reluctant to cut the prosecution off at the knees, deprive the jury of the chance to weigh in on the case.

"Denied. We'll let the jury decide that." The judge looks at his watch, leans over to whisper with the bailiff. "On that note, we'll adjourn for the day, pick up with the defense tomorrow morning at nine o'clock sharp." He cautions the jury not to discuss the case with anyone, sweeps down from the dais and through the back door, robe flying out like the wings of a giant black bird.

The courtroom is an impaled anthill, jurors scurrying from their tiered swivel seats, reporters fleeing out the main door. Ruby and John wait for the swarm of people to subside, then step out into the hall, just in time to see the Tinsdales and their entourage. Mr. Tinsdale leads his tiny parade like a drum major—a sleek briefcase his baton—across the shiny tiles, around the corner, and out of sight. Ruby gulps tepid water from a drinking fountain, waits on a heavy bench while John steps into the men's room.

John returns, retrieves his cell phone from the marshal's desk, and they take the elevator down to the first floor. Outside, the furnace is still oppressive. The air is a damp wool blanket thrown in Ruby's face.

While John steps off to the side to check messages and return calls, Ruby waits beside one of the concrete barricades that stands sentry in front of the glass doors. To her left is a McDonald's and just beyond, a bus station, and proof that Dallas is indeed populated. A cluster of black women pushes out the door of the restaurant, some with toothpick legs and scrawny bodies, some dirigibles ready to burst, all wearing tight working-girl skirts and genuine smiles. A scattering of rough-looking men, the inner-city huddled masses, hoot at the women as they pass.

Ruby feels the cooler shadow of another body step between her and the shimmering heat. She turns, expecting Little Miss Red Suit or some other pest, but finds instead Darla Tinsdale.

"I want to hate you." Darla's voice is fuzzy. "I *want* to . . ."

"I'm sorry." These are the only words that can form in Ruby's mouth. "I am so sorry."

Darla raises a hand. For a moment Ruby thinks the woman is going to slap her. Then she realizes her intent is to halt Ruby's words, a crossing guard stopping tongue traffic.

"I thought she'd come home, and everything would be all right, that it would be like she'd been there all along. She's a good kid." An almost-smile ripples across Darla's lips, then melts away. "But she . . . Philip . . . we don't *know* her." Her tranquilizer-clouded eyes shift to Ruby's belly.

"Boy or girl?"

"Girl," Ruby says.

Darla lifts her head, looks straight at Ruby. "I want you to know . . . we're trying." She tells Ruby that they are meeting with a family therapist, trying to make Lark—yes, they are calling her Lark as the counselor suggested—feel at home, trying to make a family.

This woman, Ruby realizes, is not the enemy. She's just an ordinary mother trying to do her best under extraordinary circumstances. Ruby can't hate her, either, even if she is keeping Ruby from Lark.

Darla drops her gaze to Ruby's belly again. "I want my *baby* back."

"Please—" Before Ruby can finish her sentence, Philip Tinsdale encircles Darla's upper arm with his quarterback hand and pulls her away.

What would she have asked for anyway? Please let me help you know each other? Please let me see her again? Please give her back?

FIFTY-NINE

The light is unnerving. Yellow and orange quiver against the walls; a patch of blue twitches on the blanket. And outside the window, Erector Set buildings lit up like Christmas trees. This is not a nightscape Mother Nature created.

Ruby paces the hotel carpet from bed to dresser to window. Across the street, walls of glass are fluorescent-bright; a cleaning crew works their way through a maze of cubicles, dumping wastebaskets into bulky gray rolling bins, pushing vacuum cleaners around desks and chairs. She can't hear the roar of the machines, yet her room is anything but quiet. A TV droning through the adjacent wall, creaking and clomping from above. A siren wails. No cricket chirp, owl screech, or plaintive cry of a coyote to be heard here. Though the street below is empty of cars, the humming and buzzing and throbbing of City persists.

Yet all that noise doesn't begin to dampen the clamor in Ruby's head.

Do something. The picture of Lark is indelible, there on the wall, on the carpet, on Ruby's eyelids if she dares close them for even a moment. She can't remember what Lark was wearing, whether her hair had been trimmed, but she can't forget the too-thin face, the sallow skin, those sooty crescents that have no right being under the eyes of a nine-year-old. And the words. *Do something.*

She pictures, too, Darla Tinsdale. None of this is fair to that poor woman, either. Ruby's legs are as heavy as the cement barricades lining the street below, fireplug-high cylinders that protect the buildings from crashing cars. She sinks to the floor, leans against the mattress. *Do something.* Inside her, that other life shimmies in protest.

Then, like an August thunderhead rolling across the Sangre de Cristo mountains, it comes to her. Ruby knows the *something* she has to do.

SIXTY

Ruby's body feels as if it's been through an old laundry mangle. Her second time ever in a hotel room was no more pleasant than the first. If she slept at all, she did so in meager snatches, in between reliving those precious, awful minutes with Lark.

The courtroom emanates a sense of déjà vu. The assistant prosecutor sits in another power suit behind the same stacks of files and notebooks. The jury members have reclaimed their same places, creatures of habit formed in just a day. The judge, the bailiff, the benches of reporters, it is déjà vu all over again. Except this time, Ruby will take the stand.

John wanted to call the addict's girlfriend to establish on the record that she put the baby in the trash can where Ruby found Lark, but he couldn't track her down. Apparently she didn't make it up all those steps; her rehabilitation didn't stick. They don't really have much of a defense to present without Ruby's own testimony, and John said putting her on the stand will "humanize" her before the jury, shifting the focus from statute numbers to real people. This is why Noble was so determined to show the Tinsdales' pain. But, while the prosecution cannot call Ruby to the stand directly, if John calls her as a witness, Noble can cross-examine her. And that could get ugly.

They have prepared, practiced for hours. John cautioned her about getting flustered and saying something that could be used against her in the civil case. He has left the final decision, though, to Ruby. Now he looks down at her. Ruby feels fortified by last night's resolve; finally she can take *action,* instead of letting herself be swept along by a river of events. And testifying is just the first step of the plan she formulated last night. She takes a deep breath and nods her head.

After she is sworn in, she smoothes her skirt, this one with gray diagonal stripes, and readies herself to regurgitate the answers they have practiced.

The first questions center on that morning at the rest stop, simple questions to let Ruby get comfortable—or as comfortable as she is ever going to be on a witness stand trying to justify her life. Where was the rest stop? What time of day did she pull into the rest stop? Was anyone else around? Where did she find Lark?

Then John shifts to the more narrative questions. "How old were you when you found Lark in that trash can?"

Ruby hates hearing again and again that her daughter started their life in a trash bin, but John told her it was important to keep the image in the juror's minds. "I had just turned nineteen."

John moves to the jury box, places a hand on the rail. "And why were you driving across Oklahoma that day?"

"My grandmother died. She was my only family. The house . . . it was too hard to stay there without her. So I decided to move away."

"So you were all alone, then you found another child all alone in the trash."

"Ob-*jec*-tion, your honor," Noble sputters.

John says his "sorry" as quickly as the judge says "sustained." "The jury will disregard Mr. Brainard's statement."

At the rail, John pauses before he walks back toward Ruby. He told her he would do this, make sure the jury connects the two images, the pitiful orphan and the baby thrown out, not even with the bathwater. Yet Ruby still bristles at how he makes her look like a victim.

"You were nineteen when you found Lark. Do you think you would have made the same decisions today?"

Noble jumps to his feet again. "Objection. This is asking for complete conjecture. And it doesn't matter what the defendant *would* do today; she's on trial for what she *did* do then."

"Your Honor," John says. "What Ms. Leander was thinking at the time is paramount to establishing that she did not willfully intend to kidnap a child, a required element of the crime with which she has been wrongly accused. How she thinks about it now helps flesh out how she was thinking then."

"I'll give you a little latitude here, emphasis on the *little*."

"Thank you, Your Honor," John says. "Ms. Leander, looking back on that day, how would you have responded to the situation, knowing what you know now?"

SIXTY-ONE

This is the tough one. Ruby feels as if she is abandoning Lark all over again, but she knows what the jury wants to hear. "It's hard to picture how things would have been without Lark. She and I . . . we were *family*. But knowing *everything*, how it would turn out, yeah, I would have gone to a police station in the first town."

"Thank you, Ruby. I know this is difficult. Describe for us, in your own words, your life with Lark over the past nine years."

Noble stands, objects that the question is irrelevant. "We will stipulate that the child was not harmed while in Ms. Leander's possession, other than, of course, the incalculable emotional harm of keeping her away from her real family."

John looks at Noble, then the judge. "Who's testifying here?"

The judge puts on his stern-grandfather face. "Enough, both of you. The jury will disregard Mr. Noble's last statement. But I have to agree, Mr. Brainard, that the child's well-being was adequately established yesterday. Let's move on."

John doesn't appear at all perturbed by the ruling. He exudes calm, control. "Okay then. Ms. Leander, are you in possession of any fraudulent documents related to Lark?"

"No."

"What about the birth certificate, a copy of which was presented yesterday?"

"I only used it that one time, to enroll Lark in school. Then, I don't know, I guess I misplaced it when we moved to our new house."

"And how long ago was it, since you enrolled Lark in school?"

"Well, she'll be starting fourth grade this fall, and I enrolled her in the district's pre-K program because she was so inquisitive and already reading, so that would be six years ago this September."

"Thank you. Ruby, from the moment you found Lark in that trash can to the moment you found that article, did you *ever* think she was anything but abandoned?"

"No."

"Did you intend to kidnap her, to interfere with a relationship between her and her biological parents?"

"No." Ruby shakes her head. "No. I wanted to *rescue* her."

John starts in with questions about finding the article, how terrible she felt about learning the truth, how she came forward voluntarily.

"Since Lark left . . . I only *wish* I could say I don't know how they felt when they lost their baby." Ruby's voice creaks like an old rocking chair during this telling; she swipes at tears with the back of her hand.

"Thank you. I know you're tired from this ordeal and have a baby on the way to look out for—"

"Objection," Noble shrieks.

The judge raises an eyebrow at John. "Watch yourself."

John tries to look chagrined. "I'm sorry, Your Honor." He slides in closer to Ruby. "One final question. Ruby, did finding that baby in that trash can bring out a particular memory from your own childhood?"

Noble is only halfway to his feet when John adds, "Going to the state of mind of my client, a door the prosecution opened." Noble finishes his upward bob and sinks back to his chair in one fluid motion, his mouth opening and closing with a mechanical click.

Ruby can feel the panic flashing in her eyes. They have talked about this. John said it was important for the jury to understand *everything,* that it could make a difference in how they decide her case. Ruby resisted at first. This other part is *her* story; she has owned it, lived with it all these years. Somehow using it as a play for sympathy seems wrong, diminishes it. Now, though, the stakes are even higher; she can't execute her plan from a jail cell.

"Ruby, were *you* abandoned as a child, placed in foster care?"

She wraps her arms around the bulge of her belly, as much to shelter the child she once was as the baby in her womb, and, through the answers to John's probing questions, Ruby tells that other story from long ago.

SIXTY-TWO

She climbed onto the chair and looked through the curtains. Nothing but concrete and a row of parked cars, none of them red with a roof that folded down. When her mama tucked her into the itchy sheets the night before, she said Mama and Daddy were going out for a grown-up dinner. Mama said they would be back before Ruby woke up. But now it was morning, and she was alone in a strange room. She was hungry. She was scared. Ruby cried for a while, and she waited in the center of the big empty bed.

A lady with a stack of towels found her there, led her down to the motel office. Bits of breakfast clung to the beard of the man at the desk. Ruby sat in an orange plastic chair, like the kind at the Dairy Dog, and tried to be as small and quiet as she could. She felt funny sitting there in her jammies, and she was afraid to ask the man to use his potty.

The police who came were nicer than the man. One was a man with a Frito-Bandito mustache and the other was a lady with a ponytail that swished almost to her bum like a real pony's tail. The lady took Ruby back to the room and let her go potty and put on the pretty sundress her mama had packed for her. The lady emptied out all the suitcases and looked all through the piles, even in pockets. Then she put some of Ruby's clothes in one of the suitcases and they went back to the office.

Ruby sat again in the orange chair and the police kneeled down in front of her and asked her questions.

How old was she? She was three.

Did she know her whole name? Her name was Ruby.

Did she know where she lived? Of course she did. She lived with her mama and daddy in a compartment. Except one time when her mama called her daddy a drunk and threw the bottle of whiskers at him, she and her mama took a train and lived with Nana and Grandpa until Mama got mad at them, and then Mama and Ruby took a different train and then a bus back to Daddy's compartment. But now they were all going to live in California and Ruby was going to swim in the ocean.

Did she know her mama's and daddy's other names? Nana called her mama Annie. And her mama called her daddy Jack, or sometimes Jack Daniel. The policeman snorted in his nose when Ruby said her daddy called her mama Muffin.

Did she know her nana and grandpa's other names? Her mama called Nana Mother and called Grandpa Dad. Ruby couldn't remember her daddy calling them anything at all.

The grown-ups shook their heads at one another, and the policeman went behind the counter and talked on the telephone. They took her to the restaurant next door to the motel, and Ruby ate a hot dog and the waitress wore a pink shiny dress and carried a whole line of plates on one arm.

Then they got in the police car and drove down the big road. The lady sat in back with Ruby, and the man drove. He turned on his siren for just a minute. They both laughed when Ruby put her hands over her ears. Their car passed lots of other motels and some stores. They hadn't driven very long when Ruby saw a gas station with a big truck parked beside it. And dangling from the truck, like a fish on a pole, was a red car that looked just like her daddy's. Except this one was all smashed up. Her daddy was going to be really mad if someone broke his special car.

SIXTY-THREE

John pauses his questions to ask the court clerk to refill Ruby's water. Ruby drinks and drinks, and the clerk refills the glass again before sitting back down.

"Where did the California police officers take you, Ruby?"

Ruby continues her story over the gurgling in her stomach.

The police took her to another lady's house. A chain fence made a square around the front yard. The yard didn't grow grass, just dirt and toys. The lady's hair was yellow on the bottom and brown on top. Her tummy poked out between her shorts and shirt, and her legs were jiggly. She talked with a cigarette poking out of the side of her mouth.

Lots of other kids ran around, in and out of the house and across the yard. Some of them looked mean. Ruby cried when the police started to leave; she asked them please could she go with them and promised she'd be good, but they left her anyway.

Ruby didn't like staying at that house. The lady yelled all the time. The older kids were mean to her, and the babies cried really loud and their diapers sagged with poop. She wanted her mama and daddy. She felt scared all the way to her tummy every day and every night. The lady yelled at Ruby when she cried, so she tried really hard to keep her tears inside her eyes, but sometimes at night the tears leaked out onto her pillow, especially when the big boy climbed into her bed.

After more days than Ruby had fingers, the doorbell rang at the foster home, and a lady called out to Ruby. She didn't recognize Nana at first because she wasn't at her regular house, and when Ruby did recognize her, all Ruby could do was cry.

A yellow taxi drove Nana and Ruby to a big airport, and then they flew on a plane. Ruby was a little scared and a little excited because she had never been up in the air before. But mostly she was sad, because Nana told her that her mama and daddy's car crashed and now they were in heaven.

Nana said she was sorry Ruby had to stay at the house so long, that the police took a long time to find Nana because she and Ruby's mama had different last names. Ruby knew that heaven was up in the sky, and she searched the clouds outside the airplane window.

But she didn't see her mama and daddy; she never saw them again.

SIXTY-FOUR

"Your Honor, the defense rests." John strides back to the table, takes his seat as if he hasn't a care in the world. Beyond him, Ruby catches sight of a familiar face. Chaz. Of course he came, even though she told him not to. Chaz meets her eye and gives a nod that says everything, that he finally understands.

"Mr. Noble?" the judge asks.

Noble stands, buttons his coat. His body tenses as if he is a cat readying to pounce.

"Ms. Leander, on the subject of that birth certificate, did you destroy it, burn it?"

"No. Not intentionally. But it could have gotten thrown out."

"But if we executed a search warrant of your house, it might be there? We might find it stuck in some pile of receipts or letters or something?"

"I . . . I don't know. Maybe."

Noble crosses his arms, looks at the jury, back at Ruby. "Let's say that you didn't find the article and next year you needed a birth certificate to get Lark in a different school or a camp or a doctor or—"

"Objection," John says. "Now *this* is speculation."

"Overruled. I'm going to allow it. The witness will answer the question."

Ruby looks up at the judge, over at John. They hadn't practiced this one. "I, I guess I would have looked for it or asked the school for a copy or something."

Noble unfolds his arms, nods to the jury. "Thank you, Ms. Leander.

Now let's switch gears. Did you take that child—the Tinsdales' child—across the state line of Oklahoma into New Mexico?"

"Objection," John says. "I think this has already been established, Your Honor."

"Your Honor, I am trying to establish consciousness of guilt through evidence of flight."

The judge looks at Ruby. "The witness may answer."

"Actually"—Ruby cringes a bit at using that word, Lark's word— "we crossed into Texas, then into New Mexico."

Noble's cheeks pink up a shade. "But. You did. Take that child and leave the state of Oklahoma with her?"

"Yes."

The prosecutor slinks in for the kill. "Because you knew it was wrong, because you *knew* that little baby belonged to someone else."

Ruby shrugs. "Actually"—this time Lark's word makes the inside of her mouth smile—"I was on my way to California, before I found Lark. I was just passing through Oklahoma and I, we, decided she'd come along, seeing as how she was just thrown away."

Now Noble's cheeks are cherry bright. "Your Honor, will you please instruct the witness to stick to answering the questions asked?"

The judge leans over the dais toward Ruby. His voice is stern, but his eyes twinkle. "Let's rein in the editorializing."

Ruby nods, and takes a breath. She doesn't want to come off as flippant, glib; this jury needs to like her. "I'm sorry, Mr. Noble."

Noble tugs at his tie. "And did you report to any authority the fact that you had come across this infant at a rest stop."

"Actually," Ruby starts. *Watch it*, she tells herself. "I did tell the authorities. Just as soon as I found out about the carjacking, that Lark hadn't been abandoned after all."

"I mean at the time you found the child. Did you at any time in the *almost ten* years leading up to finding that article ever tell anyone the truth?"

Ruby resists the urge to look down at her hands; John made her practice keeping eye contact. She also avoids seeking out Chaz's face in the gallery over John's shoulder. "No."

Noble fans through some papers on his table. Ruby has no doubt his actions are for show; he knows exactly what he's going to say next. "Where were you, Ms. Leander, on the morning of July 13 of this year?"

"I . . . I was here. In Dallas."

"Despite a court order to remain in the state of New Mexico?"

"Yes. I . . ."

"And just where in our fine city were you on that morning?"

"At the Tinsdales'. On the street in front of their house."

"And were you not also under a court order regarding contact with the Tinsdales and their child?"

"Yes."

Noble's "hmm" is as melodramatic as a silent-movie villain twisting the end of his mustache. "So in direct violation of not one but two separate court orders—"

"I didn't *contact* her." Ruby's words burble from her mouth despite her attempts at control. "I only wanted to *see* where she was living. I needed to see that she was all right."

"No. You wanted to kidnap that poor child all over again, didn't you?"

SIXTY-FIVE

"Objection," John says. "Your Honor, there is no evidence—"

Noble smirks his "withdrawn" before John can finish his sentence, before Ruby has to face answering that question. He struts back to the prosecutor's table, shakes his head when his assistant slides a yellow notepad his way. "That's all I have for this witness."

"Redirect, Your Honor?" John pushes his chair back from the table. At the judge's nod, he rises and walks over to the witness stand. "Ruby, who is the father of the baby you are carrying?"

Noble jumps to his feet and shouts his objection before Ruby can answer. "Relevance, Your Honor?"

"The prosecution has put Ms. Leander's state of mind into issue, Your Honor," John says. "If you give me a little latitude, this testimony goes to the heart of the matter."

Ruby can feel the judge's eyes studying her before he turns back to John. "Go ahead."

As John tosses out questions about her relationship with Chaz, she tries to quell the shame of being pregnant and unmarried. She focuses on Chaz's face behind the defendant's table, allows herself to be calmed by the trust and encouragement she finds there.

"Weren't you worried about dating a *cop*?" John folds his arms, cocks his head toward the jury. "Weren't you worried he'd find out about Lark? That he'd turn you in? Or that you'd put him in a compromising position between his job and you?"

"I didn't think I'd done anything wrong. Until I found the article."

Ruby locks her eyes on Chaz's face. "I should have . . . I didn't tell him the truth. But not because I thought I was a *criminal*."

John's voice softens. "Ruby, until the time you found that article, what was the 'truth' as you understood it?"

As if she were at the communion rail at the little Episcopal church, Ruby clasps her hands on the bar of the witness stand. "That Lark had been abandoned. That there was no one who would be looking for her."

"Did you *intend* to kidnap her?"

"No. Never."

John thanks Ruby, helps her from the stand. She knows he wants to depict her as a fragile pregnant woman, but frankly, his arm is welcome. Her legs are shaky; her head throbs. She feels, well, like a fragile pregnant woman.

SIXTY-SIX

The jurors file out the back door to make their deliberations, and Ruby stands beside John as the judge leaves his throne. Before she can sit again, strong hands spin her around, and she tilts into Chaz's embrace. Her head acts on its own, seeking out the sweet spot between collarbone and collar. "You came."

"I came."

Chaz's Adam's apple slams against Ruby's cheek. Behind them, the main doors swish open and swoosh closed, reporters stepping out to make phone calls, have a smoke. Ruby's hot tears soak Chaz's shirt. "I don't . . . I don't know why I'm crying *now*." She spits words between hiccups.

John hands Chaz a travel pouch of tissues, and Chaz mops up Ruby's face, settles her in a chair.

"This may take awhile," John says. "Why don't you two take a walk, grab a soda."

"I'd rather just sit here." Ruby doesn't want to have to walk back into this courtroom, up to this table, ever again.

"I'll go check my voice mail then." John pats her hand, stuffs some papers into his briefcase, moves through the swinging gate to the gallery.

Ruby and Chaz stay at the defense table while the court clerk removes the judge's water glass and notepad, while Noble's assistant packs her files and notebooks back into her box. Noble himself was first out the door.

When the courtroom is empty, Ruby turns to Chaz. She unravels her voice from the knot in her chest, tells him about Lark, about the Tinsdales. She omits Lark's parting words to her; these she needs to keep inside her, their razor edges cutting into her, not so much in an act of flagellation as to ward off the bone-weary numbness. If she can hold on to that burn, like a million paper cuts up and down her spine, then she can hang on to her plan.

Before she can tell him the rest, John comes back through the courtroom door. "We have to talk," Ruby says to Chaz. "Not now. But I have to tell you something."

"We've got forever to talk." Chaz brushes a straggler tear from her cheek as John steps up to the table.

John gestures toward the judge's bench, where a clerk is placing a pitcher of water. "They need us out of here. The judge has an afternoon docket call." He hands Chaz a pager, like the ones hostesses dole out at busy restaurants. "I'll be in the lawyer's conference room. You two go feed that baby of yours."

Later, Ruby sits in the conference room where she had her visit with Lark. Chaz alternates between sitting next to her and pacing the hall outside the large window. Across the table, John bends his head over a stack of papers with dense type, making notes in green ink.

Time is a snail in the stuffy room. By late afternoon, Ruby is in a stupor. She knows she ate, but she couldn't say what. She must have gone to the bathroom, several times, with a baby pummeling her bladder, yet she has no memory of leaving the conference room.

Ruby thinks about the closing arguments, John stressing that she had no intent to harm, no malice in her actions, Noble painting her as the devil incarnate. She thinks about the judge's instructions to the jury, telling them that, although they may feel acutely the pain that the parents of the child must have suffered these nine years, as well as the good the defendant thought she was doing, in the end, their decision must be grounded in the law.

She tries to think about what might happen; she tries *not* to think about what might happen. She again folds her hands, prayerlike, over her belly, but this time she actually whispers a prayer, "Whatever happens or doesn't happen to me today, just let Lark and this baby be okay."

Finally the pager beside her flashes and jiggles and spins in a circle.

Chaz and John walk on each side of her as she makes that long trek back up the courtroom aisle. The room seems to buzz with anticipation. The back doors swish and swoosh as the reporters rush to their seats. A cloud of coughing, chattering, rustling rises behind Ruby, but all noise ceases when the jury files into their seats. The room tastes metallic, like a green Iowa sky just before a tornado.

Ruby has seen this part on TV so many times that she wants to giggle at watching it live, the judge asking the jury whether they have reached a verdict, the taller black woman standing, handing the bailiff a slip of paper, the bailiff walking the paper to the judge, back to the forewoman. The scene seems so clichéd that Ruby has to force herself to remember that her life, her freedom anyway, really is defined by that paper.

At the judge's prompting, she stands up beside John. She worried about this moment, about swooning like a movie-of-the-week actress, but she feels incredibly calm.

The forewoman lifts animal-print reading glasses from the chain around her neck. "On the charge under the United States Code . . . of kidnapping, we find the defendant . . ."

SIXTY-SEVEN

John grabs Ruby's hand. She can feel the whole courtroom take a collective breath.

"Not guilty."

Unlike the TV shows, the court does not erupt after these words. The Tinsdales don't scream out or keen. And Ruby doesn't faint in relief. There is only a swell of whispers behind her.

"On the charge under the United States Code . . . of transporting a minor across state lines, we find the defendant . . . not guilty." John squeezes Ruby's hand, like a Montero amen.

The forewoman clears her throat before continuing. "On the charge under the United States Code . . . for possession of false identification documentation, we find the defendant . . . guilty."

Ruby wipes away a splatter of tears from the tabletop as the bailiff returns the paper to the judge. She drops to her chair, too numb to know whether she is crying from relief at the big not guilty or fear about the conviction for using the fake birth certificate, which still could result in jail time, especially in this post-9/11 world.

The judge sets the paper down in front of him, then dismisses the jury. The main door starts swishing and swooshing again as the reporters dash to meet deadlines. The judge turns to the clerk sitting at a desk to the side of the dais, says something or other about scheduling, jots down a few words on his notepad. He looks again at Ruby, but at the rise of belly above the table rather than at her eyes. "Mr. Noble, I will expect a presentencing report within two weeks. Now, is there anything else to come before this court today, Counselors?"

Noble stands, puts on his earnest face. "Your Honor, at this time we would move to revoke the defendant's bail—"

The judge interrupts, clearly irritated. "Surely you are trying to add levity to these proceedings, Mr. Noble. This defendant came forward voluntarily, accepted service voluntarily, waived extradition, appeared here today. Surely you are not going to attempt to convince me that she's a flight risk?"

"She's been convicted of a felony, Your Honor. It is incumbent upon this court to revoke bail."

The judge clears his throat. "Now, Mr. Noble, I'm quite sure that you did not mean to tell this court what it must do. Rather you meant to suggest a course of action."

"Yes, yes. With apologies to the court, Your Honor." Noble's head dips for a moment, like a parishioner bowing to a cross, then pops back up. "But the issue remains—"

"I understand your issue, Mr. Noble." The judge turns to Ruby. "Miss Leander, did you surrender your passport at the extradition hearing in Santa Fe?"

Amazingly, Ruby's legs allow her to stand again. "I don't have a passport, sir."

The judge chuckles. "And you don't intend to procure one illegally now, do you?"

"No, Your Honor."

"Well, there you have it. Motion denied." He leans back in his chair, folds his arms. "Now I'm going to ask both Miss Leander and the Tinsdales to go home and love their children." He picks up the wooden gavel, oak Ruby thinks, and raps it once on the benchtop. "This court is adjourned."

"All rise," the bailiff intones, and the judge leaves through the door behind the dais to the accompaniment of shuffling feet and rustling papers. The remainder of the journalists scurry out the main door.

Ruby stays seated, looks at John. He smiles, clasps his hands in front of him. "We can still appeal the birth certificate charge, argue that the five-year statute of limitations has run on your one use and that you are no longer in possession of it."

She still is too dazed to know how to respond, what to think.

"This was the best we could have hoped for," John says, "under the circumstances."

"Under the circus-stances," as Lark once said the word. Ruby pictures herself under a giant tent, striped black and white like an old-timey prisoner's uniform, and the heavy canvas of circumstances held up by her own tired arms.

SIXTY-EIGHT

When Ruby steps out onto her back porch, all she sees is flowers. Pink and red and yellow rose petals strewn along the floor, bundles in full bloom tied to the posts.

Chaz stands beside her, a sheepish grin creasing his face.

"How?" Ruby asks.

Chaz shrugs. "I called some elves."

Ruby crumples into a chair, eases her feet out of Antoinette's mangling pumps. She watches Clyde, whom the Ms must have brought back when they did their elf magic, run laps around the yard, snuffling nose pointed up in the air. The sky is a community-theater backdrop, a swag of dark burlap punched with strings and strings of Christmas lights.

"You okay?" Chaz asks.

"I don't know." She breathes in the pure air, relieved to have access to oxygen in a gaseous form as opposed to the soggy Jell-O that Texans are expected to inhale, more relieved to be here, home. She doesn't think she has ever felt this tired, every bone begging her to crawl into bed, despite the fact that she was asleep before the plane took off from Dallas, then slept again through the drive from Albuquerque.

Ruby rests her leaden head against the back of the chair, draws in an eight-count breath. *Be still and know that I am God.* She expels the air in steady four counts, pulls her rib cage against her lungs. *Be still and know. That I am God.* This was her grandmother's breath prayer, which usually presented itself when Ruby had pushed her too far.

Ruby hasn't thought about it in years, but now here it is, a bit of Nana come to tuck a heavy quilt of comfort under her chin.

She is still counting breaths when Chaz pushes his chair back, drops to his knees in front of her. He clasps her hands in his, rests them on her belly. "I know I can sometimes be an ass," he says. "But whatever happens, I'm here."

He reaches into his jacket pocket, pulls out a small square box, places it in on her belly. The black box cartwheels, seemingly in slow motion, down to her thigh, bounces, swan dives to the porch floor. Chaz grabs the box, puts it in her hand, folds her fingers around it. "No matter what. I want us to be a family. You. Me. This baby."

Ruby is too stunned for words. *Now* he proposes?

Chaz rises on his knees, draws one leg up in an old-movie proposal stance. He pulls Ruby's hand onto his bended knee, squeezes her fingers around the box. "I love you, Ruby Leander. Would you honor me, will you marry me? Please?" His eyes glisten mercury-bright in the dark.

Ruby lifts her free hand, touches his cheek, feels the hard lump, like a pistachio, that remains from his tussle with the angry gang-banger. This moment, this whole day, nothing feels real except the breath in her lungs, and the voice in her head. "I love you," she says. "I love your whole stubborn, sometimes sanctimonious, sometimes ass-acting self."

Chaz's eyes bore into hers. "But?"

"Before I can answer . . ." Ruby adds her free hand to the knot of fingers and box on her lap.

"No, you don't have to convert to Catholic." Chaz slips one of his hands from the pile, stacks it on top of Ruby's. The proverbial upper hand.

"There's something . . ."

"Anything," he says.

"This is big. Huge."

Chaz shakes his head. "Anything."

Ruby remembers reading something, an old philosopher guy who said that in every person's life there are one, maybe two, moments that define who she is. She imagines those moments as river channels, forging the course of a person's life, like water carving through a wall of rock. Her one moment, she always figured, was finding Lark. Now, she is about to jump into the raging waters of her second. She swallows, squares her shoulders, and tells Chaz her plan.

SIXTY-NINE

Chaz's body is as rigid as the post beside him. Ruby sets the ring box on the table next to her chair, stands, sits again.

"They don't want Lark," she says. "They want the baby they lost. I . . . we . . . can give them that."

Chaz sits on the porch floor, stares off into the silhouette of hills. She waits for the words to find their way to his mouth. "You can't just . . . *swap* . . . children."

Ruby slips in beside him. Her legs hang off the edge of the porch. She knows that the gentle slope of the yard is there, just beyond her toes, but in the inky dark of this night, once again she has the sensation that she is at the edge of the world. Yet this time, for the first time, she feels like she has the ability to step back from the precipice. This time she has a plan.

"I can give them back what I took from them. And bring Lark home."

Chaz's eyes flash with intensity. "Could you really, though? Give away your own baby?"

"I don't know how I'll do it." She loves this daughter inside her. She will always love this child, will miss her every second, with the persistent yet phantom pain of an amputated limb. There is more room in a broken heart after all. But the baby won't miss Ruby, won't miss someone she never knew. "I just know I have to do it."

"This is more crazy talk." He drapes an arm across her shoulders. "You're exhausted—"

"No. I mean, yes, I'm exhausted. But I know what I'm saying."

Chaz rises, retrieves the ring box, presses it into her hand again. "Get some rest. You'll see things differently in the morning."

"I won't." Ruby speaks to the ring box, as Chaz leaves her on the porch.

SEVENTY

Her plan sounded so logical, reasonable—and right—when she laid it out for him. But now, alone with this blooming life inside her… *Could she do it, could she really give away her child?* Her rationalization that she doesn't know this baby seems anything but rational when Ruby counts the ways she does know her already, how she gets restless when Ruby eats garlic, how she prefers that Ruby sleep on her left side, how Ruby's grandfather's show tunes soothe her hiccups.

Then Ruby remembers reading in *People* magazine about those switched-at-birth kids in Florida, how both families were shattered when the kids were returned to their biological parents. Didn't one of those girls end up dead?

The arguments are still spinning in her head, the ring box still in her hand, when Clyde darts around the house toward the driveway. *Crap,* Ruby thinks. John thought the media would leave her alone for now, until sentencing.

A moment later, Chaz climbs the porch steps, Clyde at his heels. "This. This is our *child. My* child."

"A child you weren't even sure you wanted," she says softly.

"A child we didn't *plan* for, a surprise. I never said . . ." His face is tight, skin stretched across his cheekbones. The pistachio pops out against the sharp bone like Ruby's belly against her hips.

Ruby stands, moves closer to him. "You thought about it. We both did."

Chaz steps back against a post as if she struck him. "For a moment, maybe. But I never would have . . . I'm *Catholic*. And now, seeing you, seeing her. She is my *child*."

"A child who would never know the difference, who wouldn't be scarred for life. A child who would be loved. Just by someone else."

Ruby and the baby inside her share DNA, but a person is so much more than mere genes. She thinks about gazing at Lark and seeing every Lark she has ever been, every moment, every experience there in her face, experiences Lark shared with Ruby. This child will grow up to be the sum total of her own experiences, shared with someone else. "We can have another baby."

"I want to have more. I want a whole basketball team." Chaz's focus shifts somewhere to the future before coming back to Ruby. "But this one—she's ours, too."

Lark's "Do something" beats in Ruby's marrow like a mantra. "I have to do this."

"It's crazy." Chaz shakes his head. "And what makes you think those people in Texas would even agree?"

Ruby pictures Darla Tinsdale staring wistfully at Ruby's belly. "It's the only way I can make things right for them."

Chaz places his hands on her shoulders, squeezes. "I love you. I want to marry you." His words slide across his tongue as if it were saturated with tequila. "But I will never, *never* agree to this." He walks down the steps to the driveway, turns back to her. "Call me. When you come to your senses."

SEVENTY-ONE

Sawdust dances in the workshop light. With safety glasses on, Ruby shoves a plank of wood into the saw's gap-toothed mouth, slicing the board in half with a satisfying screech of metal against tree. The saw snarfs board after board, pried off an old oak armoire, and regurgitates two-by-two slats into a gangly pile. Then Ruby sands and sands and sands, until each piece is satiny soft, its grain breathing healthfully once again.

When the armoire is all chewed up, she turns to a stack of unfinished deck chairs. She screws legs on to seats, her emotions threaded as tightly as the metal studs. Chaz basically handed her an ultimatum: Lark or him. She wouldn't just be giving up her baby, she'd be giving up the man she loves as well. Shouldn't a mother, though, be willing to sacrifice *anything* for her child?

Ruby thinks about what her grandmother did for her, the sacrifice to shield Ruby from just one moment of horror. "Do something," Lark implored. How can Ruby *not* do this? That is, if she can figure out how to get it done.

Sometime after midnight, she pulls her grandfather's other bible, his woodworking book, from its place on the shelf above the workbench, next to the bits-and-pieces case he crafted, using old wooden Velveeta boxes for drawers.

The time-stained pages of the book, a school textbook really, cover every aspect of basic woodworking—from selecting wood to fancy finishes to repairs—in dry, unemotional sentences. Grooved joints, dowel joints, dovetail, mortise-and-tenon, so many ways to bind pieces of wood.

Ruby runs her hand down the flyleaf, where as a child, she wrote his name. *This book belongs to Henry Leander.* And now to Ruby Leander. If only there were an instruction manual for putting a family together, making it adhere.

SEVENTY-TWO

Mrs. Levy's kitchen wall clock looks like the ones in every classroom of Ruby's life, except for the birds that circle its face. The minute hand takes its own sweet time, inching up up up on the long hard climb to twelve. The second half of the hour is passing so much more slowly than the first, perhaps a mere function of gravity rather than nerves.

Ruby watches the clock, having given up all pretense of keeping busy. Since dawn, she has done three loads of laundry, trimmed and watered the herb pots, washed windows with newspaper and vinegar, ironed to crispness the pile of limp linens that has lived in the bottom of the spare laundry basket for months if not years. Not even Clyde escaped her mania; he scowls at her through the porch door, his almost-dry red coat shiny and clean.

Finally the oriole chirps nine o'clock. Ruby waits another agonizing six minutes, so that it doesn't look like she was waiting until exactly nine. She doesn't know Mr. Tinsdale's schedule, but she figures that, with the time change, he is sure to be out of the house by ten, even if he is not a morning person. Finally, she picks up the phone and dials the number that has been reeling through her head like the news bits that crawl across the bottom of the television screen.

Darla Tinsdale answers on the third ring. Her voice is breathy, still seems detached from her body. Ruby introduces herself, apologizes for calling out of the blue.

"No, no," Darla says. "This is like one of those psychic things. . . . I was going to call you this morning."

They both speak at once, laugh awkwardly.

"You first," Darla says.

"No, you," Ruby responds.

Darla tells Ruby that she would like to get a list from her, of Lark's favorite foods, her interests. "The counselor said . . . I just want to help her settle in."

Ruby prods Darla for a report, but Darla doesn't need much prodding. She seems eager to talk, to vent even, as if she doesn't have close friends of her own. She tells Ruby that Lark is still sad, that she prefers to stay in her bedroom and read, that she acts like a guest, tiptoes around. "She won't even open the refrigerator and help herself to a snack."

"Of course I'll send a list. I'll do whatever I can." Ruby's voice catches as she tells Darla that all that matters is making this better for Lark. "Could I speak with her, would you mind?"

"Oh. Philip dropped her off at his mother's on his way to work, to meet some of her friends from the club. Sort of a sip-and-see." Darla giggles like a sorority girl. "Without the bassinet and cute baby."

The thought of her daughter on display makes Ruby cringe. Lark has always related well to older people; she begs to go along when Ruby makes her monthly rounds offering manicures at the nursing home. But this sounds stuffy, awkward. It reeks of crinoline and smocking and dainty teacups. Lark will be itchy, worried about using the right spoon.

"It's just so different from what I expected, what I hoped for all those years." Darla's voice is slick with tears, whiny even. "It's so hard." She starts to say something else, something about her husband, then swallows her own words in an audible gulp. "Maybe it's easier when you have time, when you grow with the child instead of having a nine-year-old drop from the sky." She tells Ruby that they haven't been around kids this age, that of course some of their friends have children, but they don't *socialize* with them. Her sister, who lives in East Texas, has a two-year-old son; she wishes that he and Lark were closer in age.

This slender opening is all Ruby needs to wedge in a shoulder, wrest it into a gaping maw, a door big enough for her enormous plan.

She charges through while Darla is vulnerable, and alone. "I want to give you back that baby girl, the one you missed out on all those years."

Darla is silent for a moment. Ruby imagines she can hear the pert blond brain processing the idea. When she does respond, she does so with giddiness. "We talked about adopting, after I mean. But some of the agencies didn't like our age difference. And the wait for an infant, a healthy . . . well, a baby that matched our backgrounds . . ."

Ruby is disgusted at Darla's words, thinks that if Chaz's skin weren't as light as an early-season golf tan, Darla probably would not even consider the plan. But then, Ruby thinks, don't most people want their children to look like them?

". . . Of course I'll have to talk to Philip. But, oh, this could be . . . oh!"

Ruby hangs up the phone and drops to her knees. Clyde noses open the screen door and bounds over to her, rubs his head against her chin, a poignant waft of Lark's kiwi shampoo pricking her nose.

SEVENTY-THREE

John grabs a file off his desk, eases his tall frame into the chair beside her.

"Well, it's unusual to say the least." He flips through the papers in the file while Ruby holds her breath. "But I can't find anything in case law or in state procedure—or in ethics for that matter—that would prevent it."

Ruby expels her breath in a slow, steady stream. Her body melts, molds itself into the contours of the low-slung chair as John explains the intricacies that would be required to carry out her plan. Two separate adoption proceedings in two separate states. Two separate waiting periods. Two sets of social workers.

"But it can be done?" Ruby asks. "What about my criminal record?"

"It can be done." He explains about the standard of "best interests of the child" and tells her that the Texas court is likely to appoint an attorney or advocate who will represent Lark. Lark probably would need to state on the record her preference, which can be hard on a kid, having to choose openly between parents. In New Mexico the process will be less cumbersome, because an infant rather than an older child is involved, but Ruby will still have to jump through plenty of hoops.

"I'll get my circus-poodle costume ready," Ruby says.

"I talked to the Tinsdales' lawyer. He confirmed that they are dropping the civil suit. I'll make sure they sign a broad release. And they are sending a letter, asking for leniency in your sentencing. That should carry a lot of weight. We just have to make sure that it doesn't look like all this is part of the adoption deal, that a child is being bought."

Ruby tries to focus, but her head feels overstuffed with legalese. She is thankful that she trusts John to lead her through the legal labyrinth, and that she can have Antoinette translate some of this for her later. Although if pushed, Antoinette will surely side with family, with Chaz.

"And the father?" John asks, as if reading her mind. "Chaz is on board?"

"He will be."

John closes the file, leans forward, hands clasped between his knees. "This is big, Ruby. If those media whores catch on, even friends and family... You're going to get crucified for choosing one child over another."

Ruby stands. "I know."

"Just make sure you are ready, really ready, to make that choice."

"I don't see it as a *choice*," Ruby says as John's new receptionist steps in to announce his next appointment. "I'm not choosing; I'm doing what has to be done."

SEVENTY-FOUR

The plaza is a beehive in the center of Santa Fe, abuzz with summer tourists and locals, khaki-pantsed government workers and broom-skirted retail clerks on their lunch breaks. The open green center is cut into four pie pieces by sidewalks leading to the center pavilion and is boxed in by historic buildings that house shops and restaurants and galleries. The shops used to be run by local vendors, but like every-where else on earth, even the City Different hive has been invaded by killer-bee franchises.

Along the sidewalk beneath the Palace of the Governors, Native Americans spread their silver bracelets and woven dream catchers, laid out on colorful blankets. Only the "certified authentic" Indians are allowed in the cool of the blue overhang; others set up shop on folding tables that line the edge of the green across the narrow street.

Tourists fly, drive, and bus their way to this adobe paradise, said by the woo-woos to be one of the handful of portals to some great be-yond. For Ruby, the central core is a half-mile walk down the hill, past the formidable pink Scottish Rite Temple.

Antoinette waves from a wrought-iron table when Ruby walks through the arched entryway of the restaurant's patio. Ruby weaves her way around the umbrellas that shade tables, filled with a mix of summer tourists and upper-crust locals, to join her friend. This patio is a secret garden. Adobe walls shield it from the street on two sides, and the indoor part of the restaurant completes the square. Ruby doesn't lunch here often—smack in the middle of the plaza, it is inconvenient to reach from the salon out on Cerillos Road, not to mention pricey. Yet each time she does, her blood burbles with anticipation, as if she herself were prettier, smarter, chicer just for sitting in these stunning surroundings.

The two hug while a waiter pulls out a chair for Ruby. Antoinette looks like she belongs on this beautiful-people patio; her hair is pulled back into a sleek chignon, and her work dress is liquid silk flowing over her curvy figure. No dowdy secretary clothes for her.

Antoinette is a waterfall of small talk, barely pausing to offer a flirty smile when the model-pretty waiter offers them menus. She regales Ruby with stories of her latest bad dates—the letch with Listerine breath, the Aramis cloud who turned out to be married, the self-loather. She pauses again while the waiter takes their orders, then continues with a tale of a guy who took her out to the Camel Rock casino, asked her for money, then left the casino, stranding her at the slot machines.

Ruby laughs. "For an attractive, confident, accomplished woman, you are the world's biggest magnet for the dregs of the male species." She points out a few good-looking men at other tables. "Why not him, or him, or him?"

"The blond over there sleeps with his sister, the dark brooder is obviously a serial killer, and the other dark brooder, well, let's just say that he has a teeny-weeny weenie."

Antoinette and Ruby exchange mirthful looks as a shy young busboy tries not to look at Ruby's stomach or Antoinette's breasts while he refills their water glasses. They survey the lunch crowd, create bawdy scenarios for various groups—the table of businessmen who are all wearing ladies' panties, the trysts, the improbable threesomes. And for a moment, Ruby forgets the elephant of worry crushing her chest, the elephant squeezing her bladder, the elephant on this patio.

When the waiter arrives with their food, they are still giggling like schoolgirls. He sets a seafood salad that looks like a museum painting in front of Antoinette, the braised pork special—Midwestern comfort food—for Ruby. Antoinette deftly switches the topic to her job at the courthouse, how much she enjoys working for the judge, dissecting the guts of the system.

Ruby sinks her attention into her plate, trying to taste her way back to Iowa. When she was in high school, her classmate Joe, the one who took Ruby's virginity in the backseat of a turquoise Caprice before dumping her for that cheerleader who wouldn't put out, told her that when he graduated, when he left behind that stinky pig farm that they called a state, pork was never going to pass his lips again. But for Ruby, a crisp BLT or golden pork cutlet took her right back to her grandparents' kitchen table and all the goodness there.

Antoinette interrupts Ruby's reverie. "Chaz told us about your idea."

Ruby leans back in her chair, braces herself.

"My dad, he's all for it." Antoinette spears a shrimp with her fork.

"Let the gringo give the kid away, you mean," Ruby says. "Problem solved." Ruby has known all along that Chunk is not her biggest fan. "Non-Catholic and knocked up . . . two strikes and counting."

Antoinette's chuckle comes from a place of years of pain. "Three. You're out. You're cooking a girl."

Ah, Ruby thinks. The Hispanic cultural thing, valuing boys more than girls. The Monteros' ancestors were on this land before the *Mayflower* set sail, and sometimes they seem as Hispanic as Ruby seems German, yet the culture is strong in this region. Ruby has seen it in the street kids, the machismo, the sense of entitlement, the belittlement of the girls around them. And she has seen it in the way Chunk favors Chaz over his sisters.

That is one more thing she loves about Chaz; he couldn't be more delighted to have a daughter. He would have been happy with a boy, but during the sonogram, his face radiated pure joy when the technician told them she couldn't see a penis. "That's my girl." He stroked Ruby's cheek. "I want her to look just like her mama."

"He loves you, you know." Antoinette takes a drink of her tea. "He was always such a player before. When you two started dating . . . I've never seen him stand up to my dad the way he stood up for you. He likes to think of himself as independent, the fifth generation breaking the mold. But breaking a mold is one thing, breaking up *family* . . ."

Ruby places her hand on Antoinette's arm. "And you? How do you feel about it?"

"I can't imagine," Antoinette says. "I'm not a mother. I thought I was, pregnant I mean, once. But the wonder of actually growing a life, giving birth . . ." Antoinette tells Ruby about watching a litter of puppies being born when she was young. "They were just puppies. But all of a sudden I understood God. I believed in miracles. A *child* . . . I can't imagine."

Antoinette is a good soul, cares deeply, but she is not shy about sharing her opinions. Ruby waits, but the diatribe doesn't come. Instead Antoinette tells her that she has thought about Lark and the baby, that the closest she can come to an analogy is if she were given the choice between having a hysterectomy, of never having children, or never seeing her own mother again. "I'd dump the uterus in a heartbeat."

Ruby surprises herself by playing her own devil's advocate. "But that's just giving up the possibility of maybe having a child somewhere down the road. This is actuality. This is your own flesh and blood." Ruby points to her belly. "This is your niece. Are you really okay with me giving her away?"

Antoinette squeezes Ruby's arm. "I don't know. I don't know if I'm okay with it. But Lark . . . Lark is my niece, too."

SEVENTY-FIVE

Chaz spits the words. "But Lark isn't even your own child." He sits on the edge of his bed in his striped pajama bottoms and no shirt. The late-morning sun blares through the window next to the pine headboard. His chest looks too bare without the Saint Christopher medal that he gave to Lark, and now Ruby can't even remember if Lark was wearing the necklace at the courthouse.

Ruby sets the tall coffee cup beside the pile of books on the nightstand, pulls off the plastic lid. She pushes aside a book butterflied on the blanket next to him and sits. "Try telling that to the millions of adoptive mothers out there. Try telling that to their kids."

Chaz's face is dark with fatigue and a two-day beard. He worked extra-long days—well, mostly nights—last week, played basketball half of Saturday, attended Mass and his mother's Sunday dinner. Now he is spending today, Monday, in his bed. This is what he does, runs and runs and runs until he hits the wall, then crawls into his cave to recharge his batteries. A "jammie day" her grandmother would call it. Ruby remembers one school day shortly after her grandfather had died when Nana crept into Ruby's room, turned off her bedside alarm clock and declared a jammie day. Ruby and Nana spent that day watching old movies, eating popcorn made in the heavy metal pot on the stove, and napping in the den. For Chaz, books and bed are his therapy.

On the phone last night, Antoinette filled Ruby in on Sunday dinner—Celeste is up to Russian on her gastronomical globe. And Ruby knows Chaz well enough to know that she would find him here today. She picks up the coffee cup, hands it to him. He holds it in both hands as if they were frostbitten.

"I understand, I think. How you feel." Chaz sips the still-steaming coffee, jumps as it scalds his tongue.

Ruby takes back the cup, sets it again on the nightstand. "I thought you felt the same, about Lark."

"I thought you felt like I did about our baby."

She knows the enormity of what she is asking of this man who reveres family. And she doesn't know how else to explain to Chaz that she loves the child inside her *fiercely*. That her plan is the only way she sees to save *both* of her daughters.

Flecks of dust pirouette in a shaft of sun. *Oh, to be that carefree,* Ruby thinks, *that exuberant.* At first, she and Chaz were dizzy in their love, until just recently really. All the attention he garnered from pretty girls when she and Chaz were out never bothered her a bit. For her, the attraction was instant. His tall frame, thick hair, soul-seeking eyes. A big part of the allure, though, was his love for his family, and the chance to *belong* to the whole auntsunclescousins swarm. A passport to Monteroland. As much as Chaz's laugh, even his voice on her answering machine, stirs up a flutter in her chest, that sense of belonging calms a restless place deeper inside her.

"My goodness." Ruby can't resist running a finger across the paler patch of silky skin on the underside of his wrist. "You told me you fell in love first with my goodness . . . so, what do you love now, now that you know I'm not so good after all?"

"You know I love you. . . ." Chaz takes her finger, grasps it in his fist as his voice tapers off. "We can get through this. Together. Lark's a good kid, a strong kid. She'll adjust. And when she's older—"

Ruby jerks her hand away. "You didn't see her, hear her."

Chaz stands, paces past the black-and-white photographs of New Mexico landscapes that hang along his wall. He stops at the dresser, sprinkles a dusting of food into the fishbowl; Glug, the electric blue tetra, is the only pet he can handle with his work schedule. He walks around to the foot of the bed, fusses with the thick gray duvet folded into tidy thirds, walks back to stand in front of Ruby. His torso is baby-sleek—if a baby had six-pack abs and the pecs of a gym fanatic. "I can't. I just can't give away my child."

"Maybe it could be an open adoption." Ruby tries to modulate her voice, keep out the desperation she feels. "You, we, maybe we could visit. And the Tinsdales, they want this. This is how I can make it up to them, what I did."

Chaz picks up the coffee cup, sits back down next to Ruby. "What I don't understand is this. If this is about nurture over nature, if Lark belongs with you because you have nurtured her, that she is who she is because of how you have nurtured her—" He stops, takes a slug of coffee, swallows as if swallowing the whole distasteful subject. "Well, then answer me this. What will become of *our* kid if she is *nurtured* by the Tinsdales? You don't even *like* those people."

From the beginning, Chaz has had a remarkable ability to home in right on the nagging voice in her heart. Ruby can read wood; Chaz can read Ruby. This is the rub, the stick in her craw: if those people aren't good enough for Lark, how can they be good enough for her other daughter?

She quiets the voice the way she has quieted it all these eternal nights, by reminding herself that her plan is not about whether the Tinsdales are good parents, it's about whom they should be parenting, or rather whom they *shouldn't* be parenting. She stands, pulls the ring box out of her purse, sets it on the nightstand.

"I'm going to do this." She pauses at Chaz's door. "I'm going to find a way."

SEVENTY-SIX

The Santa Fe chapter of the Sierra Club rates the La Vega trail as a moderate seven-mile hike. Moderate maybe for a nonpregnant person. Anger and confusion sear Ruby's lungs as much as the exertion.

"So, what are you thinking?" Molly asks at the top of the first steep climb.

Ruby eases herself down in the flower-studded meadow. "I'm thinking I want to be a lesbian."

Margaret sputters, spits a mouthful of water on the ground.

"Seriously. Men, they're just . . . alien." Ruby takes a long pull from her water bottle. The cool liquid sloshes around in her stomach. "You have it easy, dealing with someone from the same planet."

Molly tosses a few hunks of biscuit in the air. Gray jays swoop in to catch the pieces; the dogs leap to try to catch the birds. The Ms's little terrier mix, Dudley, jumps several times his height but barely nips at the bigger dogs' heels. "Chaz still won't agree, huh?"

Ruby gazes across the meadow. The peak of Santa Fe Baldy looms just beyond, a few patches of winter snow hiding out in crevices. "He's . . ."

"Easy?" Margaret says.

"Everything but. Or everything b-u-t-t."

Margaret shakes her head. "No, I mean us. You know us too well to think a relationship is easy because it's between two women."

"You've made it fifteen years. Even with all you went through." Ruby recaps her bottle, secures it in the loop of her fanny pack. "That's a way longer shelf life than any of my relationships."

"Well, once you get past the freak-show looks and blatant discrimination, the rest of it, the day-to-day stuff, is easy," Margaret says.

Molly stuffs the empty bread bag into her pack, helps Ruby to her feet. "Stop baiting her. You know she's just pissed at Chaz."

"Except for the toilet seat thing." Margaret stands, snakes an arm through the strap of her pack, hefts it onto her back. "You breeders are alone with that one."

The next section of the hike is downhill, a gradual descent through evergreens and aspen trees shimmering silver in the light. The Ms lead the way; Ruby follows, listening to their banter, while the dogs nose through the underbrush, darting back and forth across the trail in pursuit of chipmunks and squirrels.

Margaret raises a fist, counts off with exaggerated flicks of her fingers. "Stealing bedcovers. The endless toilet paper debate, over or under, how should that roll hang?"

Molly chuckles. "Over, obviously. Everyone knows that."

"And in-laws," Margaret says. "Let's not forget about dealing with the in-laws."

Molly looks over her shoulder at Ruby. "There is something to be said for being an orphan."

They can laugh about it now, but Ruby knows the story of when they first got together, Margaret twelve years senior to Molly's just-out-of-grad-school twenty-five. Molly's parents were livid, apoplectic, threatened to take out a full-page newspaper ad labeling Margaret a pervert sex offender. Then they cut Molly off. Shunned her, like she was an Amish girl betraying the fold. Molly had only the support of her grandmother, and the not-insubstantial trust fund from her grandfather.

After a few turns in the trail, Ruby lets herself lag behind, hoping to find a solution as her pounding heart keeps rhythm with her boots pounding the earth. She catches up to the Ms in a clearing beside Nambe Creek. Clyde and Daisy, the black Labrador, flank Ruby like soldiers attacking a foxhole. Cold creek water flies from their fur, sprinkles her legs.

She chooses a flat place to sit on the big rock where the Ms perch, stretching her legs out in front of her to ease the constriction in her calves.

"You figure anything out?" Molly holds out a bag of trail mix.

"Nope. Not a clue." Ruby frees her second water bottle from the elastic loop on her fanny pack. "I can't fathom leaving her there."

"Well," Margaret says, "if the thought of not going through with it is unbearable, then we have to find a way to do it."

"Except the thought of doing it is unbearable, too." Ruby's feelings and Chaz's points are waging a boxing match inside her. As fervently as she believes she must go forward with her plan to bring Lark home, she knows that executing the plan means losing her baby. "I want them both."

The irony is, she keeps wanting to turn to Chaz for advice, like a twist on a twisted O. Henry story. He would help her sort through her feelings. He'd do his Chaz thing and home in on the one nugget of right in all the wrong.

Molly shrieks. "Oh, Dudley!"

The smell reaches them first, then the dog, wagging proudly at their feet, his coat more green than tawny.

"Horse manure," Margaret says. "Again."

"That is disgusting," Molly says to the dog. "Look, even the other dogs are embarrassed for you."

Dudley wiggles and wags, decidedly unabashed.

"Better than dead animal," Margaret says. "Now that is disgusting."

Molly shakes a finger at the dog. "Oh, Dudley. You're not my favorite anymore." The black Lab perks her ears, as if she understands exactly what Molly said. "That's right sweet Daisy-girl. You're Mama's favorite now, aren't ya?"

Ruby knows Molly is just kidding around; she loves both those dogs with all her heart. A good mother wouldn't pick favorites.

No mother should have to choose between her children.

SEVENTY-SEVEN

The radio keeps Ruby company as she carves the wood. The AM station is static-free on this snow-globe night, confetti stars strewn across the glassy dome, the real moon paper-pale and low outside the shed door.

The words to one of her grandfather's favorites, the song playing, fit Ruby's mess like the long-lost piece to a jigsaw puzzle: if only Chaz believed in her. Perhaps theirs was only a paper moon after all. Earlier tonight, they had an ugly fight. Their battling ultimatums still hang sawdust-heavy in the shed.

The argument had started softly.

"I'm tired of this," Chaz said.

"You have to understand," Ruby said. "I love you so much."

Chaz's reply was a statement, not a question. "But."

"But I have to get Lark back. We can have more babies."

Their words escalated, sibilant *s*'s flying around the room, hard consonants smashing against walls like family china thrown in a rage.

"I've talked to a lawyer. I have rights. If you don't want our daughter, let me have her."

"You know this isn't about *want*."

"If you push this . . ." Chaz said. "There won't *be* other babies. I won't—I couldn't—be with you." He wasn't sure he could even be in the same town. Maybe, he said, he would take that job with the national gang task force, or pursue an opportunity with the LAPD.

"You're asking me to choose between you and my child."

"*Our* child. And, yeah, I am." Then Chaz stormed away.

She has been crafting a wedding gift for a young Jewish couple, commissioned by another sentimental fool. Turning a family armoire into a canopy bed that will first be used as a chuppah. The shed wasn't big enough to hold the armoire; Ruby had to disassemble it in the yard. The head- and footboards poked out of the shed door while she crafted them; days ago Chaz helped her wrestle them into the house and out of the way.

Tonight she works on the posts, carving acanthus leaves to give them an organic sensibility. Her grandfather's woodworking bible lies open on the workbench beside her. *Hollows are chamfers which have been curved with a gouge. First plane the chamfer, and then chisel the hollow with the gouge.* Ruby could swear she can smell her grandfather's pipe smoke on the well-thumbed pages, but she knows that the pungent fragrance of his favorite tobacco emanates from her memory rather than the musty old book.

As she strips away thin curls of wood with the gouge, she thinks that she may never have this, the wedding, or the marriage like her grandparents had. Maybe the price *is too dear*. But then she thinks of Lark, her ghostly pallor, gaunt face. Chaz might not be able to live with Ruby if she goes through with her plan. She can't live with herself, though, if she doesn't. Somehow, she's got to make him understand. For all of their sakes.

Clyde lies curled in a comma at the door while she works. His reddish coat gleams with gold in the wan moonlight. He seems less mournful, is eating his kibble, these past few weeks, but is hardly his old self. He lifts his head, eyes bore into her, as if to say that her plan wouldn't be make-believe if she believed in him, as if he *knows* that everything is going to work out.

"I'm trying to believe, Clyde," Ruby says. "I'm trying."

The moon is only halfway up its arc to the top of the dome when Antoinette steps over Clyde and into the shed. Her face is a melted candle of grief. Clyde whines, nuzzles Antoinette's jeans. Time freezes in this little snow-globe world of Ruby's.

"It's Chaz." Antoinette's voice is raspy, raw.

SEVENTY-EIGHT

Ruby's hand drops to her pregnant belly, a gesture of shock as much as if she were covering a gasping mouth. *Oh, God. No.* Breath is impossible. Thought is intolerable. She sets down the gouge, lines it up with the chisels, filled with an overwhelming need to make her space Chaz-tidy. She reaches over, turns off the radio. Then she pushes past Antoinette, rushes out of the shed, vomits in the flower bed.

No. No. No. She feels herself crumpling into Antoinette's embrace, a two-headed being lurching across the yard to the porch steps. Clyde is there, wedged between them, whining, licking her knees.

Antoinette starts to speak.

"No." Ruby covers her friend's mouth, stanching the words, the unbearable words, as if keeping them from being spoken will make them less true for just a moment more. Then she removes her hand, pulls Clyde against her side. Waits.

"Krueger came to Mama's. A car accident. Chaz . . ." Antoinette takes Ruby's arm. "Come on. Come with me."

SEVENTY-NINE

As Antoinette's little car speeds through the Santa Fe streets, Ruby finally manages to speak. "How bad? How bad is it?"

Antoinette looks over at Ruby. "Bad."

When they rush through the emergency room entrance, the waiting area is teeming with Monteros and cops. Celeste motions to Ruby and Antoinette. "They needed room to work."

"Kicked us out." Aunt Tia's voice comes from over Celeste's shoulder.

Celeste grasps Ruby's elbow. "But you, go." She points to a pair of metal doors.

A security guard nods and presses a red button as Ruby walks over. The doors snap closed behind her.

The St. Vincent's emergency room is one big square with a workstation in the center and curtained bays lining the three outer walls. Only a handful of the curtains are pulled; the vacant narrow beds look like lounge chairs around a pool. Wheeled IV trees cluster around the nurse's station like gossiping workers. Ruby recognizes the unique scent blend of bleach and pain from a couple of visits with Lark, a broken arm, a gash in the shin.

A petite nurse in blue scrubs directs Ruby toward a closed curtain on the left side of the room. Ruby keeps her eyes on the middle area of the curtain. *Please*, she thinks, *please let there be feet, lots of feet, below the hem. Please don't let them have given up.*

She feels all the color drain from her face at her first glimpse of Chaz through a break in the curtain. Blinking and bleating equipment and colorful scrubs swirl into an abstract painting on the white wall. The nurse holds Ruby upright with one arm and opens the curtain with the other in well-honed efficiency.

Chaz lies still, too still against the bustle around him. His clothes are a puddle under the gurney. A folded sheet covers his midsection, while doctors and nurses work at both ends. One leg is sandwiched into a splint, bound in bands of tape. Chaz's toes protrude, rouged in several shades of purple. *He hates for his long skinny toes to show,* Ruby thinks. She resists the urge to cover them with the sheet bunched between his legs.

Finally Ruby forces her eyes to focus on the face above the cervical collar. For a brief second, she wants to laugh at the features distorted to fun-house proportions. In the next second, she feels relief—that is not Chaz after all. That could not possibly be Chaz.

Lips swollen like a bad collagen job. Nose crusted with blood. One eye bulges so that the lids do not quite meet, a sliver of dark iris peering out beyond the crimson and violet skin. A doctor is stitching a seam that extends from the eyebrow to just above his ear, a black-and-blood crescent running through a pale swath of shaved skin. A nurse presses gauze to the wound as the doctor works.

"Touch him," the petite nurse says. "Talk to him."

Before Ruby can make herself step closer, the doctor at Chaz's head stands tall. "I'm done here. Move him on up."

Metal rails are locked into place on each side of the bed, yellow plastic gowns are shed, and the whole parade rolls past Ruby as she reaches out her hand.

EIGHTY

Ruby hesitates at this next set of double doors. The black-and-white sign is stark, forbidding, against the shiny metal. ICU. NO ADMITTANCE. IMMEDIATE FAMILY ONLY. VISITORS STRICTLY LIMITED TO TWO PER PATIENT. ICU. *I see you.* She feels exposed, looks down at her hands, twists her right fingers around her left ring finger.

Antoinette pushes the red button. "It's okay," she says as the doors flip open. "Mom told them you were family. They have a broad definition of spouses anyway, I guess because of all the gays in town."

Beyond the entrance, three large windows and three open doorways line each side of the short corridor, bridged at the opposite end by a nurse's station. A man in scrubs at the counter motions toward the first door on the left. Ruby places her palm on the shuttered window beside the doorway, whether to steady or steel herself she's not sure. Then she takes a deep breath, follows Antoinette into the small room.

In the pale, blue-tinged light, Chaz looks outlandish, dark hollow cheeks, gray lips. Tubes, in his nose, in his mouth, sprouting from beneath the ski hat of bandages on his head. The edge of the sheet is folded neatly over a thin blanket and tucked in along Chaz's side. Wires snake out from under the covers at his chest. As Ruby approaches, a blood pressure cuff inflates on his arm, and the panel behind his head bleats as its lights flash.

On one side of the bed, Celeste sits in a chair, her body curled into itself beside Chaz. She looks up when they enter, nods.

Antoinette pushes Ruby toward a rolling stool on the other side of the bed, then steps behind her mother. Ruby balances her butt on the vinyl cushion. She's stiff and worn out from sitting and worrying in the waiting room while Chaz was in surgery and recovery.

Chaz's arm looks waxy against the blanket. Ruby has a flash of memory—small-town funeral parlor, open casket banked by velvet curtains stiff with dust. She lays a palm on his wrist, relieved to feel the throb of veins under skin that feels warmer than her own hand.

Across the bed, Celeste strokes Chaz's swollen cheek. "They're always your babies. Always."

The man from the nurse's station steps in beside Ruby, switches out bags of clear fluid on the IV stand. Ruby gasps when he lifts a catheter bag from a hook on the bed rail. "It's common, some blood in the urine from the bruising," he says. "Just a few drops can look like a whole lot in the bag."

The exact opposite from dye in milk paint, Ruby thinks. And then thinks how once again, she's having absurd thoughts at inappropriate moments.

"I'm Walter, by the way." The man points to a small whiteboard hung on the wall behind Antoinette. Several lines in permanent black lettering. TODAY IS. YOUR NURSE IS. YOUR AIDE IS. "Walter" is written in blocky green print as the attending nurse. "I'll be with ya'll 'til six."

Ruby jerks her hand off Chaz's arm as if she's a naughty child when she hears Chunk's voice in the hall. She spins on her stool toward the door just as Chaz's father, aunt, and other sister crowd into the tiny room. Apparently, this hospital is lax about a lot of its rules.

A fortyish woman, red hair cut pixie-short, stands at the foot of the bed. "Dr. Jarveras" is embroidered in blue script on the white coat that hangs over a floral-print blouse and dark slacks. She sounds like she's reading a bad soap opera script. "We removed a small hematoma to reduce the pressure on his brain. We really won't know the extent of any permanent damage until he regains consciousness, so we're hoping we can control the swelling without further sedation. If, when, he does regain consciousness, then we can do a full evaluation. We'll hold off on the orthopedic surgery until we have that prognosis."

In other words, Ruby thinks, *if my boyfriend lives, if he's not a vege-table, then they'll worry about whether he'll walk again.*

EIGHTY-ONE

After the fifth or fiftieth attempt to budge Ruby from her stool, the Montero family settles into a routine of taking turns on the other side of the bed. Chunk paces. Antoinette and her grandmother knit their rosaries, beads sliding through arthritic fingers as smoothly as young, supple ones. Linda fidgets. Celeste strokes and pats. Tia; other aunts-unclescousins; Father Paul, the family priest whom Ruby recognizes from her times at Mass with Chaz; lots of people dressed in scrubs. The tiny room holds an ever shifting crowd.

And Ruby sits, her own breathing keeping rhythm with the metro-nomic hoosh-hiss of the respirator. Dee Dee replaces Valeria; Emily replaces Walter. And still Ruby sits. Trays of hospital food and sacks of takeout appear and disappear at her side. During Celeste's rota-tions, she shoves a handled plastic cup at Ruby's face, demands that Ruby swallow a few gulps of water. Mothering Ruby in ways that she can't mother Chaz. If Ruby could convince a nurse to give her a cath-eter, she wouldn't have to get up at all.

At some point Dr. Jarveras stops in, with another doctor in tow. "This is Dr. Feinberg. He'll be taking over while I go home and get some sleep." She pauses, points to Ruby. "Which I suggest you do, for your baby if not for yourself."

Ruby listens as the woman brings her colleague up to speed.

"Shouldn't he be awake by now?" Across the bed, Chunk places his hands on Celeste's shoulders.

Dr. Jarveras looks up from her chart. "The anesthesia from the sur-gery has been metabolized, so yes, we would have hoped to see some level of consciousness by now. Sometimes this is just the body's way, hibernating as a path to healing. Sometimes . . . it's just too soon to know."

The spaces between the doctor's words speak louder than the words themselves. *No. This is not possible. It has to be a mistake,* Ruby thinks. In her nightmares, it was always a gangbanger's knife slicing a jack-o'-lantern smile across Chaz's gut, a bullet whistling through the air. Not a car wreck, not a tree. *Not Chaz.* Earlier tonight, Ruby thought she was losing him, but not *losing* him, losing him. Such an inadequate word, to define both misplaced car keys and life.

The baby inside her punches her ribs. She should have known better. She loses everyone she loves, her parents, her grandparents, Lark. She should have known better.

EIGHTY-TWO

"Here, drink this." Antoinette hands Ruby a paper cup, the string of a tea bag dangling off the lip. "It's herbal. Tia carries around her own supply in her purse."

Ruby cradles the cup in her hands. The heat barely penetrates her skin. "We had a fight. If I hadn't . . ."

The chair across the bed squeaks against the floor as Antoinette scoots it closer to Chaz's side. "It's not your fault. It was an accident, Ruby."

Ruby sets the cup on the metal hospital tray, which has been pushed against the wall beside her. She wads up a corner of the bed-sheet, places Chaz's hand over the mound, willing his fingers to grasp the linen. "He stormed out. We didn't even say good-bye."

"He still does that? Sleeps holding the sheet in his hand? I haven't thought about that in years. I can remember . . ." Antoinette's voice goes little-girl soft as she recounts the story, a thunderstorm, crawling into Chaz's bed.

Ruby half-listens as her own mind reels with thought, with memory. *We didn't even say good-bye.*

She was nineteen, had just parked the rust bucket Ford next to the shed at her grandparents' house, returning with a box of Tide and a Hershey bar—Nana's favorite—for each of them. At first Ruby didn't notice that anything was wrong. And then she saw her grandmother, sprawled out in her chore-day clothes, a bedsheet flapping in the breeze above her, the same overwashed color as the sky.

Ruby ran across the yard and fell to her knees, pulled her grandmother's head into her lap. Her face was gray and pinched; her lips looked like wax. Nana had wet herself—an orange splotch darkened her ratty peach trousers. And she wasn't breathing.

Ruby was still doing the CPR she had learned in sophomore health class when the mailman came running over.

"Enid," he said. "Oh, God." Frank clasped Ruby's hands in his, lifted them off Nana's chest, and pulled Ruby to her feet.

Later, after Dr. Weiner and the nicer of the town's two rival cousin-morticians had come and taken her grandmother away, Ruby stored the casseroles and Jell-O molds in the fridge and piled the cookies and brownies and pies on the counter. Then she carried the box of detergent down the basement steps. And there, right between the harvest gold Sears dryer and the newer white Maytag washer—a testament to her grandmother's zeal for breeze-dried linens—sat another bright orange box of Tide, almost half full.

For the second time that day, Ruby sank to her knees, this time on the clammy concrete floor. This time Ruby cried, like the first nasty winter storm—wailing wind, pelting sleet—like she hadn't cried since she was three. Why had her grandmother sent her into town when she had plenty of detergent? If she had some premonition that her heart was about to give out, why had she sent Ruby away, to die alone in a patch of grass? Why hadn't Nana said good-bye?

Antoinette's voice pulls Ruby back into the room. "It wasn't your fault, Ruby."

Ruby picks up the cup of now-tepid tea off the tray. She tugs on the string, watches the darker amber liquid nearest the bag swirl into the rest of the water. "I should have known better. I lose everyone I love."

EIGHTY-THREE

The Ms lead Ruby to a bench outside the hospital. She shifts the blanket draped over her shoulders, surprised to find it there until a vague memory surfaces, of enveloping warmth, of an aide telling her she was shivering.

"What do you need?" Margaret asks.

Lark. I need Lark, Ruby thinks. *I need Chaz to be okay.*

"Lark should be here," Molly says, as if reading Ruby's thoughts.

Ruby can only nod. For the first time since Antoinette came to the shed, she allows herself to sink below the flood line of grief. She tries to catch her breath between sobs. Her head pounds. Bile burns her throat. Her intestines feel as if they are turning inside out as she dry heaves. And the Ms hold her until the tide recedes.

Margaret's voice slices through the cool evening air. "You. Go away."

Ruby lifts her head from Molly's shoulder, recognizes the reporter. Little Miss Red Suit. Only tonight she is dressed in jeans and a sweatshirt, her blond hair not exactly unkempt, but far from the perfect helmet that has shadowed Ruby throughout her ordeal.

"I'm sorry." The reporter looks down at her feet. "I just had to come. To say I'm sorry."

"Sorry for what?" Ruby's own voice sounds as husky as the reporter's.

The story comes out like Little Miss Red Suit is reading a teleprompter. "We followed him. To that restaurant with all the piñatas. I just wanted some color, some B-roll footage for a follow-up piece." Her cameraman, Benny, waited in the van. She took the barstool next to Chaz, sipped a margarita while he slammed several beers. She chatted him up, flirted a little, spun a tale about boyfriend troubles. He flirted back, bought her a drink.

"And then, I don't know, he must have realized who I was or that he was nearing a line he didn't want to cross." A single tear digs a trench through the reporter's makeup. "It was just flirting. He taught me how to dip chips Christmas-style, in both red and green chili sauce. Nothing happened between us, I swear."

"You," Margaret says. "You chased him. *You* caused the accident."

"It's Princess Di all over again," Molly mutters.

"No. No!" the reporter says.

The Monteros' priest pauses on the sidewalk in front of them until Margaret assures him they are all right. Ruby watches Father Paul walk toward the parking lot as the reporter talks.

"He just bolted out of there. By the time I paid my tab, reached the door, I heard the screech of tires. The horrible crunch. Benny said he raced out of the parking lot, pulled out right in front of a car. Then he accelerated to avoid the collision. And lost control."

Ruby withers against the slats of the bench. "No, it's mine. It's my fault." If she hadn't fought with Chaz, if she hadn't let him leave... Hadn't he *told* her she was pushing him away? "It's my fault." She rubs her belly in small circles, trying to soothe the baby with touch as well as her thoughts. *When I said I would find a way, I didn't mean this. I never meant this.*

EIGHTY-FOUR

The elastic panel of the lavender skirt is stretched tight across Ruby's belly. Her second-day court outfit hangs like different clothing from how it did in Texas last month. She digs a mascara tube from the back of the bathroom drawer organizer. When she unscrews it, the wand is clogged with dried gunk. She tosses it back in the drawer, onto the pile of old lipsticks in shades that shouldn't have seemed like a good idea even at the time.

Antoinette squeezes in beside Ruby at the small counter, digs her own makeup bag out of her crammed-full purse.

"Thank you," Ruby says. "For spending the night, for going with me today."

"I wouldn't let you walk in there alone." Antoinette empties the contents of her zippered bag onto the counter. "He'll always be a part of you."

"I know."

Antoinette holds up an eye shadow case. Ruby shakes her head.

"At least a little blush," Antoinette says.

Ruby takes the small brush from her friend, swabs a slash of color across each cheek.

"More," Antoinette says.

Ruby startles. Then sighs, weary from all that has transpired in such a short time.

During those hours sitting vigil beside Chaz's bed, Ruby kept thinking how much she needed him. She might as well take a sledgehammer to her attempts at salvaging her own life if she lost him in the process. She was half-dozing in the chair beside him when the noise made her jerk alert.

"More," Chaz repeated, his voice raspy and raw. "And stop biting your lip."

In the few days he was hospitalized, he sailed through the mental facilities examination and surgery to repair his leg, and even when he was crotchety, restless, and in pain, Ruby was just too relieved that he was *there* to think about anything else.

As the fear-pumped adrenaline subsided, though, Ruby could again distinguish individual particles in the complicated swirl of her emotions, like sediment in roiling water. The silty flakes of missing Lark, pervading every molecule. The coarser grains of wanting Chaz, poking at delicate membranes. *Both*, Ruby thought. *I want—I need— them both.* And in those first days, when the shock of his accident made Ruby and Chaz more tender, even tentative, toward each other, she thought they would find a way to work it out.

But even sediment in the roilingest water will eventually begin to separate. And as the water cleared, Ruby and Chaz were right back to their old stalemate. That tenderness didn't stick around long.

Their fights were bitter. Maybe it was a side effect of painkillers, but postcrash Chaz exhibited a cruel streak Ruby had never seen before. He was appalled that Ruby would still even consider her plan. "After I almost *died*?" His warnings about her pushing him away intensified into threats that she was *driving* him away.

And when he lashed out at her, when he dug in his own heels, Ruby could easily curb her own guilt about his wreck and hold her side of the rope steady. Once she even lashed back at him, "Thank *God* I didn't make some stupid bargain with God when I worried you might die!"

Chaz spent several hours a day in physical therapy, stretching and strengthening his healing leg. And if, when evening rolled around, he told her he was tired, was turning in early, she didn't push him, relieved to have a break from the arguing, from him. She was tired, too.

EIGHTY-FIVE

Ruby's own doctor's appointment had been six or so weeks into Chaz's recovery. Afterward, she had driven straight to the physical therapy center. She needed to talk with Chaz; she hadn't yet been able to process what the news might mean for any of them.

She walked into a suite of several small rooms with examination tables and followed a hall to a large area with a few stationary bicycles and treadmills. With all of the colorful balls, mats, long bands, and other "toys," the place looked like a day care center at first glance.

Ruby spotted Chaz across the room, lying on his back on a floor mat, a trim, ponytailed therapist on her knees beside him. Ruby couldn't see his face, only his clasped hands pressed into the back of his head, elbows winged out to his sides. One knee was bent, the other leg extended, lifting and lowering in a steady rhythm. Ruby passed an older woman slowly riding a bicycle, her feet strapped to the pedals. *Stroke,* Ruby thought. The half-face sag and the struggle were unmistakable from her visits to the nursing home.

And then she didn't *think* anything at all. She *knew.*

She stood at the edge of the mat, watching them, and she knew. It was nothing so obvious as the woman on the bike, nothing blatant at all. But it was just as unmistakable: the therapist's hand a little too high on Chaz's thigh, a fleeting look crossing her pretty, young face, a crackle of electricity in the air.

Ruby sounded like a clogged vacuum cleaner as she swallowed her gasp. Then she turned and walked away as fast as her belly would allow.

"Ruby. Ruby!" His sneakers squeaked behind Ruby in an uneven gait.

He caught up with her in the parking lot, grabbed her arm, and spun her around, pinning her to the Jeep. "It's not what you think."

Ruby stared at him, willing her lips not to tremble.

"It's not what you think."

But just from his denial, Ruby knew it was exactly what she thought. Chaz had cheated on her. "Let. Go. Of. Me."

He took a step back. His face looked stricken, as if the vehemence in her voice were a slap, the pale yellow of the last fading bruise suddenly mauve again.

Ruby opened her car door, climbed into the seat.

"Ruby. Ruby, please."

She closed the door, started the engine, and backed out of the space. In the rearview mirror, she watched him, standing in the lot. His haircut still looked like a crazy person had taken scissors to it, the patch of scalp that had been shaved now a bristly burr. A brace stretched from thigh to ankle over one leg of his sweatpants.

She was almost home before she remembered that she hadn't even told Chaz the news.

By the time she got into the house, her answering machine was clogged with entreaties from him. For the first day or so, the messages were pleading. *It just happened. It didn't mean anything. Please.* Then they mutated from contrition to demands. *Pick up the phone. You have to understand.* Later, his voice seethed with anger and transferred guilt, as if she were to blame that he and his physical therapist had screwed. *Maybe if you hadn't been so unavailable, so stubborn about this whole Lark thing.*

"The Lark thing?" Ruby screamed at the machine. "My daughter is a *thing*?"

A few days after she witnessed his "physical therapy session," Clyde barked Chaz's arrival before the doorbell rang. By the time she reached the door, Clyde had pushed it open and stood on the porch, sniffing at Chaz's legs. For a moment, Ruby wondered if betrayal had a scent, but the dog was more likely reacting to the strange odors of the brace and doctors' offices.

"I can't do this anymore." Chaz thrust a sheaf of papers toward Ruby. "They're all signed."

She took the adoption forms and consents from him, riffled through the pages, keeping her eyes on Chaz's face. The anger that had creased his brow was gone. All she saw was weariness and something that she hoped was self-reproach or regret but might have been simple chagrin that he had been caught with his hand in the cookie jar.

"Louie'll be happy." Chaz pointed to the bat hanging at the top of the wall.

He started to walk away, then paused and turned back to her. "What was it, why did you stop by PT that day?"

Ruby clasped the papers against her chest. "It doesn't matter anymore. I just wanted to say . . . to tell you that the baby, he's a boy."

Chaz looked up into the sky then back at Ruby. "You're right. That never mattered to me." He continued down the driveway before pausing once again. "I'm sorry."

"More," Ruby said softly as Clyde whined at her side.

EIGHTY-SIX

Now Ruby watches Chaz's sister, who unwittingly mirrored that final "more."

Antoinette's hair crackles with static as she brushes it. "Thank you for still being my friend. After everything."

Ruby sits on the closed toilet lid, fiddling with the toilet paper roll. "Like any of this is your fault."

"Well, I did push you into meeting my brother." Antoinette twists her hair into a knot at the nape of her neck.

"I don't regret that. Just . . . how it ended is all." Ruby folds the toilet paper into a hotel triangle. What she doesn't say is that she didn't know it would be this brutal, even with the excitement of knowing Lark will be coming home.

Antoinette stabs a bobby pin into her bun. She talks through another pin that she holds in her lips. "Well, this could have been awkward. Between you and me. Friendships have ended over less."

"But we were friends before."

Antoinette finishes her hair, holds out a tube of mascara. Ruby shakes her head, and Antoinette leans over the counter toward the mirror, applying the wand to her own lashes, little-boy long like Chaz's. Her mouth opens into the O that seems to be a reflex in all women. After she sets aside the mascara, she combs her lashes, then starts in on her brows. "You know you don't have to go today. This is just a preliminary approval of the motion. And just . . . just for the baby." Antoinette wields more tools at her eyes and brows than Ruby uses in an entire pedicure. "You'll have to go to Texas, for the final hearing on Lark's adoption next year."

"I know." Ruby plays with the knot Antoinette tied in the shawl she insisted Ruby wear. "I just feel like I owe it"—she dips her chin toward her belly—"to him. To be *present*, you know."

"He'll always be a part of you." Antoinette pulls Ruby to her feet. "This is the right thing. You're doing what's best."

The curl of son inside Ruby's belly is still too fragile to survive outside her womb. Yet that is what she is doing today, really, tossing him from that watery, safe house into the mean, broken world beyond. "I'm sorry," she whispers to him. She doesn't know whether his soccer kick is in protest or benediction. "I'm doing what I have to do."

Antoinette's elbow in Ruby's side is softer than the tiny foot to her kidney. "Come on, girl. This is one step closer to Lark coming home."

"Yeah, it is." Ruby smiles at her friend.

"What did Darla say?" Antoinette tucks her rosy blouse into the waistband of her tweed skirt, slips on the matching jacket.

"I . . ." Ruby plays with the fringe of her shawl. "I haven't told her yet."

"*What?* The hearing is *today*."

"I know that." Ruby shrugs, shakes her head. "But what if after all this what if they don't want to go through with it? They wanted a baby *girl,* to replace the one they lost. I told them I would give them that."

Antoinette stuffs her makeup bag into her purse, tosses the purse over her shoulder. "Then, girl, you better find out. Before this goes any further." She leads Ruby like she's a recalcitrant child, out of the bathroom, down the short hall, and into the kitchen. "Call. Now."

EIGHTY-SEVEN

"Hi, baby."

The snuffle travels the distance from Lark's nose to Ruby's heart in an instant. It is a stoic snuffle; her daughter is trying as hard not to cry as Ruby is. "I know Darla's standing right there, so I'll just ask questions, okay?"

" 'Kay."

"Are they being nice to you?" Ruby leans against the kitchen counter.

"Uh-huh."

Ruby glances at the bananas hanging by a hook over her fruit bowl. "Are you eating?"

"Yeah."

Ruby pauses to think about what else she can ask. She wants to be careful about what she says. From the beginning, Ruby asked Darla not to say anything to Lark about the plan. Darla is probably not the most reliable secret-keeper, but Ruby would rather risk Darla slipping than the devastation that would rain down on Lark if Ruby told her and then something were to happen, a legal snag, or if the baby . . . if something happened to the baby.

"How's Clyde?"

The dog at Ruby's feet pricks up his ears. "He misses you. He's not eating very much, either. I tell you what, if you promise to eat more, then I'll make Clyde promise to eat more, too."

"Okay."

"Have you been reading, or painting?" Darla told Ruby her mother-in-law was "way into" art and had given Lark some canvases and paints.

"Um, some."

"Do you know how much I love you?"

Lark's voice sheds a handful of years. "To the moon."

"And back," Ruby says. "And back, baby bird." Before she starts crying herself, she asks Lark to put Darla back on, hears Darla telling Lark to go play in her room.

"I've got some other news." Ruby puts a hand to her throat, not sure of how the words she is about to speak will be received. "The baby . . . it's, he's . . ."

"He?" Darla says. "It's a boy?"

"A boy."

"A boy," Darla squeals. "A boy, oh boy." The rest of what she says gushes out with an almost-manic laughter. "Philip is going to flip. In a good way, I mean. Philip . . . and he'll be not much younger than my nephew. It's, *he's* a boy! I have to call Philip right now."

EIGHTY-EIGHT

Ruby storms past the reception area and barges into John's office. "They served me with papers. A constable came right into the salon. In front of everyone." She presses her palms to her cheeks. Just when she was starting to feel like everything was going to work out. She *knew* better than to jinx herself that way.

"Let me call you back." John sets the phone receiver in its cradle as he rises. He walks over to Ruby, puts a hand on her shoulder. "I left voice mail at your home and a message at the salon. I just found out that they had filed this morning." He guides her to a chair.

The receptionist, a younger woman than the receptionist who was here when Ruby was here before, enters the office with a tall glass. The woman stumbles, spills water on the geometric-patterned rug, then hands the dripping glass to Ruby. John lets out an exasperated sigh and waves the woman away as Ruby wipes the glass on her pants.

"But what does it mean, the lawsuit?"

John sits across from her, rests his elbows on his knees. "The Monteros are seeking an injunction to prevent the adoption of the baby."

"The judge already approved it, though. Chaz agreed. Can they go against him? Can they stop me?"

"They can try. Anyone can file a lawsuit for anything," John says. He explains that the first step is a hearing for a temporary restraining order to stop her from turning over the baby to the Tinsdales when he is born. "A judge *might* give them that, just to maintain the status quo until he can set an evidentiary hearing. I've got someone researching this, but I would be shocked if even the temporary order were granted, and I don't see how they have standing to win a permanent injunction."

"Then why? Why are they doing this?"

John scratches one ankle with the other shoe. Loafers without socks today. "My guess? This is a ploy to build a case to seek visitation rights, a gesture for evidence of how much they care."

Ruby sets the glass on the table. "Oh, shit. Oh, shit shit shit." She shifts her weight in the chair as the baby kicks her.

"Ruby, their chances are really slim. It's highly unlikely—"

"The Tinsdales." Ruby shakes her head. "If the Monteros ask for visitation, Philip Tinsdale will blow a gasket." She looks at the ceiling, at her lap. The Tinsdales wanted *Lark* to themselves, cutting off all contact with the outside. She can't imagine that they'll accept anything less with their new baby. The papers for Lark's adoption haven't even made it to preliminary approval in the clogged Texas family court; the Tinsdales could still change their minds. Ruby puts her head in her hands. "Chaz's family is going to screw the whole thing up."

John leans back, crosses a leg on his knee. "Let's just take it one step at a time."

"I can't believe that Antoinette . . . she didn't even warn me." Ruby chews her lip hard until she can feel the pain at her mouth separate from the ache in the rest of her body. She folds her arms against her chest, feels that looser second skin of grief from losing Lark, like a shirt of an old boyfriend that a woman wears around.

"Ruby, listen. I think I should call the Tinsdales' lawyer, give him a heads-up. Better that they hear it from us."

"They'll freak, they'll friggin' freak." Ruby tries to gird herself for yet another battle. She knows that winning means losing something—someone—too. But losing? That cannot happen, not for Lark, and not after all Ruby has been through.

EIGHTY-NINE

Little Miss Red Suit is waiting on the driveway when Ruby steps out to go to work. "Just give me a minute."

This siren, who *almost* lured Chaz to the cliffs, is a scarlet reminder as vivid as Hester Prynne's A of his betrayal. "I don't have anything to say to you." Ruby brushes past the reporter, heads for the Jeep.

Little Miss Red Suit scurries after her. "Woman Chooses Foundling Over Biological Child!" Her whisky voice is somewhere between normal talking and clarion. "Nurture Trumps Nature!"

Ruby stops, turns to her. "Please. Just leave me alone."

"The story is out there," the reporter says. "Grant me an exclusive, and I'll do it right. I won't exploit you or your daughter. You don't want those other headlines."

Ruby leans against the side of the Jeep, her belly like the heavy medicine ball her grade-school teachers made the kids throw around the gym on snowy days. "How did you hear?"

The reporter steps in beside Ruby, her skinny red hip resting against the car. "The grandparents."

Of course. Ruby just might vomit this news onto the driveway. The Tinsdales are already squirming at the possibility of a legal battle. If the Monteros fight through the court of public opinion . . .

"Mrs. Tinsdale already agreed to an interview."

Ruby shakes her head. "She wouldn't, Darla wouldn't . . ."

"Not the trophy wife," the reporter says, "the mother, his mother." Little Miss Red Suit tells Ruby that old Mrs. Tinsdale of the high tea and crinoline, a woman who would tell you that a true lady's name is in print only three times in her life—her birth, her marriage, and her death—rather liked the buzz she generated at her stuffy Dallas country club because of the trial, doesn't mind stirring up a bit more interest.

Ruby drops her chin to her chest. She can't face another media madhouse, can't put the salon through it again. And what about Lark, if the press gets hold of her? "I can't . . . I won't."

Little Miss Red Suit shoves a card into Ruby's hand, squeezes Ruby's fingers as if she is kneading bread. "Call me. I promise to be fair." She strides down the driveway, a vulture in search of her next carrion. "You don't want those headlines."

Ruby groans herself off the Jeep. She takes the crisp white card and tears it into snowflakes, a little flurry of winter there on the late-summer ground.

NINETY

"Don't you think?" Ruby's client asks.

Ruby looks up from her nail station, where she holds the client's hand, brushing each fingertip with I'm Not a Waitress red. "Sorry?"

"Don't you think a Russian theme for the Chamber Music Festival party would be fun?"

"Oh, yes." Ruby takes the client's other hand, bracing her own hand on her other pinkie, a manicurist trick for steady polish strokes. She has learned over the years; clients want pretty nails and an hour to vent to a good listener. The hand-in-hand intimacy of the manicure chair opens the floodgates. All that is required, desired even, from Ruby is a few "uh-huhs" and nods along the way, which is a good thing at the moment, because she is incapable of cogent thought.

She makes the occasional "mmhhh" noise as the client continues her monologue: it's Shostakovich after all; they could hang jewel-toned fabrics from the ceiling, faux Fabergé eggs on the tables, create a whole Hermitage feel.

Ruby finishes the top coat on Mrs. Kremlin, then sends her to dry under the ultraviolet light with a comment that the Chamber Music Festival event surely will be a smash. She motions to Zara that she is ready for her next appointment, then readies her station, changing out the towels, laying out clean instruments, returning the bottle of polish to the rack on the wall.

When she steps from the back room with a fresh dish of warm sudsy water, Antoinette is sitting at the nail station. "You've been avoiding me."

"Yeah, I guess I have." Ruby sets down the shallow manicure bowl, places Antoinette's left hand in the suds. "I'm sorry. I . . ."

"No, I'm sorry," Antoinette says. "For my family's behavior. I didn't know about the lawsuit. They didn't even tell me. I had to hear it from a friend in the clerk's office." Antoinette shakes her head. "You didn't think I had anything . . . you know I would have called to tell you."

Not long ago, Ruby assured Antoinette that their friendship could survive anything. But this is a whole lot of anything, for anybody. "I don't blame you. It's just hard." The ache of missing Chaz is still such tender skin. Being with his sister is like fingers picking away at bits of scab, making Ruby bleed again and again and again. And now a court battle with his family. Antoinette glances over at Margaret, who is sweeping a patch of already-swept tile around her station. "He left, you know."

Ruby holds Antoinette's right hand, squirts cuticle cream around each nail. "Left her?"

Antoinette takes her other hand out of the soaking dish, wipes it on a towel. The linen is marshmallow-white against Antoinette's vanilla-cream skin. "No, left town."

Ruby moves the dish to the other side of the table, dunks Antoinette's right hand in the suds. She squirts the cuticle cream on Antoinette's left hand, massages it around her fingernails, then nudges the cuticles with an orange stick.

Antoinette rubs her nose against her upper arm. "Left all of us. Phoenix. He quit the force and took a job with a company that helps people find runaway kids. Works for a guy he knew from that gang task force stuff."

A bounty hunter of children. Chaz, too, is still a rescuer, trying to bring babies home. "How did your family, how are they about . . ."

"The prodigal son?" Antoinette's cheeks flush with emotion. "They're sure he'll return someday to claim his rightful place. Just like the Bible story."

Ruby dries Antoinette's hand, sets the soaking dish aside. "I never understood that story."

"Me neither."

Ruby knows Antoinette refers to more than just a parable. She trims the cuticles on Antoinette's other hand, files the nails into the squarish ovals that Antoinette likes, and lets her talk. The anger is directed at Chunk for not caring about Ruby's baby—even wanting it to go away—until he found out it was a boy. All the pain that Antoinette has managed to bury through the years has burbled to the surface, of feeling slighted, held back, because she was a girl. "I just don't know how to be around any of them right now."

Ruby's belly feels leaden, like a wrecking ball that has cut a swath of devastation through the Montero homestead before coming to rest again in her lap. "These are my problems, my actions. They shouldn't drive you and your family apart." Ruby lifts the lid of the apothecary jar, slips her clippers and metal files into the green antibacterial solution, replaces the lid.

"None of it should have ever happened, not to you or to Lark." Antoinette hands Ruby a bottle of peachy nail polish. "My dad's not going to let go of it. The suit, I mean. He's a dog with a bone."

NINETY-ONE

The Ms' cabin on the Pecos River, just on the other side of the Santa Fe ski mountain, is a refuge. Dense pine forest blocks the view from the road behind Ruby; the river is a moat in front of her. She sits in a canvas soccer-mom chair, watches the dogs as they play. The big dogs jump from rock to rock. The terrier runs back and forth along the riverbank, barking at foam and floating sticks.

John's warning that the press would crucify her was an understatement. Ruby is the fodder for the twenty-four-hour news machine. The street in front of her house is a parking lot of vans sprouting satellite dishes. If this were just about a gross invasion of privacy, like being raped in a public square, Ruby could bear it. She would be bruised, battered, but she would bear it.

But the Tinsdales are livid. John told her Philip is ranting about all kinds of legal action, against Ruby, against the Monteros. He'd sue God Himself if he could serve the papers. Ruby has left messages for Darla, but she hasn't returned Ruby's calls.

From the chair beside Ruby, Molly pats Ruby's arm. "This will all blow over. It'll be forgotten before the next news cycle."

"A deal breaker. John said they're calling it a deal breaker." Ruby almost has to shout to be heard over the swift water.

"Chaz's family won't win. Your lawyer said the court wouldn't grant them the injunction, right?"

"Wasn't *likely*." Ruby shakes her head. "There's no such thing as a sure thing. But it's not just the legal stuff that will kill the deal. The media attention . . ."

All the criticisms that have blared from the television now scroll across Ruby's mind. The biology junkies argue that Lark belongs with the Tinsdales, and this baby with Ruby. The family-first activists are screaming about grandparents' rights. Ruby has her moments when she wonders if they are all right. Maybe they are right.

She tries to quiet the arguments against the swap by focusing on the arguments she made for the deal in the first place. This baby won't miss her, but Lark is withering in Texas. Giving her baby to the Tinsdales is recompense for keeping Lark after Ruby found her. But those reasons will be worthless if the Tinsdales back out of the agreement.

Clyde and Daisy bound past Ruby, showering her with icy river water. She jerks around.

"Relax," Molly says. "It's just Margaret."

Clyde runs circles around the chairs, and Daisy escorts Margaret from the cabin. Dudley never shifts his attention from the river foam he is determined to bark into submission.

Margaret hands a portable telephone receiver to Ruby. "It's John."

NINETY-TWO

The inside of the Albuquerque airport looks like the face of the Mexican pyramids in the photos Ruby has seen. Two pairs of escalators and two wide staircases rise up to the middle tier. Beyond a few shops and restaurants at the second level, two more sets of escalators frame the stairways to the departure lounges above.

Ruby looks over her shoulder once again to make sure she hasn't been followed, rides the escalators, up, up, up until she reaches the skylit top of the hill. She joins the short line winding through the security checkpoint, shows her gate pass to the first agent, walks through the metal detector.

"You got any contraband in there?" The security agent on the other side of the detector points to her belly. Ruby gives him the scantest of smiles in response, not wanting to engage him in the inevitable "when is it due, what is it, when my wife gave birth . . ."

At least he doesn't try to touch her. She has realized through all of the mauling—by clients, by strangers on the street—just how much she values her personal-space bubble.

The plane is pulling to the jetway as Ruby arrives at the gate. Its orange and mustard nose sniffs at the window. A tide of people gushes through the tunnel. First out are the businessmen, wielding briefcases like shields as they push past the people milling around the gate area.

Next comes the old lady with the walker, holding up the line, probably the same way she does with her big Buick on her hometown streets. When she finally steps out of the jetway, people stream around her like river water around a rock, more businesspeople dragging their black suitcases, vacationing families laden with backpacks and strollers. Ruby doesn't think traveling with cranky kids would be much of a vacation for the parents.

The stream sputters to a slow trickle before Ruby sees her, walking with a flight attendant and a young boy. For eighty-eight days, Ruby has prayed for this moment, not daring to hope too hard that it would actually happen. Yet now, when the time comes, she can't move. She is frozen in place like a fat statue while a dad walks over to the attendant, signs the paperwork for the boy, ruffles the boy's hair as he steers him past Ruby. The flight attendant looks at Ruby, tilts his head in a question. And still Ruby doesn't move.

Finally, Lark drags the flight attendant over to Ruby. Ruby shows her ID, scribbles her name, and drops to her knees. She sweeps Lark into her arms, squeezes limbs, sniffs skin, strokes cheeks, laughs. And cries.

Until Lark scrabbles out of Ruby's reach. "Mo-om. You're making a scene."

Those are the sweetest words Ruby has ever heard. She wants to clamp her hands over her ears, trap the sound in her head forever.

NINETY-THREE

Lark tugs Ruby to her feet, pats her belly. "Ho-ly moly. That was some watermelon seed you swallowed."

Ruby chuckles through her sobs, but she can tell her daughter's joking is forced. Lark was so stiff when Ruby hugged her, like a Barbie-Lark, with hard plastic skin and limbs that don't quite bend. Then Lark smiles, a real smile, an imp smile. Her daughter is undoubtedly damaged, yet a Lark is still stirring underneath that shell.

Watching Lark walk down the stairs in front of her makes Ruby practically giddy. She still has to fly to Dallas for the sentencing hearing in a couple of weeks, but the presentencing report has been filed with the recommendation of the minimum fine and no jail time, and John is confident the judge will rubber-stamp the prosecutor's terms. Ruby has been so caught up in fighting the Monteros and the public outcry that she hasn't even noticed that a prison gate is no longer looming over her head like a guillotine.

Funny how the Monteros' tactic of going to the press was actually the impetus for the Tinsdales to send Lark home. "It will quiet things down, take the press heat off her," Darla said on the telephone. Off *you*, Ruby thought.

Yesterday, John had called with a trifecta of news: as expected, the New Mexico court ruled that the Monteros had no standing to stop the baby's adoption and denied their motion; the Texas court signed the preliminary order for Lark's adoption; and John and the Tinsdales' lawyer had finalized the release of all civil claims. "The Monteros still could seek visitation rights through the Texas courts, but precedent is against them," John added.

Darla's call came this morning. "It's not like we need to keep trying to bond with her after all."

Ruby looks up at the big clock above the stairway. The conversation with Darla took place only seven hours ago.

"There really is no reason to wait," Darla said. She would put Lark on a plane that afternoon. She would pack Lark's things, ship them to Santa Fe. Ruby could taste the woman's relief through the telephone. If Ruby hadn't been so relieved herself, she might have been offended at Darla's eagerness to rid herself of Lark. "I know you're anxious to get your daughter home."

Her daughter. Home. These are more words Ruby wants to roll around in her head, savor.

As they cross the passenger pickup lane on the way to the parking lot, Ruby takes Lark's hand out of habit. Lark doesn't pull her arm away, protest that she is not a baby anymore. Instead, she squeezes Ruby's hand and holds it all the way to the car, as if she, too, is afraid that this moment will vaporize into a dream if she lets go.

Ruby maneuvers the car out of the airport exit and onto the interstate. Traffic through town is heavy; the exit lane to I-40 is backed up with workers heading home to the suburbs. As the Jeep passes under the freeway interchange, she thinks about that day almost ten years ago, when her car was new and she got mixed up at this intersection, before the swooping Big I, as the locals call it, was complete. Ruby looks over at Lark and sees the infant who rode backward in her carrier as well as the nine-year-old with gangly legs almost reaching the floor. That was a wrong turn that turned out right.

NINETY-FOUR

"Is it really over?" Lark's voice is laced with anxiety, and some healthy anger.

"I think so, baby bird. I pray so." Or, over but for a few minor details. For Lark, all is over but the healing. Ruby still must attend her sentencing, deal with any fallout from the Monteros' antics, give birth, give away her other child.

The drive toward Santa Fe passes in a haze. Lark is quiet, almost shy, as Ruby tells her little things, lighthearted salon and flea-market stories from the weeks she was away. Ruby restrains herself from asking questions about the time in Texas. Lark will talk when she's ready.

They each get lost in their own thoughts as the New Mexico sky melts into one of its trademark sunsets. Then, as the old Jeep wheezes up that last big hill, Lark points out the sign for Las Vegas. "Let's go," she says.

Ruby grips the steering wheel, closes her eyes for a second. *Thank you*, she says in her head. Thank you for this moment. Thank you that Lark's scars can soften enough, even temporarily, to make the old family joke about Ruby thinking she was headed toward Las Vegas, Nevada, that day long ago. Thank you that her daughter is here to make the joke—Ruby glances at her belly wedged against the steering wheel—even if her son is going away.

They have just exited the highway onto Old Pecos Trail when Lark asks about Chaz.

"He had a bad accident, but he's okay now." Ruby tells Lark about the car wreck, Chaz's injuries.

"It's my fault." Lark tugs at her neckline, lifts out Chaz's Saint Christopher medal.

Ruby pulls over at the entrance to the Elks Lodge. "It is so not your fault. And he's fine, he's fine now. But . . ." Ruby tells her that he moved to Phoenix for a new job. She doesn't go into details; she's still trying to sort out the best way for Lark to hear that her mother is swapping the baby in her belly for her own return. "We decided not to be together anymore."

"It's my fault." Lark fingers the small medallion as she begins to cry. "It's all my fault."

"Oh, baby." Ruby slides Lark over the console and onto what remains of her lap. In a way, she's relieved at her daughter's tears; emotion, even raw emotion, is so much better than that stony resignation. And as she tries to convince Lark that neither Chaz's accident nor the breakup was her fault, Ruby's voice echoes in her own head and starts to chisel away at the frozen block of her own guilt.

Lark wearing a piece of metal was not to blame for the wreck, and neither was Ruby trying to get Chaz to agree to her plan. Someday, maybe both of them will be able to embrace the hard truth that they can't control random events, instead of the more consoling idea of vindictive gods and bad karma.

As Lark's own tears subside, she lays a soft hand against Ruby's cheek. "Oh, Mama. Your heart must have been attacking you really bad."

Molly, she'll cry at anything. Movies, music, dog food commercials. But Ruby has never seen Margaret cry until today. Which may be because Margaret is not a pretty crier. Southern belle Molly just opens her eyes wide, and the dainty waterworks trickle out. Her tears wouldn't even smudge mascara, if Molly wore any, that is. Margaret, though, is a blubberer. Swollen face and snorts and snot.

The house was quiet when the Jeep crunched up the driveway; the covered windows glowed opaque and muted. No decorations outside this time—the Ms were careful not to tip off reporters or even neighbors. But walking into the house was like climbing into the netted play area at McDonald's. Untethered balloons, bright green, orange, pink, and Lark's favorite, purple, dotted the living area. Some filled with helium slithered across the ceiling; the ones with plain air bounced around the floor.

Clyde was so excited that he peed on the rug when Lark came into the house. Ruby figured that was his own way of crying at her return. Then he went on a tear, doing figure eights around the kitchen table, around the coffee table, around and around, pausing to head-butt balloons along his path. Lark's giggle sounded as if it had been shredded in a blender.

The Ms brought pizza and bright-colored cupcakes and bubbly drinks. Ruby drank half a glass of champagne for the toasts—to Lark, to Home, to Forever—then switched to sparkling cider. Antoinette called not long after the toasts. Ruby invited her over, but her friend demurred, telling Ruby that Lark needed a night just with family.

And Antoinette was right. After Lark's crying spell in the Jeep, the shy-stranger persona returned. She isn't quite tiptoeing around like Darla said she did, but she's not acting all home-sweet-home, either. She sits now in the center of the sofa, sandwiched between the Ms. Poor Lark is going to shed a layer of skin after all the hugging and rubbing from both of them. Clyde, exhausted from his seal act, is sprawled across their laps while the Ms make plans for the next century or so.

"You can come to the opening of my show at the gallery." Molly wiggles with happiness.

Margaret has abandoned her champagne flute, clasps the bottle by its throat. "Let's go on a trip." She pauses to take a swig as if the Moët were a longneck beer. "All of us together."

"You're drunk." Molly speaks in a Minnie Mouse voice.

Margaret tucks the champagne bottle between her knees, reaches across Lark to grab the balloon from Molly, sucks helium from its snout. "I'm verklempt. Ver-klempt."

Lark just sits there between them, a swipe of lime green icing on her cheek. She exudes more relief than happiness. Ruby remembers reading about POWs, how the army put them through a multistep reintegration after their release from war camps. And they weren't sent to prison by their mothers, weren't mad at their mothers before they even left. Ruby has some heavy-duty reintegration to undertake.

NINETY-SIX

Long after the celebration has ended, after the Ms have cleaned up the mess and left, after Lark and Clyde have tumbled into an exhausted slumber, Ruby sits on the edge of Lark's bed. The moon is a bright orb outside the window. Ruby worries about photographers, night lenses, but just for tonight, she has opened Lark's shade, needing the affirmation in the splash of yellow moonlight on Lark's serene face, as if God, too, is saying, "Yes, this is our beloved child. Here is where she belongs."

The moon was full the night before Lark left, too. Ruby can't quite believe that all of it, Lark leaving, Lark returning, and everything in between, has transpired during a scant few lunar cycles. "To the moon and back," Lark said tonight before she drifted off. *I love you, too,* Ruby thinks now, *to the moon and back.*

She sits and watches. Clyde lifts his head, nods at Ruby, nuzzles back into Lark's neck. He and Lark have fallen right back into their old tangle of limbs and sheets. Ruby remembers a cat that used to sleep with her like that, cheek to cheek, a paw thrown over her chest and the rest of her nestled in her armpit. Her grandmother had a firm rule about cats in the house; "They're called *barn* cats for a reason," Nana would say. But this particular feline attached himself to Ruby from the time he was an itty bitty kitty. Determined and curious, the cat learned how to squeeze around the loose screen on Ruby's open bedroom window and leap onto her bed.

Ruby's grandfather knew. He would spot the cat in Ruby's bed when he peeked in on her as he was heading out the door, after bringing

Nana's morning coffee to her bedside, as he did every morning of their marriage. He would whistle softly, and the cat would jump down, follow him out to the yard. Ruby isn't sure why this particular memory surfaces now, but it makes her smile.

Lark stirs, settles back against Clyde. Ruby wonders what her daughter is dreaming this night. How much will her ordeal change already cautious Lark? Will little pieces of the horror cling to her mind like smoke to clothing, surfacing at random moments, like tonight with Ruby's cat memory, only without the smile?

Ruby hums the daffy song to the dark room. She thought she might crumble when Lark asked to be tucked in tonight with her baby lullaby. But tonight Lark needed to be a baby, to be cocooned in mother love.

Ruby never has been much of a singer, and her repertoire is limited. In those first few sleepless nights with Lark in the apartment above the salon, though, this was the song that popped into Ruby's head. She sang it over and over while she paced that small room with the bundle of miracle on her shoulder.

The song became a tradition with them. During her toddler years, Lark would start chanting "The daffy song, the daffy song" before she hit her bed. She would change the words up every now and then, but Lark would give a sleepy giggle and say, "No, Mama, it goes like this."

Daffodil, daffodil, daffodil-dilly.
Sleep baby, sleep; the moon's in the sky.
Daffodil, daffodil, daffodil-dilly.
Sleep sweet one, sleep, for morning draws nigh.
Dream, baby dream, of flowers and sunshine.
Dream, sweet one, dream, oh, daughter of mine.
The moon's in the sky, love. The moon's in the sky.
Close your eyes to today, love. Morning draws nigh.
Sleep sweet one, sleep baby, sleep daffodil-dilly.
We'll share tomorrow and tomorrow and tomorrow, you and I.

Ruby isn't even sure where she learned the song. It certainly wasn't something her grandmother passed on to her; Nana wasn't the sentimental, bed-singing type. Ruby's grandfather sang constantly, while busy at his workbench, while out in the fields, even at the supper table until Nana would give him a look. But he didn't sing this one. No, Ruby likes to think that maybe, just maybe, her own mother sang it when she held Ruby in her arms.

After the moonlight shifts from Lark's face to the edge of the bed, Ruby heaves her swollen torso to standing, shakes the creaks out her knees. She gives Clyde a pat on the head, brushes a strand of hair off Lark's cheek. "A million tomorrows," she whispers. "We have a million tomorrows, you and I."

NINETY-SEVEN

Lark sits at the kitchen table, Clyde at her feet. The avocado pit has sprouted long tendrils of roots while she's been gone; Lark caresses it, talks to it, then places it in a clay pot. "Do you think he will grow, here I mean?" She sprinkles more potting soil into the container.

Ruby sets down her water glass—she's trying to follow doctor's orders to drink extra liquids; in the high desert, hydration is imperative. "I don't know. Santa Fe is not exactly California, but you're giving him every chance."

In the week or so that Lark has been home, she has traipsed over every square inch of the house, running her hands over walls and furniture and doodads. She acts like a cat sniffing out new territory in every nook and cranny. Ruby understands the impulse. When she touches Lark, any skin-to-skin contact at all, she can feel a thousand coils unwinding in a sacred serpent dance along her spine. She tries not to hover, but she breathes better when Lark is in her sight.

Lark climbs onto the kitchen counter next to the stove top, opens the cabinet where the spices are stored. "You expecting an extra big visit from the Easter Bunny this year?"

Ruby looks past Lark at the shelf, and the stack of food coloring boxes from the pie-safe project, each missing a red squeeze bottle at one end.

"Ladies and gentlemen, Miss Smarty-Pants is back in the building." Antoinette steps through the side door.

"Wonnie!" Lark yelps, jumps from the counter, and bounds across the room. These days, she reminds Ruby of some of the dementia patients at the nursing home, greeting everyone like a long-lost relative with the same exuberance, even if she sees them several times in a day.

"Whatcha cooking there?" Antoinette asks.

Lark untangles herself from Antoinette and holds up a spice jar. "I'm burying Brad. I'm gonna put some garlic in the dirt to make sure he grows into some go-ood guacamole."

"Brad?" Antoinette asks.

Ruby shrugs. "Wait for it . . . wait for it."

Lark skips over to the table, opens her arms with the flair of a magician's assistant. "Pit. Brad Pit, my avocado."

Antoinette's laugh bubbles up from her toes. Lark holds her position with a satisfied smirk for a beat or two before dissolving into giggles herself.

"Oh, little girl, I'm gonna want me some of *that* guacamole," Antoinette says.

Ruby holds her belly with one hand, pinches her side with the other. Their laughter is out of proportion to the joke, but at least the tone of Lark's giggle has descended from dog-whistle range. "You two are going to make me pee my pants."

"She's a peeing machine," Lark says.

Antoinette nods. "Yep. And that gas. Whoo-ie."

"Make fun of the fat person, why don't ya. I'll be right back." Ruby waddles across the room to the hall, listening to the laughter, music that has been missing from this house for too long. She and her daughter, they're both going to be okay. She wipes her eyes with her hand, wondering what that African language would call tears of joy.

When Ruby steps out of the bathroom, Lark is in front of her, heading out of her bedroom. Ruby pauses at the doorway to the living area, takes in the scene.

Lark and Antoinette stand facing each other, Antoinette's hands wrapped around Lark's. Clyde, as usual, has his nose in the middle of the action.

"Tell him." Lark speaks quietly; Ruby can barely hear the words. "Tell him I'm sorry. That he had his wreck." Lark pulls her hand away, and a thin gold chain dribbles from Antoinette's palm, dangling between her fingers.

"I'll give it back to him if you want, Larklette," Antoinette says. "But he gave it to you; he wanted you to have it."

Ah, now Ruby understands what's going on. The Saint Christopher medal. *Chaz's* medal.

Lark drapes an arm around the dog's neck. "I'm safe now. And he'll need it in his new job, because he doesn't have his gold shield anymore." She glances over her shoulder, spots Ruby. A sheepish shadow falls across her face.

"It's okay." Ruby walks into the room. "You can talk about him in front of me." Since their conversation in the car, Lark hasn't asked any questions about Chaz. Ruby didn't doubt that Lark sensed there was more to the story than she was told, yet she seemed to accept that he was gone. She also must have sensed Ruby's sadness. His absence lurks around the house—jumping out to slap Ruby across the face at odd moments—and the rest of the time simply lingering, like a scent of aftershave in the air, as she moves through the days. "You don't have to pretend he doesn't exist."

NINETY-EIGHT

A horn toots in the driveway. Ruby turns off the faucet, leaves the breakfast dishes to soak. The waffle iron sits open-jawed on the countertop, drips of crusty, brown batter and a blur of melted rainbow sprinkles on the sides.

"Come on," Ruby calls. "Shoes. Backpack."

She thought about taking Lark away, hiding out at the Ms' cabin, but Lark needs a semblance of normalcy. She needs her first day back to class with her friends. When Ruby called the principal to warn her about the media, the principal was resolute; no reporter is going to get anywhere near this child on school property.

But Lark has a better chance of avoiding detection if Ruby stays far away.

When Ruby peeks through the paper covering the door panes, Margaret's tinted-window SUV is pulled right up to the edge of the front porch, doors flung open wide to block the view from the street.

"I'll be fine," Lark says as Ruby hugs her. "Mama. Let go."

Ruby forces her arms to separate from Lark's back, like prying magnets apart, and opens the front door. As a screen, Molly stands on the porch with Margaret's golf umbrella held out beside her like that dancing fool in *Singin' in the Rain*. Lark gives Ruby a little-girl wave, dashes alongside the umbrella, and into the car.

As Lark's head disappears behind the closing door, Ruby resists the urge to call out to her to come back. She isn't going to cause Lark to miss school, even if it takes old-movie antics to get her there. But she doesn't even try to quell the panic pounding in her throat as she watches her child disappear from her sight once again.

NINETY-NINE

Lark kneels on the sofa, bends the blind slats to make a peephole. "They're still there. Three of them." She spins around, throws herself down onto the sofa. "This sucks."

Ruby swipes her own forehead. They've never before needed a swamp cooler, but the room is stifling, stale without the cool air circulating through windows. She doesn't even bother to caution Lark about her language. The press siege is wearing her down, too. The reporters are relentless. The phone is unplugged. And the answering machine. Anyone who needs to reach them will know what's going on.

Clyde jumps up on the sofa, takes Lark's place at the window, his chubby paws on the cushion top, nose under the blinds. "Get down." Lark tugs his collar. "You don't want to end up on national TV." The dog flinches at Lark's unusually harsh words. The way he puts his head on Lark's knee is worthy of its own Oscar.

Little Miss Red Suit showed up at the salon yesterday after Ruby left. Margaret said she never imagined that ohm-chanting Zara knew so many four-letter words. Among other invectives, she told the reporter that if she wasn't gone in five seconds, she would walk out with a curling iron up her cute little skirt. One of the other hairdressers recognized the reporter; she's a talking head for a court cable station, all luridness, all the time. Red is her signature color, the magic carpet she hopes to ride to prime time.

Ruby offered to stay away so that the salon's business wouldn't be disrupted, but Margaret shrugged off the suggestion, told her the ladies love the intrigue. Then she posted a REPORTERS WILL BE SHOT

ON SIGHT sign on the front door and let it be known that anyone, staff or clients, who talked with the press about Ruby and Lark would be included in the firing line, or at least shunned for life. The latter threat carries some real weight; Margaret still hasn't forgiven a cousin who borrowed her car and racked up several hundred dollars in unpaid parking tickets twenty years ago.

And today the reporters are gathering outside their house. Just a small camp, not a full-fledged army. Not yet anyway. Now Ruby knows how Chaz's fish felt. No, this is worse. Glug at least got fed. Ruby and Lark just get violated.

"How about a game before bed? Scrabble?"

Lark doesn't answer, just recrosses her arms against her chest. Lark loves Scrabble; she routinely trounces Ruby. Lark can see words in the mess on a rack, while Ruby just sees mess. But not even the chance to skunk her mom tempts Lark today. "How 'bout just bed."

Ruby follows Lark into her bedroom. "They'll lose interest soon. Last time—"

Clyde startles Ruby out of her words as he scuttles past her, growls at the window. She rushes to his side. Maybe tomorrow she'll nail plywood over this window, batten down the hatches to protect Lark from the media storm. But for tonight, she double-checks the latches, tugs at the shade to make sure it covers every speck of glass. That is when she sees the shadow.

Ruby runs out the front door, Clyde at her heels. She grabs the garden hose, turns the spigot on full blast, and aims the cold gushing water at the cameraman skulking along the side of the house. The man shrieks, curses, covers his lens with his jacket. And runs down the driveway with Clyde snarling at his heels. The crash of camera against asphalt, plastic and glass chattering, shattering, is gunshot-sharp against the evening quiet.

At Ruby's whistle, Clyde comes bounding up the drive, his teeth a flash of grin in the dark. Ruby follows him in through the door, locks it behind her, pats the brown grocery sacks taped over the glass panes to make sure that they are secure. She storms to the phone, plugs it in, and calls Chaz's ex-partner, Krueger.

He probably can feel the blaze of her words through the phone line. "Hold on," he says. She hears him on his cell phone, calling in a favor from the police captain. "They'll be right there," he says to Ruby through the landline as he thanks his boss on the other phone. "And the cruisers will drive by all night."

When Ruby walks back into Lark's bedroom, Clyde stands guard in front of the bed, where Lark sits cross-legged, her face a mask of shock and indignity, her pj's clenched to her chest. Ruby sits down beside her. "I think Clyde helped himself to a cameraman's bum for a bedtime snack."

"Good boy, Clyde." Lark strokes the dog's head, and he looks back at her with a mixture of complicity and adoration. "I wish you could eat them all."

Ruby takes Lark's pajamas from her, pulls the top over her daughter's head. "All this make you want to go back to Texas?"

Lark leans her head against Ruby's arm. "How 'bout maybe next never?"

How does a person explain the inexplicable to a nine-year-old? At first, Lark was so relieved to be home that she didn't ask why or how. Ruby unplugged the television, didn't bring newspapers into the house. But, of course, kids at school talk, and now the questions come. Lark is an old soul, in many ways wiser than Ruby. Yet this is a lot of albatross to hang around her skinny neck.

They sit on the rug of the living area, Ruby and Lark and Clyde. This carpet picnic is borne out of feeling vulnerable rather than adventuresome. Ruby hasn't been to the salon in a week. The commotion became too much for everyone, that and the fact that Ruby's belly gets in the way of her nail table.

Ruby has been pacing this cage of a house, feeling so much like a zoo attraction even with every pane of glass obstructed. When she and Lark moved into Mrs. Levy's house, Ruby felt as if she was crawling into Nana's big iron bed after a thunderstorm, but today she finds no comfort anywhere. Her ankles are swollen, her back aches, she's just downright grumpy.

She tried woodworking, but she is too ungainly to be around sharp objects. Besides, Margaret heard from one of her clients that the people in the house behind Ruby's have rented out a second-story window to paparazzi, and Ruby doesn't want a shot of herself waddling to the shed at every cash register in America.

So here they are on an otherwise glorious fall Saturday, or glorious as far as Ruby can tell from quick peeks out the window, picnicking on the carpet instead of under a canopy of brilliant gold and orange leaves.

The baby kicks at the tender spot between her separated ribs. Over the past months, Ruby has been so caught up in an emotional whirlwind that she hasn't paid nearly enough attention to this baby. In the torrent of the trial, the details of getting Lark back, the devastation of breaking up with Chaz, this burgeoning life has been anything but nurtured. Yet now, when Ruby most needs the detachment in order to do what she has to do, the baby's presence, its sheer physicality, is consuming.

As Clyde shifts his sprawl across their legs, Lark giggles. She pokes at Ruby's protruding belly button, visible through her shirt. Ruby takes her daughter's hand, rests it on the steep side of the mound, where a ropy appendage writhes.

"Ooh," Lark says. "Does that hurt?"

"Sometimes." What Ruby doesn't say is that the physical discomfort is nothing compared to where her mind keeps taking her. Her third-trimester nesting instinct has kicked in, and she can't eat away the hours readying for the baby she won't be bringing home.

And now Ruby needs to explain to Lark about the swap. She sets her tuna sandwich on the blue willow plate, tucks a wisp of hair behind her daughter's perfect ear, and begins. If nothing else, she wants to make sure that Lark doesn't think that she was rejected by the Tinsdales, that they preferred someone else's infant over their own biological kid.

The trick is how to make Lark understand without her realizing that Ruby essentially made the same choice as the Tinsdales, swinging back to smack Ruby in the face.

"I get it, Mama." Lark pats Ruby on the knee. "I think. They wanted me, but you wanted me more."

Ruby starts to interject; she doesn't want Lark to think this was some competition for her love. No child should have the burden of being anyone's whole world. But before she can say anything, Lark continues.

"I didn't know how to dotter around those people. I know how to dotter with you."

Ruby puzzles over Lark's words. Did the Tinsdales subject her to one of those overachiever-kid schedules, with no time for dawdling, meandering around?

"And you know how to mother me better than they do."

Finally, it is Ruby who gets it; her sage child really does understand. *Daughter*, not *dotter*. Daughterhood creates as much of an action verb, as much of a sense of place in the world, as being a mother does.

Finally, the press siege has wound down. Ruby thinks of that Sinatra song about a fickle friend blowing in. Not that the media was ever her friend, but indeed it was fickle. After the reporters' collective thick skull finally absorbed the fact that Ruby was never going to speak with them, the story petered out. There just wasn't enough *there* there to feed the voracious appetite. Little Miss Red Suit did ride her crimson carpet to the big leagues, though; Zara saw her behind the desk on a network early-bird news program.

Lark sits on the kitchen counter, her feet in the sink. She trims the leggy ivy cuttings, nips some brown edges off the basil. Ruby looks at her supple form bent over her knees, imagines the day when she can even *see* her own knees again.

"You ready?" Ruby puts a hand on Lark's back.

"I don't want any of it." Lark slides off the counter and onto the floor. "I don't want to even touch that stuff."

"That just means a bigger bonfire."

They walk together out the screen door to the back porch, or rather Lark walks while Ruby lumbers. The boxes are lined up against the house, where Lark demanded the deliveryman carry them. She was adamant that they not enter her bedroom, her house. She said she would need to burn incense just to cleanse the porch. That comment prompted Ruby to respond that perhaps the two of them had spent too much time in Santa Fe amid the seekers and reincarnates and general crazies.

Ruby slices open the first box and lifts out frilly dress after frilly dress, piles them to one side. Then she hits the rock-star clothes—slinky fabrics, sequins, spangles, outfits that Ruby doesn't think belong on any nine-year-old body. "Was Darla schizophrenic?"

"Skiza what?"

"Never mind. I just can't imagine the same person buying these two extremes of clothes."

Clyde noses open the screen door, pads over to Lark before her giggles subside. "Actually, Dingbat Darla bought the trendy stuff," Lark says through a face full of fur. "And the creepy grandmother gave me the others." She stands up. Clyde nuzzles her belly.

Ruby doesn't scold Lark for her language. The counselor whom John recommended told Ruby that this is a way for Lark to work through her anger.

"Can I go now?" Lark's voice is colored with desperation. "Please, can you just do this?"

"Pick out two outfits, one from each pile. We'll burn those and give away the rest to children who need them."

Lark points to the most hideous of each, avoids touching any of them. "Now?"

"Now." Ruby rubs the spot between her breasts, trying to soothe the heartburn that is her companion these days. "But don't—"

"I know. Don't talk to anyone. Blow my whistle and run if I see any cameras."

Although Ruby hasn't spotted a reporter in several days, she's still skittish. She can't keep Lark cooped up forever, though. She watches her daughter and Clyde bound down the driveway. They look more like puppies on the loose than a nine-year-old girl and an at least five-year-old mutt. When the last shimmer of head bobs out of sight, she turns back to her task.

The bonfire was Lark's idea. Each September, Santa Feans gather in Old Fort Marcy Park and set fire to a three-story marionette. They burn Zozobra in effigy for all of the bad things that have happened in the past year, throwing scraps of paper that list what they each want to put behind them. The festival started out as an ancient new year's ritual—the Aztec calendar, like the Jewish calendar, starts each year in September—but has morphed through the years into an excuse for teenage gangs to rampage. The gang kids Chaz used to try to help.

With Zozobra just around the corner, Lark decided they should have their own ritual burning, of everything that even touched anything in Texas. Ruby sets aside the two outfits Lark chose and sorts the rest into garbage bags that she will deliver to local charities.

The scrapbook and CD that Molly sent to Lark are wrapped in a flowery sweater at the top of the second box. Ruby will store them for later; Lark may want them when her emotions are less raw. The rest of that box contains hair bows and headbands in various colors, prissy nightgowns—Lark must have hated sleeping in those leg-constricting things—and sexy-girl panties that Ruby would be embarrassed to wear.

Finally, when she reaches the bottom of the third and final box of more and more clothes, she finds what she is looking for. There, nestled all together in a corner, lies the photo of Ruby and Lark, the note she slipped into Lark's duffel bag. And the giraffe.

Ruby lifts them out reverently. She smiles at the photograph, vows to take Lark up to the top of the Chamisa Trail before the fall colors fade, even if she needs to be hoisted by a crane to get there. The letter has been folded and refolded so many times that it feels like tissue paper. Ruby opens it carefully, lays it across the patch of lap that the baby has not overtaken, which most people call "knee." The ink is smeared, words here and there obliterated, others barely legible. Ruby didn't want to read it anyway; she doesn't want to be reminded of what she wrote.

Lark, alone in a room in the huge state of Texas, crying over this note. Ruby tears up herself as that picture forms behind her eyes. She refolds it carefully, sets it with the clothes to be burned. This will be her own offering to Zozobra, to satiate the beast of bad days.

She picks up the giraffe. Just touching it brings a flood of memories. Those first weeks with Lark, Ruby was terrified she would break the baby, harm her somehow. Yet she also remembers feeling, right from the beginning, that they were supposed to be together, that Lark was a sudden gift of fate.

She lifts the giraffe to her face, rubs it against the tip of her nose like baby Lark did while sucking her thumb. Ruby closes her eyes, inhales deeply through her nose. And she could swear that it is there, a tiny trace, the merest hint even, of talcum powder, of formula, of Larkness.

"Tough day, Mama?" Lark tosses her backpack onto the rear seat and climbs into the Jeep. "You look tired."

Ruby drives away from the school. "I am tired, baby. I'm gonna have to stop doing pedicures. My big fat belly gets in the way." She will never get tired of hearing Lark's giggle, which is sounding closer to normal. "How was school?"

"Not as bad as stinky feet. The afterschool part was fun. We played games in the gym. And I aced my spelling test."

"Of course you did, my little prodigy."

Lark sits up straight, clasps her fingers together at her chest, arms triangled out at each side. "Prodigy. P-r-o-d-i-g y. Prodigy."

"And how do you spell smart aleck?"

"M-o-m," Lark says.

Ruby smothers a yawn with her laugh. "You got me."

"Good thing it's pizza night. Or you might fall asleep at the stove."

"That," Ruby says, "is why God created pizza night." The sun is sliding into the cleavage of the mountains when she stops the car at the foot of the driveway. Sunset is arriving noticeably earlier each of these late-fall days. "Hop out and get the mail. I'll send Clyde down to greet you."

Ruby stomps the pedal to give the Jeep a shot of gas; tired, too, the engine needs a boost up the driveway. She enters the house through the back door, lets Clyde out behind her. "Go fetch the girl, dog. Go fetch."

She kicks off her shoes, drops Lark's backpack on the table, then plods over to the phone to call in the pizza order. She's still on hold when Lark and Clyde tromp in. Lark lays the mail on the counter beside Ruby. Bills, probably. And catalogues. No matter how many opt-out services Ruby tries, she can't get off those mailing lists. Most of them are still addressed to Mrs. Levy, who was apparently quite the catalogue shopaholic.

Lark makes a beeline for her bedroom. As the pizza guy comes on the line, Ruby snaps her fingers, points to the backpack. Lark retraces her steps, slings the backpack over her shoulder. When she turns again, Ruby spots the tan envelope poking out from between Lark's arm and side. A small Bubble Wrap mailer, it looks like.

After Clyde has devoured the last of the pizza bones, as Lark calls the crusts, and they are settling in to watch a movie, Ruby asks about the envelope. "What did you get in the mail?"

Lark points the remote at the television screen, fast-forwards through the dire FBI warning. "Nothing really. Just one of those stupid doodads from Girls Inc."

Ruby swallows a stream of questions before she can give them voice. Her daughter is not fessing up to something.

The hospital room is standard-issue. Ruby wonders which genius decided that pale green was a soothing institutional color. At least she has the room to herself; it's a slow birth day here at St. Victims, and the hospital wanted her in a private room anyway, to keep the media at bay. She is beyond exhausted, can't figure out how limbs can be spaghetti and lead at the same time, and her virginia, as Lark coined it when she was seven or so, feels like it has been turned inside-out and bathed in astringent.

St. Vincent's encourages rooming-in to foster the bond between mother and infant as well as for security purposes. They wouldn't want a baby going home with the wrong mom, after all. But in the case of adoptions, the hospital's policy is to keep the infant in the nursery.

Ruby wonders whether this rule is to ease the pain of the mother, to avoid sticky change-of-mind situations, or because they worry that a baby human, like a gosling, will imprint on the first face it sees.

Ruby was allowed to hold the baby after the staff completed their poking and prodding and printing. She knows that in the barbaric days, a child was whisked out from between his mother's legs and out the door, never to be seen again. The hospital social worker met with Ruby soon after the birth, and with her approval, the nurses have brought the baby to Ruby's room a couple of times.

The door swings open and Margaret strides over to the bed. Her entire body seems to vibrate. She has been gliding on a druglike high of having coached Ruby through the birth, witnessing the first breath of a new life. It's the closest she'll ever get to motherhood, she told Ruby when Ruby asked her to be her Lamaze partner. And giving birth was amazing, really, despite the whole virginia-inside-out part.

But now Margaret radiates anger rather than awe.

"What is it?" Ruby pushes the control button to raise the head of her bed. "The baby?"

The baby is fine, Margaret assures her.

"Lark? Did something—"

"Lark is fine, too. Molly will bring her by later."

"Then what?" Ruby asks.

Margaret's words come out like the hiss of a snake, a really pissed-off snake. "They're out there."

Ruby's medicine-numb brain churns. The Tinsdales declined to be present for the birth. Darla laughed, said Philip was more the Hugh Hefner, cigars-in-the-waiting-room type. Ruby considered going to Texas for the birth, so the baby could make that trip in the security of her womb, but some wrinkle between the two states' adoption laws made it simpler to give birth here. Ruby called Darla last night when her water broke. The Tinsdales are coming in a day or two, whenever the baby is released; they aren't supposed to be here now.

Margaret repeats herself. "They're out there at the nursery window. The Monteros. The whole bunch of them."

Now Ruby understands. Despite its growth over the past decade, Santa Fe is really just a small town, St. Victim's a small-town hospital. And the Monteros are one big family. Somebody must know somebody who knows somebody who. Ruby rubs her forehead with her fingertips, draws her palms down until they support her chin. She peers out through her spread fingers, as if a carnival mask will separate her from the situation.

"Chaz? Is Chaz here?" Ruby remembers calling out for him during one of the last contractions before her epidural, thinking that if this were a movie, he would rush into the delivery room as she made her final push.

"I didn't see him," Margaret says. "I'll call security."

"No. No—"

A gentle rap interrupts them before Ruby can formulate the rest of her thought, and Antoinette steps into the room, approaches Ruby's bed. "Hey, girlfriend."

Ruby looks over Antoinette's shoulder, expecting an incursion of the Montero tribe.

"It's okay," Antoinette says. "They're not coming in." She sits half her butt on the edge of Ruby's bed. "How are you? How do you feel?"

"Like I just gave birth to an elephant." Ruby's tongue feels as fuzzy as her brain. "But the drugs are good."

Antoinette fiddles with the edge of the thin blanket, pulls at a loose thread. "I want, I need to ask . . ." Her eyes remain downcast as she speaks; her fingers pick at the blanket's stitching, unrolling the hem. Ruby tries to focus on Antoinette's words, but she keeps thinking how her friend really, really needs a manicure.

It would mean so much to the family, Antoinette says, if they could do just this one thing, if they could have their priest come to baptize the baby before he is sent away from them. "You know, so they won't all worry that he'll end up in limbo or hell."

All of it, the exhaustion, the emotion, the reality that she is giving up her child, is an insidious fog that creeps in and shrouds Ruby as tightly as her baby was swaddled. She says something, she must, because Antoinette squeezes Ruby's foot then disappears. Margaret holds a big plastic mug to Ruby's lips; she drinks from the straw, feels the cool water trickle down her throat. Margaret lowers the bed. And Ruby closes her eyes.

Candles throw their golden light everywhere. Rows of flickering votives line the ledges that run down both sides of the little room and balance on the railing in front of the pews. Two tall candelabra stand like many-armed goddesses on the riser just beyond the railing. The candles transform the plain, institutional chapel into a garden of light.

This whole thing was organized in a brief few hours while Ruby slept. She climbs out of the hospital-regulation wheelchair at the doorway, walks gingerly beside Margaret down the aisle. She can't help compare this feeble processional of two to what she had imagined for her wedding day.

Ruby eases down beside Lark in the first pew, squishes her daughter in a sideways hug, kisses her head. Margaret takes a seat in the row behind them, next to Molly. The other side of the aisle is crammed full of Monteros. In the front row, the immediate family.

Ruby scans the small crowd. Chaz is not there. She doesn't know whether she feels relieved that she won't have to face him, or sad that he didn't come to meet his own child.

Before she can sort through her feelings, the heads of the entire Montero side turn in unison and emit a collective sigh as a nurse carries the baby up the aisle. Ruby almost expects them to stand, throw rose petals in the nurse's wake. Father Paul steps out into the aisle, takes the bundle of baby from the nurse, walks through the gate at the railing and up onto the riser.

With the baby in the crook of one arm, the priest pours water from a weary plastic pitcher into a gleaming silver bowl. He sets down the pitcher, picks up a small glass vial. This water, he says as he empties the vial into the bowl, is from the River Jordan. The vial disappears into a pocket of his billowy robe as he clears his throat.

"What is the Christian name of this child?" Father Paul sweeps his eyes across both sides of the room, waits. "This situation is a bit out of the ordinary order of service, but we need to name this child before God."

The room is so silent that Ruby feels as if she can hear the candles breathing their carbon into the air.

"Charles Henry. Charles for his father, Henry for his great-grandfather." The name comes from Ruby's mouth unbidden. She had consciously, deliberately refused to think of her baby with names or endearments since the moment in Texas when she thought up her plan, and all the names she and Chaz had discussed before then were for girls. She looks across the aisle, wondering if maybe the Monteros would object to using Chaz's name, but she sees only nods of approval.

Father Paul proceeds through the short ceremony of baptism, then ends with a prayer. A rustle rises up from the Montero side as they reach across pews to make a chain of hands for the amen squeeze.

"Wait!"

Lark is on her feet before the reverberation of the amen settles back over the pews. She walks up and through the gate, takes the baby from the priest as if she has been holding newborns her entire life. Father Paul steps aside, looks down at her.

"When Mama said yes to this, she said, 'But let's do it right.'" Lark pauses, looks past Ruby to the Ms. "So we, well I, decided that besides a baptism this would be sort of a farewell, not a party because it's too sad, but a nice good-bye."

Lark walks with the baby through the gate, stops in front of Celeste. The priest glides past her, slips into a pew behind the throng. Lark explains what she has in mind, shuffles the baby from her arms to Celeste's, and returns to her seat next to Ruby.

Celeste sits there for a moment, looking down at the child of her child. Then she stands, walks to the railing, turns to face the small group. She cradles the baby in her arms. "What I want for you"— Celeste's voice quivers—"is for you to never for a moment forget that you are loved, by many, many people." She motions to Chunk, who comes up and takes the baby, then Celeste picks up a votive, blows it out, carries the candle back to her seat.

The father of three gazes at that infant as if he were the first baby on earth. And Chunk cries. His tears roll like mercury down his fat cheeks, splash on his grandson's face. The baby shudders, limbs jerk; during this second baptism, arms escape the tight swaddling.

Abuela approaches next, her crepe-soled shoes squeaking on the industrial flooring. The old woman takes the baby as casually as she would take a loaf of bread. She holds him upright, a hand at head, a hand at bum, and brings the baby's face to hers. She holds the infant like that, nose to nose, for several minutes, then she settles the child at her neck. Abuela leans her head into the bundle, and she whispers.

Ruby remembers a story that her grandmother used to tell, about why people have that little cleft just below their nose. Before a baby is born, she said, it knows all the secrets of the universe, and just before it enters this world, God puts a finger to its lips, says, "Shhh, don't tell." And the imprint of God's finger remains forever, to remind our souls to keep His secrets.

Maybe Abuela tells this infant about his father and all the history of the Monteros so that he will always know where he came from. Maybe she tells him stories, folklore. Maybe even that Abuela will someday be his guardian angel, will always watch over him. Ruby doesn't know what Abuela says, only that this baby whisperer whispers for what seems like a very long time, until Antoinette steps forward and puts a hand on her grandmother's shoulder.

Antoinette looks straight at Ruby as she speaks her wish. "May you be blessed with friendship, even one true friend, because that will make you rich no matter what is in your piggy bank."

And so it goes. The Monteros move up to the railing one by one, tell the precious child their hopes for his future, blow out a candle, and return to their seats. A tidal wave, of words salty with emotion, crashes into Ruby. A few voices tremble, but most resonate in the tiny room. To know God, to know happiness, to know himself, to know football, the wishes go on and on.

Ruby is rapt, wrapped in the warmth in the room. She doesn't notice what Lark is doing beside her until a yellow scrap of paper floats to Ruby's feet. She reaches down, picks it up, hands it back to Lark. Her incredible old-soul daughter is writing down the wishes on colorful strips of paper, in careful schoolgirl script.

When each of the Monteros has taken a turn, four glowing candles remain on the rail. Lark and the Ms couldn't have known how many to place there, how many Monteros would attend. This is just one of those God things.

Margaret and Molly walk up to the rail together. Margaret takes the baby first. "May you always love people for who they are inside, not for their race or gender or sexuality. May your heart always be open to new ideas, new ways of doing things."

Margaret hands the baby to Molly. "And may you always nurture both sides of your brain, both your intellect and your creativity."

Then Margaret looks at Ruby, nods to her.

For a moment, Ruby isn't sure she can do it. Then she stands, pauses to place a palm on Lark's head. That Lark, not Ruby, should be last to speak feels as right as the rest of this ceremony. Her knees are shaky, and her virginia winces in pain. She takes the baby, her baby, from Molly, waits as the Ms each take a votive, blow them out in unison.

Ruby holds so, so many wishes for this child, too many to be captured on a scrap of paper. She wishes Chaz were here to take part in this ceremony, that the ceremony didn't need to happen in the first place. Finally, she holds the baby up Abuela-style, peers into his eyes. "My hope is that someday you understand, that one day you forgive me." As Ruby speaks, the baby stares back at her, as if they are looking further than just into each other's eyes.

"Imprint this, all of this, in your heart, baby goose," Ruby whispers.

Lark joins Ruby at the railing but doesn't take the baby in her arms. Instead she reaches out, grabs that impossibly tiny fist in her own tender hand, leans in close to the baby's face. "I wish that your other mother will take care of you in lots of special ways, like our mother takes care of me."

Then Lark reaches both hands around the baby's neck, and when she steps back Chaz's Saint Christopher medal hangs from a tiny gold chain. "And this is from your daddy. He asked me to give it to you." *The mysterious package,* Ruby thinks. When the wash of tears clears her eyes, she is surprised to find that she still is upright.

Too soon, the hospital social worker steps forward to take the baby from her. Ruby instinctively clenches the bundle against her chest, as if she were saving her infant from a fall. The pull is visceral, starting somewhere deep in Ruby's sore gut and coursing to her arms. The woman peels Ruby's hands, finger by finger, from the blanket, and takes the baby into her own arms. Ruby swallows a scream as her uterus contracts, this time pushing her child not out of her body but out of her world.

As the social worker walks away with her baby, the emptiness in Ruby's arms is only a fraction of the hollowness in her core. Yet the feeling is almost comforting in its perverse familiarity. Loss, a guest, albeit unwelcome, too often has visited before.

In her haze, Ruby feels a nudge at her elbow. Lark, the one sweet miracle Ruby has wrested away from that festering guest, hands her a votive. Mother and daughter, too, blow them out in unison, and Margaret helps Ruby back to her seat.

The chapel now is lit only by the two candelabra. They cast their light higher, paler, than the votives. In the dim room, Ruby tries to recognize something profound in how a dozen or two tiny lights can make such a difference, but her brain refuses to grab the thought.

Lark still stands at the rail. "Take these candles home with you," she says, "and light them when you want to feel a little bit of Charlie." The nickname flows smoothly from Lark's mouth and feels natural in Ruby's ear. "And maybe," Lark continues, "he will feel a piece of you, too."

After Lark returns to her seat, the Monteros file out of the shadowy chapel like good Catholics—one row at a time, front to back, with a curtsy and the sign of the cross at the first step out of the pew.

In the faint light of the empty chapel, Ruby sits beside her daughter while Lark folds each strip of paper into thirds, places it reverently into the treasure box that Ruby made when Lark was six or so. What up until now has held a rabbit's tail, a few pottery shards, a handful of special rocks, will be the repository of all those wishes. Ruby doesn't remember what she mumbled this morning, but even through the ache in her gut, she recognizes that the dear Ms and her amazing daughter created a sacred garden for the farewell Ruby didn't know she needed.

A powder-sugar dusting of snow sparkles in the bright sunlight. The air is razor-sharp, stings Ruby's lungs. On her skin, it tingles, how she imagines her grandfather's Old Spice felt slapped against his just-shaved skin.

She walks away from Lark's school, back toward home. Ruby used to enjoy this walk from the little school on Acequia Madre, sometimes stopping at the nearby bookstore café, where she would read the newspaper and Clyde would beg for pastries from people as if he had never been fed in his life.

These days, though, Ruby can barely manage to command herself to crawl out of bed, shove a cereal box across the counter, and trudge along beside Lark. The walk, her very life, feels like a forced march. She has whittled down her voluntary motion to the barest of necessities, bathing when she reeks, eating when her stomach thunders, speaking when spoken to. She curses her body for tormenting her with its involuntary actions, breath, pulse, brain waves. Only pain, and sleep, are welcome.

The thought she can't seem to stop bouncing around her head is where she would be if she had never found the magazine article. She pictures the game Mousetrap, a relic from her own mother's childhood that Ruby found in a closet when she was young. Blue and red and yellow pieces of plastic snapped together on a board, creating a rickety course for a metal ball to travel, ultimately knocking into a rod on which the domed mousetrap perched, sending the red trap skittering down the rod to capture some loser's mouse.

If Ruby hadn't found the article, Lark never would have been sent away. Ruby never would have been put through a trial. Ruby and Chaz wouldn't have broken up. And Charlie would be with all of them now. Ruby can't stop feeling like a little plastic mouse peeking out through the bars of a cage, wishing she had never started the ball rolling in the first place.

She tells herself to chase away the black dog, the mean reds, the colorless funk, whatever this is that haunts her. She tells herself she has to pull herself together for Lark, just as she did for the baby while Lark was away. She worries that Lark might think Ruby regrets her choice, wary of making her daughter believe she needs to earn a place in Ruby's heart continually.

Lark's birthday is coming, the holidays, too. Ruby wants, needs, to make those days special. Her doctor says to be patient, that her hormones are still adjusting, that postpartum depression is common, especially when no baby comes home.

The gardens along the road that were summer-lush just a few months ago are now a nuclear winter, dead-brown stalks, leaves black and mushy from frost. Ruby's grandmother used to say that this was faith, hacking away your plants for winter in the belief that spring would come and grow them back. "And spring always comes," Nana said.

Even though this November day is August-bright, spring seems a long, long way off to Ruby. She knows that winter is hanging out around a corner, a kid loitering in front of the Rexall, waiting to come blustering through. And she is having difficulty gathering the faith, like the squirrel collects the last pieces of nuts from under the tree beside the road, that winter will require.

She tells herself she should be used to the sadness. This is just one more on a long list of loss. The hurt of her breakup with Chaz is still there, a layer of scar-tissue ache under her acorn shell. But she carries the absence of her baby in her gut, a weight as if she has yet to give birth at all.

As Ruby and Clyde cut behind the art galleries that line Canyon Road, she happens upon the detritus of a party. Melted ice bags are in a limp pile by a tree, reminding her of the witch in *The Wizard of Oz*. A hill of trash bags is buttressed by liquor boxes, flattened, bundled, and tied. The pieces of an Erector Set party tent lie waiting to be carted off.

Something about the whole scene pricks Ruby with sadness, the kind of sad of an opportunity lost or time marching too quickly. When she sees the balloons, though, she crumples to the ground, as a knife stabs her chest. Clusters of pink and red and white balloons hanging limply over tree branches like someone's forgotten laundry. She sits there, not crying, not feeling anything but the knifepoint in her chest. She sits there until the cold, hard ground finally penetrates the numbness of her skin, until Clyde practically knocks her over with his worry.

By the time Ruby trudges behind Clyde up the final hill, her own driveway, the feathery snow has vanished, some down into the earth to nourish the slumbering plants, some up into the cloudless sky to come again another day like the childhood rain song. If only the snow in her head could dissipate as easily.

She just didn't expect it to be this hard. Yes, she rescued Lark, brought her daughter home. Yes, that was worth any price. But she didn't expect the payment to hurt so much. She feels the phantom ache each time she reaches for her belly, finding a barren plain instead of the mound she expects.

In a perverse way, Ruby needs to hang on to that pain, even knowing that her hurting has got to be hurting Lark. As fiercely as she loves Lark, as surely as she knows she did the right thing, Ruby doesn't want to lose the pain of losing her other child.

Her nail polish a shimmery burgundy, Antoinette blows on her fingers. "Berry tones, they're all the rage this season."

"Again already? Who decides that crap?" Ruby asks.

Antoinette picks up her purse with the tips of her fingers. "They, the proverbial *they* do. Come on, I'm driving. *You're* drinking."

In the car, Antoinette looks Ruby over with an exaggerated head-to-toe nod. "We got us some *work* to do. Margaret's blitz attack on the hair helped, but we still got us some work to do."

"That's redundant, you know," Ruby says. "Blitz attack. It's like saying 'baby puppies' or 'with au jus.'"

Antoinette shoots Ruby a look. "Yep, we got us some work. We'll start with margaritas."

Ruby gives her a wry smile. "You know, alcohol is no cure for depression. Not even a Band-Aid."

"Maybe the Band-Aid's not for you, but so the rest of us don't have to look at your ugly sore."

Ruby's laugh is almost a guffaw. The mere fact that her friend can joke about it, that Ruby even gets the joke, tells her that she's going to claw her way out of her black hole.

The traffic signal turns red as Antoinette approaches the intersection of Cerrillos and Paseo de Peralta. To the right is their usual restaurant, where Ruby met Chaz, where Chaz met the reporter. Relief is a warm flush through Ruby when Antoinette turns left. She may be seeing some glints of light these days, but she's not quite ready to see those piñatas, or the tree that bears Chaz scars more visible than her own.

Antoinette doesn't miss Ruby's sigh. "Gotta get back on the horse someday, girl. My mama would say, 'Don't ya think that tea bag has steeped long enough?'"

"Wallowing," Ruby says. "Nana called it wallowing." As if rolling around in sadness were a pleasure, like the Ms' Dudley writhing in manure. "She'd set a time limit, two hours, two days, depending on the cause." And when time was up, wallowing was put aside, tucked away like a forgotten handkerchief in a drawer. "I wonder how much time she would give me for this, for giving my baby away."

Antoinette cocks her head. "I'll give you, oh, about a third a pitcher of margaritas."

In the backseat of the Jeep, Lark and Numi chatter as Ruby drives down Canyon Road after picking them up from dance class. With her friends, Lark seems almost normal these days. She peels away a layer of the reserve that still hangs between her and Ruby.

Both girls wear black leggings and shirts. Ruby is wistful, thinking of the days of pink tights and tutus, strands of Lark's hair escaping the bun no matter how many bobby pins, how much gel. But the wistfulness is quickly replaced by sheer gratitude that she has *these* days about which to grow wistful in the future.

Ruby glances in the rearview mirror. "I like your shirt, Numi."

"Thanks, I, uh, put it on backward."

Over her leotard, Numi wears her green T-shirt from Girls Inc. camp, indeed backward. Laddering down from the "I am," oversized, polka-dotted capital letters spell NUMI in the middle of other words:

I am
daNcer
fUnny
toMboy
kInd

"Tomboy," Ruby says. "There should be a word for girls who like to play outdoors that lets them still be girls." Her gender-image musing receives no response from the backseat. When she looks in the mirror,

Numi is rummaging in her backpack, and Lark is staring out the window, all her layers of reserve tucked up tight under her chin.

Ruby knew she was whacking at a hornet's nest when she mentioned the shirt. The last time she checked, Lark's own "I am" shirt was shoved to the back of the dresser drawer. At least it was *in* the drawer; that is progress.

Lark will never be the same person she was before she went to Texas. Yet, while Ruby thinks of each distinct segment of her own years as a separate "life," she hopes that someday Lark will be able to knit her ordeal into all the ways she defined herself before. Like a mended bone, stronger after a fall from a tree.

The art gallery teems with an opening-night crowd. The boldface types are factions from the arts councils, Chamber Music Festival, opera, ballet and local charities, and of course artists and art lovers and art sellers. Ruby recognizes many faces from the salon and from Molly's previous shows.

Ruby clasps both hands around her plastic cup of wine—white only; no gallery would risk a stumble and splash of cabernet on the works. Tonight's opening is a big deal for Molly here in the third-largest art market in the country. Molly's pieces are showcased in the front room; glossy white walls and precision lighting make her large collages shine. In the next room, stark sepia prints by a young American Indian photographer expose the third-world conditions of the sparsely populated pueblos just north of the excess and abundance of the city.

"Girl, you are looking fine." Antoinette steps around a cluster of patrons. "How is it fair that my stomach balloons out after a big plate of pasta, and yours is flat after giving birth?"

"Cheers." Ruby taps her cup against Antoinette's. "And thank you, for the confidence boost."

"De nada." Antoinette studies the artwork behind Ruby, a background of thickly painted fragments of a plantation house, a column here, a crumbling cornice there. "That would look so *good* in my bedroom."

Ruby shakes her head. "Horrors. Don't talk about matching artwork to your bedspread around here. Artists have killed for less." She pauses to look at the piece again. Over and around the architectural components, Molly has layered strips of paper with typed text, like they have been torn from oversized pages of *Gone with the Wind,* and antique fabrics cut into the shapes of icons of her Southern upbringing. A drapery-brocade tree drips with Spanish moss that is tea-stained lace. "And you're too late; this one is sold." Ruby points to the red dot beside the collage.

Through the throng of people, Ruby catches glimpses of Molly, like patches of barn flashing through a field of grain. Her red top is a rebellion against the black that is de rigueur at these events, black turtlenecks or sports coats over jeans for the men, sophisticated black pantsuits or dresses for the women. No loud-print broomstick skirts or squash-blossom necklaces in this crowd; those are reserved for tourists and the storeclerks who cater to them.

Margaret breaks away from a group of her clients and joins Ruby and Antoinette. "Lark's over at the buffet table with some Olivia kid from her school. Have you eaten anything? The crab cakes are good."

Margaret and Antoinette make small talk, pointing out people here and there, tossing Ruby morsels of their lives. The whole scene seems a bit surreal; Molly's opening is Ruby's first real outing in months. She feels as if she should be draped in one of Molly's debutante-gown fabrics instead of her good jeans and dressiest top.

"Don't look," Antoinette says. "Over my shoulder, nine o'clock. The guy is checking you out, girl." She whisper-squeals, "I said don't look!" when Ruby and Margaret, of course, both snap their heads.

"The granola-cruncher?" Margaret asks. "Looks like he lives in a cave with a bear?"

Antoinette smacks at Margaret's shoulder. "The *other* nine o'clock."

Ruby swallows the last of her too-warm, too-ripe wine, trying to be discreet as she gazes across the room over the top of her glass. "I'm sure he just recognizes me. From, you know. Or else it's you he's checking out."

"No," Antoinette insists. She leans closer to Margaret and whispers, "Does he play for our team?"

Margaret rolls her eyes. "Darn. I left my gaydar at home."

Ruby risks another glance in the direction of the man—tall, forty-ish, silver-strewn hair. She feels her face sizzle when she meets his eyes.

"No wedding ring," Antoinette says.

Ruby shakes her head. "No matter. I am so not ready to even think about it. He's all yours."

"If you insist."

As Antoinette slinks off like a bad-movie spy on a winding route toward the man and his friends, Margaret raises an eyebrow at Ruby. "Soon."

"Right," Ruby says with sarcasm. "When Lark's in college, maybe then."

Clyde's head bobs up and down, and a silly grin erupts on his face in between barks. Ruby would like to think that he's keeping time to the music, but she knows he is just trying to shake off the party hat strapped to his head. For Lark's last birthday, she wanted a bowling party. For her sixth, they threw a grown-up beauty party at the salon, complete with hairdos, makeup, and, of course, manicures. This birthday, though, called for nothing but silliness.

Lark, Numi, Olivia, and a handful of other kids dance around Jay's friend Brigham as if he were a Maypole. They shake tambourines and maracas and castanets, all with ribbons flailing, while Brigham does his one-man-band thing in the center of the circle. Antoinette, the Ms, and Jay contribute clapping and laughter and mostly out-of-tune singing from the sidelines.

Ruby leans against the kitchen island, shoves a streamer out of the way. She didn't dare risk balloons after her meltdown behind that gallery, but the banners and confetti are festive enough. She refills her glass of champagne; the chains of bubbles race one another, burst at the surface, like upside-down fireworks. She takes in the scene, absorbs it through every pore in her skin, and her heart hums. What a marvel that this much silliness, this much joy, can exist in a room, in a world, that was shrouded in so many different shades of darkness, such a short time ago.

Lark's old inquisitive, imaginative self is back, but tinged with a sad worldliness, like a shadow of a stain on cloth. Although they now know her actual birth date—Ruby was off by sixteen days—Lark was insistent that they continue to celebrate on December 6. Ten years old; Ruby's baby bird isn't a baby anymore.

As for Ruby, her postnatal hormones finally have leveled out. Her pain for her son is a jagged hole ripped in the crazy quilt that she pictures as the stitching together of her lives. Yet she is learning that she can let happiness share the space, live this fourth life, without feeling as if she is betraying her love for him. This is her new-normal.

Brigham finishes a song with a toot toot toot of his air horn. Ruby grips a glass drawer knob on the gloriously barn-red pie safe. The drawer slides open smoothly on its new wooden bottom. Behind the screen doors, blue willow plates stand out against the whitewashed back panel. Ruby takes out a book of matches and calls for everyone to gather around the table for cake.

Ruby is a decent cook, but she has never been a particularly adept baker, which makes the result of this particular effort fit perfectly with the party's theme. The three lopsided layers of gloppy chocolate icing and confetti candies look like a mud sculpture gone awry. The icing is extra thick in the spot where the top layer caved in, and toothpicks hold a broken chunk of the second layer in place. This is truly a cake of love and joy and silliness, and thankfully the burning candles, ten plus one to grow on, distract from the chaos below.

After a raucous round of "Happy Birthday," complete with "cha-cha-chas," Lark blows out the candles with a single billowy breath and just a little spit. Ruby doesn't know what Lark wishes for, her nose scrunched up to her squeezed-tight eyes, but Ruby makes her own wish on those candles, for many normal, quiet, even boring, days in the year to come.

Margaret carves the cake like she is parting hair to apply highlights. Molly scoops ice cream, and Antoinette distributes the garish paper plates to eager hands. Brigham declines dessert. "This place needs more ambience," he jokes as he picks up his harmonica.

Once again, Ruby steps back toward the living room and just enjoys the scene. A now-hatless Clyde steals a plate off the corner of the table, scoots it across the kitchen floor as he licks it clean of ice cream. Margaret and Molly lean into each other, exchange a look of sheer comfort that reminds Ruby of her grandparents. The kids snicker and point at each other with purple plastic forks flecked with frosting and drippy with melted ice cream. They chatter in grade-school shorthand, telling tales on each other over the honks and rattles of Brigham's rendition of "Hey Jude." Ruby can't imagine that any place on earth is better than this home at this moment.

The sudden silence breaks her reverie first. Then she sees Lark's bleach-white face. *The Heimlich*, Ruby thinks; Lark must be choking on the chalky cake.

"I'm not going back." Lark's voice sounds tiny, scared. "I won't. I'll take Clyde and run away." The next few seconds pass in clicks of slow motion: Molly flashing to Lark's side, wrapping a protective arm around her; Clyde whimpering, whining; Ruby following Lark's stricken eyes to the glass-paned front door.

Ruby's first reaction is confusion, seeing someone out of context, out of place. Then the primal instinct to protect Lark from an intruder pulses in her veins. What follows is a worse thought, that something awful has happened to her other child. Finally she commands her body to move to the door.

"I forgot why I was driving around that night in the first place." Darla's face is streaked with tears. "In all the commotion after, I forgot." Her tongue stumbles over too many words gushing from her mouth all at once. She is sorry; she tried to call from Albuquerque, but no one answered. She is sorry; she forgot what it was like, what Philip was like, with a fussy baby. She looks down at her feet.

Ruby's head follows Darla's, and there he is. Ruby's whole body tingles with the disorienting sense of déjà vu. A carrier. A baby, in footed onesie pajamas—blue this time.

Then Ruby bends down, picks up her other child, carrier and all, and brings him inside.

Everything seems to happen in an instant. Parents arrive to collect children—thankfully, the cake was the finale of the party. Molly takes a quaking Lark to the safety of the Ms' home. Brigham and Jay pack up the percussion instruments into a big wicker basket, haul it away. Margaret and Antoinette make quick work of kitchen cleanup and disappear.

Ruby holds herself ramrod stiff in a chair beside the sofa, where Darla sits like a two-year-old in time-out, the baby sleeping in the carrier on the floor below her.

"It's just so hard." Darla's words come in awkward, embarrassed bursts. Philip is uneasy around babies, children at all really. He worked his way through his first marriage, long hours at the office, business trips, late-night meetings. The frailest of threads link him to his adult children. When he married Darla, and Tyler came along, he said he wanted to be a real parent with his second family.

Darla's words are almost drowned out by the questions pounding in Ruby's head. She stares across the room, keeps her eyes away from the baby—her baby—sleeping at Darla's feet.

"Philip *wanted* to be a father. But his work was so demanding. He needed his rest." The night of the carjacking, Darla had been driving around and around, not as much to lull a teething baby to sleep as to keep the shrieks away from Philip, to keep the peace. She drove around until her gas tank hit empty, then she stopped to fill it up. "He blamed me. But looking back, I think he was relieved at the same time."

Darla doesn't say it, but the rest of the sentence hangs in the air between them: *And Darla was relieved, too.* Ruby can picture her, the beleaguered wife trying to keep her fussy baby from flaring her husband's temper. Then, overnight, she turns into a poster child for mothers of lost children. Not that anyone sane would ever choose the role, but a power, prestige even, exists in victimhood, the identity that Darla has owned for more than nine years.

Ruby squeezes shut her eyes, opens them. She forces her ears to suck in the woman's words, an attempt to crowd out the hope prickling at the edge of her brain.

"The truth is . . . Philip is miserable around babies, the mess, the noise, the disruptions to his routine." Darla's face reddens, with chagrin at confessing her perfect husband's imperfections, or at the fact that she is talking about her own inadequacies, resentments, as much as his. "It's awkward, him suddenly having an infant when all his golf buddies have empty nests."

Why did he even take Lark back in the first place, or go along with the plan to adopt the baby? Ruby wonders. She wants to believe he acted out of love for his wife, knowing how badly Darla wanted a child, but more likely his motivation was about vengeance, to punish Ruby for taking what was his. When Darla pauses, clenching and unclenching her hands, Ruby decides that she must voice one of those pulsing thoughts, get it out of her head before her skull explodes.

"I'm so sorry that you are having such a hard time, but, well, we're not trading back."

From the doorway to the hall, where he guards Lark's turf from this intruder, Clyde lifts his head, growls softly, more from his tail than throat, a mild warning that he, too, won't let Darla take away Lark again.

"No, no," Darla sputters. "I wouldn't dream . . . is that why Lark ran? You thought . . . no, no, I don't want her back."

Ruby bristles at Darla's words, not "I didn't come to take her away," but "I don't want her." Thankfully, Lark is not in earshot.

"Then what *do* you want?" There. Ruby breathes easier after she lets the question barge into the room.

"I . . ." Darla slouches down farther; the deep cushion envelops her in a down-feather embrace. She sobs like, well, a baby. A baby who makes rather unfortunate belches when she cries. The noise wakes the real infant in the room, who joins Darla's chorus.

Ruby averts her eyes from the carrier. She doesn't want to see re-crimination, or Chaz, staring back at her. She waits. Darla does nothing. Finally, Ruby rummages through the diaper bag beside Darla, finds a bottle filled with water, a spice jar with a dollop of powdered formula. She dumps the formula into the bottle, shakes. Scoops up the baby and plugs the bottle into his pursing mouth.

The baby settles down immediately in the crook of Ruby's arm. She repeats her whispered "There, there," like a mantra. She can't bear to call this child by the name the Tinsdales gave him, the name

Ruby put on his birth certificate as they instructed. Thinking of Lark as Tyler was impossible enough, but naming this second child after the daughter they lost that night at the gas station seems to burden his tiny shoulders with huge expectations before he can even stand.

Ruby coos, and the baby squirms his way closer to Ruby, as if he remembers her voice and wants to crawl back into the womb. That other thought shrieks for attention inside Ruby's head as she watches him suck down the bottle, sigh, and go limp with sleep. She sets the bottle aside, lifts the baby to her shoulder, burps him, brings him back down to her lap without him stirring a bit.

"I . . ." Darla clears her throat of clogging tears. "I want you to take him."

Ruby leans back in her chair, too stunned to speak. The thought that she didn't even dare to think solidifies from a vapor of hope to real possibility.

"I want you to have him." Darla bounces herself out of her sinkhole, balances on the edge of the sofa, wraps her arms around her chest. Philip wants to travel, she says. He wants to be a doting grandfather, not a parent. "And I want Philip."

The fireflies shooting around Ruby's head amazingly don't disturb the slumbering infant in her arms. She walks with the baby to the kitchen phone, calls John. She catches him at his office as he is walking out the door after Saturday preparation for a Monday trial.

John is at her door in minutes, a thick file in hand. He looks back and forth between Ruby and Darla, shakes his head. He sits in the chair opposite Ruby, sets the file on the old cedar chest that serves as a coffee table. "Does your husband know you are here?"

Darla nods with vigor. She is older than Ruby, yet she seems like such a child. "You can call him." She pulls a cell phone out of her pocket, holds it out to John. Ruby isn't sure what kind of Darla-child she is, a smarty-pants daring him to make the call or a suck-up trying to be helpful.

"I'm going to do that." John turns to Ruby, tells her he doesn't want to waste anyone's time or create false expectations if this is not on the level. Ruby winces at his lawyerly words. He's trying to protect her, she knows, but she wants to scream out, *Don't make her mad. Don't make her change her mind.*

The conversation is short, just a few uh-huhs and I see's on this end. John snaps the phone shut, hands it back to Darla. "Well, then." He explains that the waiting period is still running, that the Tinsdales can withdraw their petition for adoption at any time. "But you need your own lawyer to draw up the papers. I want this so aboveboard that it knocks on the floor of heaven."

Heaven, Ruby thinks. *Can this really be happening?*

Darla goes outside to her car, steps back inside the doorway with two Neiman Marcus bags stuffed with stuff. "Is that hers?" She sets the bags down and points to the artwork on the wall beside her. "Is that Lark's?"

"Yes." Ruby puts the baby in his carrier and walks over to the painting, a bright red O'Keeffe-sque poppy, stands protectively beside it. "She gave it to me for Christmas last year."

"I had one framed," Darla says. "One of the canvases she left behind."

Ruby won't tell Lark about that, not yet anyway. Lark still would dig a Grand Canyon between her and Texas if she could. But she won't tell Darla about Lark's attitude, either.

The two women walk outside and hug awkwardly at the door of the rented SUV; one zigs while the other zags.

"Tell Lark, if she has any questions, wants to know anything . . . she can call." Darla fumbles with her purse as she speaks, its contents spew to the ground. Her forehead almost collides with Ruby's as they both squat, gather up pens and credit card receipts, a couple of pill bottles, sunglasses.

"Tell her . . . tell her I'm sorry."

Darla stands, gets in the car, backs down the driveway. Ruby isn't sure what to make of a woman who seems to have everything yet is happy with none of it. *Maybe Darla is ill,* Ruby thinks, remembering the pill bottles. Maybe she is using Philip as an excuse. Wherever the truth lies, Ruby does believe that underneath the trophy-wife veneer, beneath the excuses, is a mother who loves *two* children enough to give them away.

Back inside, Ruby sits in the chair beside the baby—her baby. Clyde, confident that the Lark-zone is secure now that Darla has gone, abandons his post. He pads over and gives the baby a big lick, then lies down alongside the carrier.

"What happens if they change their minds—again?" Ruby asks John.

He shrugs, then talks her through the procedure: the Tinsdales sign and file a petition to withdraw the adoption papers here in the Santa Fe court. The judge sets a hearing and rules on their motion.

"But what if he says no?" Ruby looks down at the baby, panic rising like gorge. "And what about me? I signed the papers terminating my rights. And there *is* that pesky felony conviction."

John makes some notes on a yellow pad. "We'll just have to see."

Ruby needs a moment to make herself breathe before she again can find her voice. "If this works, if this really happens, what do we have to do to legally change his name?"

"Let's not get ahead of ourselves." John gathers his papers. "This is not a done deal."

"Keep them closed, Mom. Don't peek."

Ruby lets herself be led across the uneven surface, her eyes squeezed shut. She clenches Lark's hand, hoping that she, too, isn't peeking. Ruby wants to experience this in one big moment, together with her daughter.

"Okay," Molly says. "One, two . . . open!"

Ruby hesitates for just a second, then she opens her eyes. She doesn't speak; she just looks. And looks. Beside her, Lark musters only a "Wow."

"Well?" Margaret asks. "What do you think?"

"I think . . ." Ruby says, "I think it's incredible. All those pictures, all those movies . . . but this, this is incredible." Ruby stares out at the pewter expanse before her. The sheer vastness of the ocean, the power of the crashing waves, is more than she could have imagined.

Molly steps up beside her, and Charlie reaches out from Molly's arms, falls into Ruby's grasp.

"And what do you think?" Ruby asks her son, who giggles a reply.

Ruby stands at the foamy edge of the water. Her toes make sucking noises as they sink into the sand. She watches Lark and Molly as they dash, shrieking, in and out of the waves curling into the beach. She marvels at the more ferocious breaks of surf farther out. She laughs as Charlie crawls around the silky sand, chasing crabs and water bugs, Chaz's Saint Christopher medal swinging against his throat.

Then, for a long time, Ruby just sits on a blanket. Lark and the Ms build a sand castle fit for *Architectural Digest*. A sleeping Charlie is delicious weight in Ruby's lap; the face in repose pure Chaz. The carpet of water unfurls, closer and closer to her every time, until the sun drowns itself in the horizon.

Ruby plays the what-if game. What if she hadn't stopped for a drink at that rest stop? What if she hadn't made that wrong turn in Albuquerque? What if Margaret hadn't been in that parking lot? If Ruby had driven here, to California, back then, this would be her life, sand and ocean and salty breeze. Maybe she never would have seen the magazine article; maybe she and Lark would be happy surfer girls.

Though then she wouldn't have Charlie. Ruby wouldn't choose to go through all the pain of the last year to get to where she is today, but this fourth life, which she built from the pile of rubble her last life left behind, feels as if it were supposed to be.

Charlie is thriving. Lark is doing well. At Ruby's urging, Lark called Darla to interview her for a class genealogy project. And—shock—the older Mrs. Tinsdale invited Lark up to Taos for an afternoon while she was there for an art retreat. Ruby has seen the Monteros a few awkward times. They want to be part of their grandson's life, but they and Ruby need time. The water under that bridge is full of acrimony and blame and recriminations, from their legal challenge, from Chaz moving away.

As for Chaz, Ruby hasn't spoken to him. Sometimes she feels angry that he wants nothing to do with his own child, after he fought her plan so hard in the first place. Sometimes she imagines she'll one day hear a knock at the door, and . . .

Perhaps, someday, he can be part of Charlie's life, or maybe that rift will never heal. This isn't a happily-ever-after fairy tale after all.

Mostly, Ruby feels peace. No, she can't imagine the California life that could have been. She doesn't even mind that she can't feel the slightest hint of her mother here amid the trillion grains of sand.

Tomorrow, Lark's masterpiece of a sand castle will be gone, turrets and spiral stairways and all. Tomorrow this beach will be washed clean. But Ruby's life is a mountain life. She lives with every crag, every crevice carved from the hours, good and bad, of her days.

Ruby's grandmother used to sing a hymn on wash days, an old African-American spiritual. "I've got peace like a river. I've got joy like a fountain. I've got love like the ocean." Ruby understood the joy part from the beginning; at times she felt for herself the burble of joy rising inside her, like a spray of fireworks or a champagne bottle blasting its cork. And the vast waters before her now surely do express the love part, unquenchable, uncontainable, forever love.

But the river part always confused her. The rivers that Ruby has known are anything but peaceful. They gush and surge and spill their banks. When she was young, Ruby imagined that the writer of the song must have had some quiet swimming hole in mind.

But now, she sits on this shifting, sandy beach with her mountain family and smiles as Lark pulls her green "I am" shirt over strawberry shoulders. And Ruby thinks she was wrong back then. She thinks that the hymn writer had in mind those same rivers Ruby knows. For even in a roiling, battering river, peace can be found. Even, especially, there.

Reading
Group
Gold

MOTHERS AND OTHER LIARS

by Amy Bourret

About the Author

- A Conversation with Amy Bourret

Behind the Novel

- "A Muse Named Johnny"
  An Original Essay by the Author

Keep on Reading

- Recommended Reading
- Reading Group Questions

A
Reading
Group Gold
Selection

For more reading group suggestions,
visit www.readinggroupgold.com.

 ST. MARTIN'S GRIFFIN

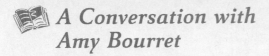

A Conversation with Amy Bourret

A question authors seem to be asked the most is what parts of their work are autobiographical. And your answer is?

That is easy. No, I have never found an abandoned baby, never given up a child for adoption. Probably the strongest link is Ruby's Midwestern sensibility and sentimentality. My grandparents, to whom this novel is dedicated, were proud Iowans. And I have very fond memories of time spent with them, working in the garden, "helping" my grandfather refinish furniture, and partaking in family races to see who could eat the most corn on the cob. The tool chest made from wooden Velveeta boxes is real; it sits on my own workbench now. My grandfather died while I was in law school. A decade later, I received the honor and profound gift to be able to move into their home to be with my grandmother during her last months.

What was your inspiration for this book?

This sounds kind of wacky, but I was on a walk when a "what if" popped into my head: *What if you built your whole life on a certain assumption and then years later discover that the assumption was wrong?* I am intrigued with exploring the personal past and discovering how it informs the present—the road not taken and all.

You have a background in child advocacy. Is the novel based on an experience you had in the field or a case you may have worked on?

Not any specific case, really. It's more just the general experience. A child builds her own life from the foundation of her family experience. If that environment she grew up in is abuse or neglect or incest, when she is removed from the situation she faces reshaping her life with a new definition of "normal." I think my experiences of working with scared and scarred children are wrapped into the reasons my protagonist, Ruby, makes the choices she makes.

About the Author

This is your debut novel, and you have created characters that are complex, believable, and ones the readers will really root for. How did you come up with their stories?

I've been told since I was a young kid that I have an "old soul." I study people, try to figure out what makes them tick. I know the people in my own life very well, and my characters seem to be a patchwork of lots of different pieces of them and of me. That and pure invention from my arguably warped mind. Writers are lucky; they can call the voices in their heads characters while the rest of the world calls them crazy.

I'm glad the characters seem believable to the reader, because they became very real to me. My friends tease me about the time I was shopping for Christmas presents and didn't realize until I was up at the counter that I had picked out a gift for Ruby.

The subject of the book is very sensitive. What are you hoping readers will take away from *Mothers and Other Liars*?

Ruby faces some choices that make readers think about what they would do in that situation. People have strong feelings about her story; some tell me that they could never make those same choices, others that Ruby's path was the only one she could have taken. I'm thrilled that the story makes people think and engage in lively debate. In addition to their opinions about Ruby's choices, I hope readers also take away a different sense of what makes a "family." It is a privilege to be invited into peoples' homes, to have them give my story a chunk of their own limited time. I'm honored when they feel that their reading time was well spent, that the story sticks with them after they finish the book.

"I've been a writer since before I could hold a pencil."

You were a partner in a law firm before you published this book. What made you decide to become a writer?

Oh, I've been a writer since before I could hold a pencil. *Mothers and Other Liars* is my debut novel, but my first publishing credit was a poem called—I kid you not, but my family kids me about it plenty—"Where Buffalo Where." It was a plaintive ode about the disappearance of buffalo due to overdevelopment of their land. I guess Lark gets her green streak from me. As a child, I also wrote short stories and kept journals. In high school and college, I was a writer for and editor of yearbooks and newspapers, and I think there still exist somewhere out there beside my parents' bookshelf a few copies of my college thesis, published by the university press. And in my law practice, I wrote a lot of legal documents and articles.

I probably shouldn't admit this, but when my parents moved a few years ago, I went home to clean out my stuff and found notebooks full of my old writing. There were these journal entries from when I was eight and nine where I wrote dreck like "I am a writer. It is who I am. It is the destiny of my soul." I asked my mother if she had seen that stuff and when she said she had, I asked her why she didn't get me into therapy!

At the same time, though, I've always been very analytical. "Dogged" and "Type-A" are some of the nicer ways I've heard friends and family describe me. Hence the law part. I guess I've just kind of lived in the middle space between my left and right brain, drifting back and forth from time to time. But my lifelong love affair with words, as my eight-year-old self knew even then, is what defines me best.

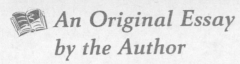
"A Muse Named Johnny"

I went to law school because I wanted to be a child advocate. Yale has a terrific clinical program where students can take on real-life cases. My very first assignment was representing a twelve-year-old boy. Let's call him Johnny Doe. A teacher had recognized signs of abuse in Johnny's younger sister, and—warning, there's an ick-factor here—an investigation had revealed that Johnny had been sexually abusing her. Johnny was being prosecuted in juvenile court for child molestation. And I was his lawyer. The kicker was—and this one really puts the "ick" in "kick"—that the children's mother, a single parent with mild retardation, was sharing her bed with the boy. Johnny had clearly committed a crime, but he was no criminal; he was only doing what was "normal" in his little world.

In an instant, that boy's little world imploded. He was taken away from his mother, his sister, his school, and thrown into a juvenile detention center. When I met with him, all I could see was a skinny, scared boy peeking out of a too-big orange jumpsuit. Johnny was book-smart. He excelled at science. And he didn't understand why he was being punished for something he was "supposed" to do.

It's been more than twenty years, and that boy's story is still vivid in my mind, along with Janie, whose mother's boyfriend found sport in dipping her in scalding water, and every other Johnny and Jane who I represented. Stories are never pretty in child advocacy. But the children, they were all beautiful enough to break a heart. Every time. Which is how I ended up practicing corporate law, and taking on one pro bono child advocacy case at a time—that was as much breaking as *my* heart could handle.

Over the years, more than just the details of those stories has stayed with me. The cases made me wonder, what would I do if one day my whole world changed? What if I discovered that the assumptions upon which I had built my life were wrong? The cases also made me think about nature versus nurture. Johnny's actions were surely a product of his environment—he learned at the hand (or other body parts) of his "nurturing" mother. Or were those actions "nature"? Maybe both Johnny and his mother were hard-wired that way and would have acted accordingly in any environment.

And what about me? I have tight bonds with my family. When my sister's friends meet me, of course they notice the dimples. No doubt my sister and I swam in the same genetic pool. Yet people also comment on how we make similar gestures, how our voices have the same timbre. I have my mother's eyes, and her sense of humor. My interest in furniture refinishing is a piece of my grandfather that I carry around like a precious family heirloom. So which of these are nature, threaded through that double helix, and which are nurture, mere products of the times our family has spent together? Yes, I've been told a time or two that I think too much.

Like my character Ruby, I left one life behind and moved to Santa Fe. That area is like a candy store for a hiking lover such as myself. My meanderings are prime musing time—I ponder as I wander, so to speak. And somewhere along the way in those dalmation hills, spotted with piñon bushes, and beneath the shivering gold of the Aspen trees, I noticed that other voices were chiming in to the conversations in my head. Either I was in the midst of a psychotic episode, or all of those musings about nurture and nature and what is family and lives changing in an instant were weaving themselves into a story. I decided on the latter.

Recommended Reading

Reading Group Gold

Amy's List

Bird by Bird by **Anne Lamott**

For me, the best book about writing but also a great read about life in general. I'd recommend any of her books, especially her collected essays.

Upgraded to Serious by **Heather McHugh**

When my work is "young," I read poetry rather than other novels so that I inspire but don't interfere with the fragile voices of my own story. Heather McHugh and Pablo Neruda are two of my favorites. *The Best American Poetry*, an annual publication, is a great book to find poets who inspire you.

Day Hikes in the Santa Fe Area

This is the Sierra Club book that Ruby carries on hikes (as do I). You can find it in Santa Fe bookstores and gift shops.

The Furniture Doctor by **George Grotz**

Ruby used her grandfather's book, *Principles of Woodworking* by Herman Hjorth, but I find this Grotz book more accessible. First published in 1962 and revised several times, this is my woodworking bible.

The Best Interests of the Child: The Least Detrimental Alternative by **Joseph Goldstein**

Speaking of bibles, this is the bible of child advocacy, written by my law school professor.

Keep on Reading

 *Amy's Favorite Book Club Reads*

The Double Bind by Chris Bohjalian

Superb writing and a masterfully-executed twist.

The Widow's Season by Laura Brody

This is not another *Good Grief*. It's an engaging look at the winding road through the shadow and light of life.

Wildflower by Mark Seal

I was fascinated with this true story of Joan Root, a wildlife filmmaker, kind of *Great Gatsby* meets *Out of Africa*.

Lamb: The Gospel According to Biff, Christ's Childhood Pal by Christopher Moore

Wet-your-pants funny and a very interesting take on history. Don't be put off by the title; my book club, which includes Jews, Christians, and nonbelievers, had a great discussion about this one.

To Kill a Mockingbird by Harper Lee

My book club picks one classic to read each year. I could read this one every year. I also enjoyed the new biography of the author, *Up Close: Harper Lee* by Kerry Madden. Two timely reads for 2010, the fiftieth anniversary of the novel.

 *Reading Group Questions*

1. People seem to feel very strongly about Ruby's choices. What would you have done in her situation? Do you think her acts were selfish or selfless?

2. The theme of nature versus nurture is woven through this novel. Ruby believes Lark is the person she is more because of their shared experiences than because of Lark's biological heritage. Which do you think is the stronger component of a person? Which parts of your own character do you think are based on nurture and which come from nature?

3. The theme of water also "runs" through the story. What do you think about the contradiction in how Ruby sets out to find a piece of her mother on an ocean shore, yet she builds her life with Lark in the arid high desert of Santa Fe? In which parts of the story do the river themes resonate strongest for you? Where do you find your own peace, in a river, an ocean, a mountain, a person?

4. Chaz has strong ties to his family, yet he leaves not only Ruby but his entire family behind. Why do you think he did not return for his own child's baptism? Do you think that someday he and Ruby will have their fairy-tale ending? How is his leaving similar to and different from Ruby leaving her "second life" in Iowa?

5. Speaking of family, after her grandmother's death and until the end of the book, Ruby's own "family" is comprised entirely of people to whom she is not related. How do you think her story would have unfolded if she had not met Margaret in that parking lot?

6. Ruby talks about how every person has a pivotal moment that changes the direction of her life. Ruby identifies two, finding Lark at the rest stop and then putting into motion her plan to give up her biological child in exchange for Lark. Both of these moments, though, also drastically changed the course of others' lives. What moments can you identify as pivotal in your own life? Looking back, how do you think those moments impacted others?

7. Do you think Ruby's grandmother had some idea that she was dying when she sent Ruby to town? How do you think Ruby's own choices would have been different if, say, her grandmother had died after a lingering illness, with Ruby at her side?

8. Why do you think the author chose to tell the story from Ruby's point of view rather than from an omniscient or alternating point of view? What aspects would have changed with different perspectives?

9. How do you feel about the choices of Darla, the "other" mother? In what ways does she exemplify the distinction between what we want and what we think we want?

10. Okay, go ahead and confess. What is the biggest lie *you* have ever told?

AMY BOURRET is a graduate of Yale Law School and Texas Tech University, and a former partner in a national law firm. Her pro bono work with child advocacy organizations sparked the passion that fuels *Mothers and Other Liars,* her debut novel. She lived for several years in Santa Fe and now splits her time between Aspen, Colorado, and Dallas, Texas. Visit her at www.amybourret.com.